Revenant

Stephen B. Pearl

Also by Stephen B. Pearl

Worlds Apart

The Ray McAndrues Trilogy
Nukekubi
Revenant
Lycanthrope (forthcoming)

Revenant

Stephen B. Pearl

Dark Dragon Publishing
Toronto, Ontario, Canada

REVENANT

ISBN: 978-1-928104-20-9
eISBN: 978-1-928104-21-6

Cover Design and Author Photo
© by Evan Dales
WAV Design Studios
www.wavstudios.ca

Dark Dragon Publishing
88 Charleswood Drive.,
Toronto, Ontario
M3H 1X6
CANADA
www.darkdragonpublishing.com

For more information on the Stephen B. Pearl
www.stephenpearl.com

I dedicate this book first to my wife, Joy, and to my editor at Dark Dragon, without whom it would never have come into being.

I would also like to dedicate it to the volunteers that make the fan conventions and other such events come about. Your hard work and dedication creates places where writers, who are largely solitary, can meet and discuss our craft without having people fall asleep or roll their eyes while looking for exits. Your efforts contribute to the rich tapestry of writing, much like a bee contributes to a field of flowers. Hardly noticed but allowing for pollination of thought that otherwise wouldn't occur. I thank you one and all.

I'd also like to make mention of the staff of the Royal Botanical Guardians, who work diligently to preserve and restore the beauty of nature. To you and others who preserve nature in the city, be blessed, you are life-givers, hope givers, and I cannot thank you enough.

Chapter 1

Blood In The Water

CATHY'S SLENDER FORM pressed tight against me as I unlocked the pool office's outer door. We stumbled into the dimly-lit room, my hands slipping to the areas covered by her, barely, street-legal bikini. The light should have been my first clue. The dingy, ten by ten space with its battered metal desk and old park bench, folding chair and steel filing cabinet had no outside windows. It should have been pitch black.

We pulled apart to take a breath of the humid, chlorine-saturated air.

"Are you sure you won't get into trouble for this?" Cathy stared at me with emerald eyes in a face that would have done a Celtic Goddess proud. Her fingers played across my bare, sweat-soaked chest, then down to my Speedo swimsuit. The part of my brain that worried about getting canned left the building.

"Carl takes midnight swims. He can't nail me for something he does himself. I… Crap!"

"What?" Cathy smiled then nuzzled the base of my neck. Her shoulder-length, red hair tickled my chest.

"Cath, please. The lights should be out. Carl must have

brought a date here."

Cathy traced her fingernails over my broad back. "Maybe you just forgot to turn them off."

"No, half of them are—Ooooon. Cath! We aren't alone in here." I grabbed her hand to stop her explorations. Loving Cathy involved accepting that she had her own rules regarding appropriate behaviour. Fun rules, but her own.

"Maybe we could watch?" Cathy shifted so she could stare out the windows over the deck of the large pool.

"Cath, really, come on. We'll…" I began to object. Catching Carl having a midnight swim probably wouldn't get me canned. Technically, it was more legal for me to be in the pool area alone than him, since I had a current National Lifeguard Service rating, but he could make my life hell.

"Ray! Look." Cathy grabbed my arm, her pale hand contrasting with my tan complexion, and pointed at the left side of the tiled pool deck.

A naked, middle-aged man sprawled by the pool halfway down the deck. A reddish cloud stained the water by the man's submerged wrist, and his chubby body was pale.

"Ra's beak! That's Carl."

"Lady Bast! We have to—" began Cathy.

I caught Cathy as she tried to push past me to the door onto the pool deck.

"Get the blanket and pillows from the cupboard." I wrenched open a large drawer on the desk and pulled out the first aid kit as Cathy moved to the filing cabinet against the office's outer wall opposite the desk.

The pool deck looked safe, so I used my master key to unlock it and raced to Carl's side. An open pocket knife lay beside him, and a pile of clothes was on the floor by the wall.

Opening the First Aid Kit, I pulled on nitrile gloves then rolled Carl away from the pool. His slashed wrist came out of the water. I griped over the wound, squeezing it tightly.

The spurts of blood stopped, but my boss looked horribly pale.

ABC: I checked his Airway, making sure it was clear, then

looked, listened and felt for Breathing. It was shallow and fast. The pulse in his neck fluttered against my fingertips, fast and thready: Circulation.

Cathy ran up with the blanket and pillows.

"He's still alive. There's an oxygen cylinder and airway kit in the desk's bottom drawer. Get it for me, then call 911, tell them we have a patient, massive blood loss, respiration depressed and to use the pool's emergency door. First aid is in progress. Don't leave the phone until they say you can but tell them you're my only help here." I reached into the first aid kit and pulled out a pressure dressing while Cathy hurried back to the office.

"Live, damn it! I don't want your job."

I let go of the wound. Blood spurted, leaving a trail of red across my chest, so much for gloves. I clamped the dressing down on the wound with my hand. The bleeding stopped again, and I wrapped the bandage strips of the dressing around Carl's wrist. I let off my grip, and the bleeding remained stopped. I folded his arm so that it rested on his chest.

Cathy set the oxygen tank and airway kit beside me and streaked back to the office.

The pillow went under Carl's legs to encourage the blood to flow back to his heart, and I covered him to maintain body heat before starting high-flow Oxygen with a re-breather mask.

"The ambulance is coming," announced Cathy.

I glanced up. Cathy stared at the blood with an expression of horror.

"Cathy, prop the emergency door open."

Cathy can take a lot, but it's a different type of tough to deal with someone's insides. I'd trained for it, she hadn't.

She'd barely reached the door when someone started pounding on it. She hit the emergency bar. The door opened, admitting two ambulance attendants who rolled a gurney up to my side.

"Severe blood loss from a wound in the left wrist. Arterial involvement. Unconscious." I passed on the history.

The paramedics grunted, half pushed me out of the way, and then proceeded to repeat my body check. I stood back and watched as one of them started an I.V. while the other laid out a pair of Medical Anti-Shock Trousers.

They rolled Carl out of the pool area on the gurney. Pulling off my blood-soaked gloves, I ran my fingers through my short, brown hair smoothing it. For several moments, I stood with my back against the wall listening to the sound of my own heart.

"That was…" Cathy stood transfixed by the puddles of blood on the pool deck.

"Definitely not how I wanted the night to go." I took a deep breath. "I better leave a message on the city's answering machine and hang the closed for maintenance sign."

If it had been my YMCA gig, I could have cleaned up the mess and shocked the pool, but the city is a union shop. Playing with chlorine is forbidden for us lifeguards. Truth to tell, I had no objection to a morning off anyway.

I made my calls, cleaned myself up and locked up the pool. In minutes, Cathy and I walked the quarter block to our apartment building. The shortness of the walk made changing out of our swimwear seem useless. Besides, I liked the view, and Cathy knew I did.

Cathy took my hand as we walked. "You were amazing."

"I hope it was enough." I keep reviewing the scenario in my head.

"Don't you always." Cathy smiled. "And for the record, you usually do pretty well for yourself." I could hear a trace of her flirty teasing coming to the fore, but it rang hollow. Her hand shook, and her face was paler than usual.

"It's okay to let it get to you. It just means you're human," I comforted.

"I know him. Your boss, he's a regular at *The Gold*. I've danced for him." We stopped on the street.

I stroked her arm, "It's harder when you know the person. No surprise that Carl likes strip clubs."

"Will he be all right?" Cathy pressed into the crook of my

arm. With home so close, I never showered at work. I knew too much about what happened in those change rooms to want to. We started walking again.

"Probably. He was pinking up when the paramedics took him. That's a good sign."

Cathy's pulled me to a stop at the front entrance to the seven-story apartment building we both lived in and kissed me. "Thank you for listening. I'm being silly, making it about me, but… medicine's my mother's thing. Blood creeps me out."

"Hey, it's what you do when you're in lo—"

"No!" She held me at arm's length. "You know the rules. I don't want to hear it until you're secure enough to get over wanting to own me."

"Please don't start that, not now." I pushed down on the ire that had been growing for almost as long as I'd known her.

"Fine, I guess some slack is in order." She tweaked my nose.

I felt a little bubble of resentment. Slack, like I always gave her. How much slack does it take to hang yourself? How much slack for the other men that shared her bed pushing me aside? "Thanks."

"Why don't we go to my place to cool down?"

"Cool down?"

"At first. I do like washing your back in the shower."

"Sounds like fun." I kissed her. I could never stay mad at Cathy.

She unlocked the building's door, and I followed her to the elevator. "So, sixth floor?" she asked.

"Crap!" I buried my face in my hands.

"What?"

"I have to fill out an accident report. It has to be now in case they try to sue me for something."

"Fine, go to your place, type one up and shower there. I'll have something hot waiting for you when you're done." She stepped onto the elevator. I followed. Cathy pressed the buttons for the fifth and sixth floors. She kissed me before I got out on my floor.

The common hall of my apartment building was simple, clean and utilitarian. My apartment was simple and utilitarian. Barren and spartan also works.

I went straight to my combination study/temple room and turned on my outdated computer. As it booted up, I showered and composed my thoughts. As the stress reduced, I analysed the event. There were things there that I didn't notice before. Many of the skills of the wizard are simple mental disciplines.

Yes, I used the W-word. I've studied the mystic arts for longer than I can remember. First, with my grandfather—may Osiris bless and keep him safe and joyous in Aaru— then, on my own. Magic is part of me and has proved useful in dealing with things like poltergeists, Nukekubi and various ghosts. It's part of what kept Cathy and me together. I like to call her an enchantress. She prefers priestess. Both are accurate.

In any case, part of my skill set is a technique for remembering. There are thousands of details in a memory. Most of us remember, remembering. We recall the stories we tell ourselves and others more than the initial event.

With cool water flowing over me, I could focus on the actual memory. An odd scent like vanilla and strawberries on the edge of perception, but it couldn't be a smell because the ever-present chlorine stench would have drowned it out. A sound that wasn't a sound, it was an echo from a sense beyond the physical senses. It sounded like a bird call crossed with a flute. I recalled feeling chilled, but I had been too busy to acknowledge it.

I finished my shower, dried and sat down at my computer. The air felt good against my bare skin, better than clothing anyway. One of the great things about having my own place is I didn't have to dress in the middle of a heat wave. I typed my accident report, added a date and time, and printed it off for Cathy to witness. While it printed, I checked on the grey, orange and white ball of fur that is the other female in my life. Sekmara lay stretched out on the bed. She turned her head towards me, flicked her tail twice, then rolled over and went back to sleep.

The sense that there was something I couldn't put in my official report nagged at me, but Cathy was waiting, and I had earned a reward, so I pulled on a pair of shorts and went up to her apartment.

Chapter 2

Once More Into The Breach

SHORTLY AFTER DAWN, I was once again drenched in sweat from vigorous physical activity. This time, I wasn't complaining.

Cathy lay beside me in her queen-sized bed. The only contact between our two naked forms was my hand on her waist. At thirty degrees centigrade, that counts as cuddling.

It was too hot to sleep and far too early to get up, so I closed my eyes and focused on the memory. Breathing deeply, I stilled my thoughts, relaxed my body and entered a meditative state. I let the memory play in my mind. First, I sifted out the struggle to save Carl and the emotions that were part of that.

The background noises came to the fore. The hum of the lights, the gurgle of the pumps, the slosh of the water. The malfunctioning pump made a tell-tale sound if you knew what to listen for. I pushed this level aside. The scent that wasn't a scent touched my awareness: strawberries and vanilla. The bird call crossed with a flute, barely at the edge of perception. The feel of my energy flowing into Carl. It was like something had sucked the energy from the man. I looked at the memory of Carl's aura. Dingy, muted blue, green, and orange pulled tight against his body.

Carl is a natural salesman. His aura tends to crowd the room with bright colours. Short of a major emotional trauma, I couldn't think of what could tarnish an aura so quickly. What I remembered from the pool was the aura of a chronically depressed person. Carl wasn't introspective enough to be chronically depressed.

Somewhere between my exhaustion and the meditative state, I fell asleep.

I woke to the beeping of Cathy's alarm and turned it off. She'd set it for me. Pulling on the shorts I'd worn between my place and hers, I took the stairs to my floor and entered my apartment.

My place was, as I said, uncluttered. I had a TV, stereo, couch and my reclining chair in the living room. The TV and stereo stood on an entertainment cabinet I'd salvaged from the roadside and repaired with scrounged wood and screws. The couch was a parental hand-me-down that was nearly as old as I was, but with a bit of plywood between the dead springs and the cushions, it got the job done. My dining room consisted of an arborite table with two mismatched chairs in the little area that came off the galley kitchen.

I poured myself a bowl of cold cereal and a glass of orange juice. I considered coffee, but the thought of anything hot made my eyes water. I put down food for her feline majesty, who appeared long enough to walk figure eights around my legs and get her morning petting.

The phone rang at 8:35 AM. Just in time for someone to get to the recreation department office and listen to the messages.

The call was straightforward. The pool was closed. Aside from coming in to fill out the city's incident report and answer some questions I had the day off, without pay of course.

I stripped and went back to bed. Two hours of restless stewing in my own juices and obsessive thought later, I came to two conclusions. One, I had to buy an air conditioner. Two, there was something fishy about Carl's suicide attempt.

After that, I think the powers that be decided I was on the right track because I slept for a whole two hours.

I awoke to a noise from the hallway that connected my bedroom, temple room and bathroom to the living area of my apartment. I got up, pulled on my shorts and took the ritual sword I kept beside my bed in hand.

Live my life, then you can judge.

Creeping into the hall, I heard clicking and clunking from the kitchen.

A beautiful Asian woman in short-shorts and a tight T-shirt stood at my sink doing my dishes. I sighed as she glanced my way.

"Fuck, Ray, paranoid much? What's with the sword? I thought you'd be at work."

"Long story, the pool's closed." I lowered my blade.

Kama continued to do my dishes as I tried not to stare. "Mind if I do the vacuuming?"

"Go ahead. I'll be in the temple room. The cash is in the usual place."

"I fought the Nukekubi too. Why the big, strong men were the ones who got to keep the money, I don't know." Kama looked up at me in mock annoyance.

I snorted. Kama had helped, but Kuno and I had done the heavy lifting on that job. Everyone involved knew it. Truth is the money was poison. If the cops could prove I had it, it would connect me to the murder of a Japanese business executive, and they weren't about to listen to the truth. The business executive had been a Japanese goblin who had feasted on the people of the Golden Horseshoe and damn near had me for an entrée. My friend, Kuno, and I had saved each other's lives too many times to keep track dealing with that creature, and still, there'd been a body count. All neatly explained away as drug overdoses. The upshot, I could trickle the money out in things like Kama's under-the-table wages, but it had to be kept quiet.

I shuffled to the second bedroom of the apartment and opened the door. The room was cut in half by free standing bookshelves. My computer desk and chair were closer to the door, pushed against the wall. The books on this side dealt with topics from Archaeology to Zoology, and too many novels. I walked through the opening at the end of the bookshelves into another world. This side of the room had dark blue carpet. A waist-high, flat-topped, wooden dresser draped in purple silk pressed against the flat back of the bookshelves on the eastern side. On the dresser sat the ritual tools of the Egyptian path: Crook, Flail, Sistrum, Chalice, Winged disk and Mirror of Hathor. Smaller shelves flanked the chest with statues of various Egyptian Gods and Goddesses on them, amongst other mystical tools and paraphernalia. Candles holders topped these slightly shorter shelves. My pride and joy, the north and south walls of the temple were covered with full two-metre-tall bookshelves. Above the shelves, Papyrus prints of Egyptian artwork covered the rest of the wall.

Despite the open windows, the room was stifling. I wanted to get this job over with.

I bowed to the four quarters then opened a wooden box on the shelf by my altar. Inside was a broken pair of sunglasses. Carl had tossed them in the trash when I was watching at work. I mean, it's like dangling catnip in front of a tabby. I'd never done anything with them until now, but it's always good to have insurance.

Holding the glasses, I cleared my mind and prayed.

"Lady Nephthys, Goddess of Divination, Lord Thoth, God of all Wizardries, Lady Isis, Goddess of all Sorceries, I call on thee to open my mind.

I let my thoughts merge with the glasses. Psychometry is potent but risky. Still in all, I didn't expect Carl to have any special occult defences. I felt him as an incarnate life. That answered my first question. I focused my thoughts on the previous night. I tossed the glasses onto the floor when I was hit with a wave of depression, shame and guilt.

I envisioned a white light flowing into me from above my head and let it push the negative emotions out while a tendril of green rising from the ground sucked up the negative energies. Opening my eyes, I stared at the broken sunglasses on the floor.

"Curiouser and curiouser." Using a purple silk cloth I kept on the shelves by my altar, I picked up the glasses and returned them to the wooden box. Given the pool's location, there was only one ER they would have taken Carl to, so I didn't need to divine his location.

"I thank thee, my Lords and Ladies."After bowing to my altar, I returned to the kitchen. The sound of laughter told me that Cathy had heard Kama vacuuming through the open balcony doors and came down to visit.

I rounded the corner into the living room, and there they were, drinking two of my beers, thumbing through my video collection and laughing like maniacs.

"Independence Day, really?" said Cathy, as I entered the room. She wore white short-shorts and a yellow T-shirt with a tabby cat on it.

"It was on sale," I countered.

"You paid too much." Cathy tossed the disk case and all at me.

"It was a really good price."

"You still paid too much," added Kama.

"Aren't you supposed to be cleaning?" I crossed the room and put my DVD on the top of the entertainment cabinet.

Kama turned to Cathy. "You owe me a loony."

"I should have known better," remarked Cathy.

"You're betting on me?" I looked at the two most important women in my life.

"Oh, Ray, we always bet on you." Cathy stood and gave me a kiss. "Thanks for letting me sleep."

A moment later, she pulled away.

"I'm going to see Carl. Do you want to—"

"Is he alright?" blurted Cathy.

Cathy cares. It's part of why I love her. Part of why I put up with so much.

"He's alive, and I'm pretty sure they would have taken him to St. Joes. Cath, I think there's something woggy going on."

My voice became serious.

"Then I'm coming with you for sure."Cathy's demeanour changed from concerned to determined.

"You two are fucking nuts. Smart people run away from the monster." Kama rolled her eyes.

I smiled at Kama. "To each their own." Turning to Cathy, I continued, "Just let me get a shirt."

"Right, don't want to make some cougar drive her fucking car up a tree." Kama winked at me. "Though I couldn't blame her."

Cathy shot Kama a sidelong glance that contained a flash of jealousy.

Kama was like a sister in most ways, but as she was getting older, that could change. Cathy's insistence on an open relationship didn't encompass women I could form an emotional attachment to. In other words, anyone I'd want to sleep with. I don't think she even knew how lopsided her rules were. I smirked as I went to grab a shirt.

Cathy and I chained our bikes to the rack by the hospital's multi-story parking. If you live in Hamilton, you soon learn not to park near the hospitals. The time and money I saved made the sweat soaking both of us worthwhile.

Entering the air-conditioned hospital lobby was like diving into cold water. The reception desk behind its sliding glass panes was staffed by a middle-aged woman with long, brown hair and a muscular build.

She looked up at me, and then her eyes centred on Cathy. "Cathy, what's it been, a year? No, it must be longer. Last I saw you, I was working at Mac?"

"Hi, Jazzmen. I'm surprised you remember me."

"Are you kidding? You look just like your Mother."

Cathy plastered a false smile on her face. "Lots of people say that."

"Are you still, umm, working at the Solid Gold?" Jazzmen half-whispered the bar's name.

The muscles in Cathy's jaw rippled as her aura became a band of dark colour. If you've ever been on the leading edge of a thunderstorm, you get the picture.

"I'm still dancing. It covers tuition and books."

"If you ever want to change jobs, my brother manages the Home Depot. I could put in a good word for you."

Despite the pleasure I derived by Cathy being reminded that one, she did bear a striking resemblance to her mother—I take my life in my hands to mention that the similarities were more than skin deep— and two, her mother didn't approve of her dancing, and three, she could count on hearing all about it from any number of her mom's friends and co-workers. I decided to come to the rescue. Whether I was rescuing Cathy or Jazzmen was the only question.

"Excuse me, but we're looking for Carl MacMillan. He was admitted last night." I smiled.

"Just a moment, I'll check."Jazzmen typed in the name on her keyboard. "Room 327. I'll tell Andrea you said hello when I see her at book club."

"Thanks, but I'll probably see my mom before that." Cathy turned away, and we walked to the elevators in silence.

As the large, metal doors closed and the elevator jerked up, Cathy grumbled. "I hate going into Hamilton Hospitals."

"Your mom does seem to know a lot of people," I reflected.

"She's been a nurse forever." Cathy could have been sucking on a lemon for the look on her face.

"She's good people, and she loves you." I knew we were on eggshells, and I wanted Cathy focused for this meeting.

She glared at me, and then took a deep breath. "I know. I just wish she wouldn't go on to her friends about my dancing, and…." Cathy looked at me and sighed. "Other things. I mean, it was her sleeping around and lying about it that broke her and dad up. If only she'd been honest with him. If only she had owned up to what she really needed, dad could have given her that space. He obviously needed it too. They were both cheaters. If they'd only been honest, they could have opened their marriage and Tabby and I… We wouldn't have been in the middle so much." Cathy took a deep breath as we stepped out of the lift onto the third floor.

"I can do this solo if you need time." I stroked her arm. I understood her pain. She'd been a pawn in a nasty divorce between two people who had flushed away the trust between them. I suspected they still loved each other; only love could make people as crazy as Cathy's parents got. On the other hand, I'd been patient for years and had to wonder when what I needed was going to matter? She took a second breath, then a third, and smiled and patted my hand.

"I'm fine."

"Okay, I'll go in first. I want to scan his aura before he sees you."

"Why?" Cathy looked surprised.

I allowed my eyes to slowly track up and down her body. Short shorts and a T-shirt damp from the ride over. "Let's just say, I think you would affect the energy fields of ninety-eight percent of the male population."

Cathy grinned. "Flatterer. You go in first; I'll follow."

I moved onto room 327. It was private, painted cream but descending to beige with grubbiness. A hospital bed filled most of the space, and the morning sunshine streamed in through windows that could stand a good clean. Carl lay in the bed with an IV flowing into his arm. His left wrist was encased in bandages. A half-eaten tray of hospital, I guess you can call it 'food', occupied a roller cart to one side of his bed.

"Hi, boss." I stepped into the room.

Carl forced a fake smile. His aura was pulled in tight and still looked dull. "Ray... I'm glad you came by. I... They tell me if it wasn't for you, I wouldn't be here. Thanks, I guess."

"Anytime." I moved to his side and placed my hand on his shoulder. At the same time, I focused on my heart chakra and envisioned a golden light pouring out of me into Carl. Something hungry gnawed at the energy. I activated the brow chakra and added blue energy to the mix. It helped. But it wasn't enough. Anything I added drained away.

"I have someone I'd like you to meet," I spoke aloud, and

Cathy entered the room.

Carl's eyes went wide as I felt a trickle of orange sexual energy come from his root chakra. The orange energy seemed to slow the drain.

"Cat? You know Ray?" Carl forced some vitality into his voice as he tried to sit up.

"It's only Cat at the bar because of the weirdoes. Out here, it's Cathy. How you feeling?" Her voice became softer for the last.

Carl's eyes devoured Cathy. Drawing on my own root chakra, I added orange to the energies I fed into Carl. The energy drain almost stopped. It was like wrapping a shorted wire with electrical tape then adding a new battery. Carl began retaining energy, but he was depleted. There was something dark inside him. I knew the moment I left whatever was draining him would be back.

Cathy kept Carl occupied as I mapped out his damage and tried to plan.

"How do you feel?" Cathy swayed her hips and smiled coyly.

"Better with you visiting. Do you know what happened to Maryann?"

Cathy moved to Carl's other side and lightly touched the back of his hand. I sensed that she was adding her own power to the fray.

"Who's Maryann?" I watched his aura. It was still dingy and closed in, but sparks of brighter colours began to appear.

"The hotty I was with." Carl's eyes closed, and his aura dimmed as he thought about the woman.

Conventional wisdom would say don't think about her, but the dark energies were like an infection. Purging the poison was the only way to make any healing last.

Cathy and I shared a knowing look; she'd seen it too.

"I didn't see anybody," remarked Cathy. Her eyes focused on me. I pointed to Carl's shoulders and made a back-and-forth gesture across his chest.

Cathy bit her lip and nodded. With her free hand, she

tapped over her brow and heart chakras. I nodded and tapped over the base chakra as well. Cathy smiled and mouthed the word, 'Kinky' before her expression became serious.

"Why would she leave me like that?" Carl opened his eyes, and his voice was sad. His aura dimmed further as his eyes closed again. I thought of dropping my questioning until we could stabilize his energies, but I needed to know what happened. If something was out hunting sleaze-balls, well, there is such a thing as perspective. Carl was slimy, but he was no rapist and women who went with him pretty much knew in advance what they were getting into.

"What happened?" I pitched my voice softly and pushed empathically to make the man chatty. Cathy sat beside him and moved her hand to his shoulder. His aura pulsed as the grey energies fought against the brighter hues Cathy and I pumped in.

"I don't know. One-minute life was great, the next I... it was like drowning in mud, and there wasn't any way out. I..." Carl clutched Cathy's hand with his good hand.

"Take it at your own pace," she soothed.

I placed a hand on his shoulder. Mentally, I reached down through the floor into the earth, forming a ground, and then I centred my thoughts. Focusing on Cathy, I pushed energy towards her. This is the advantage of being regular working partners. You get each other. We formed a circuit between us cycling through Carl. The negative energies were drawn into the flow, and we expelled them through the grounds. The cleaned energies flowed back through Carl to the other pole of the circuit. Blue, gold and orange energies coursed through my boss, who would never have been my choice for any kind of threesome, but what you gonna do? I'd do the mystical equivalent of bathing in bleach later.

Carl started talking. "I think I need to talk about it. I don't get why I did this."

"Start from the beginning." Cathy's voice was angry.

I searched my own emotions. I felt depressed, dirty, guilt, shame. I focused on the ground, but there was so much of it coming from Carl, I couldn't clear it all. Cathy and I both kept working.

Carl's voice became dreamy. With the energy flowing through him, it was a testament to how depleted he was that he wasn't making a mess of the sheets.

"I was at the bar, and this hotty came up to me. She had black hair, looked a little Mexican, maybe twenty, twenty-two, legs that went up to her neck and a rack you could ski down. She reminded me of what Linda looked like when we first met. I figured she must be a pro, but with what she's packing, I'm not too proud.

"She sits down beside me. I offer to buy her a drink. You know what she says to me?"

"What?" I asked.

"Says, a drink isn't what she wants. Then she takes my hand, and I ain't gonna pass this up. We get to the parking lot, and she's all over me. I said I had a place we could cool off and have some fun. She says, 'good.' We grabbed a cab. Damn cabby kept trying to cock-block me. Talking to me like Maryann wasn't there.

"We get to the pool and start striping. She is so hot. Not a blemish on her. She stepped back, and I just started feeling wrong. Like nothing would ever be good again.

Carl's voice changed. The inflexion wasn't his. The tone became decidedly more feminine with a cruel undertone. There was a flood of negative energy. The ground couldn't keep up, and I hurt. It was like every time I'd been dumped. Like when Cathy took up with a new boy toy. I felt gutted, and I was only on the edge of the attack. I kept processing the energy because I knew if I didn't in a day, or a week, Carl would try to kill himself again. Whatever did this to him was powerful. I couldn't just let it slide. It wasn't in my nature. Maybe Cathy is right, and I do need therapy.

The words that came out of Carl's mouth weren't his, but I knew they were exactly what had been said, and they had been chosen to play on the man's personal fears and doubts. "She stared at me and said, 'You're gay. You're a loser in a dead-end job. Why would any woman want you? The girls in high school knew what you were all about. You're just a sleazy old man, nothing, a loser. What will you ever contribute? You're a fraud. You can't even do your dead-end job right. Even your mother thought you were a loser, just like your old man. That's why Linda left you. You aren't man enough. You're scum. A rapist, an abuser, you don't deserve to breathe.'"

Carl shuddered, and there was another surge of dark energy. In hindsight, I should have set up a circle, but we were in a hospital with a non-believer, and I didn't expect energy of this magnitude.

I looked at Cathy and cringed. Rage, coupled with intense concentration, filled her features. Whatever she felt was different from the depression that enveloped Carl and me. I focused on the green grounding line; splitting it, I pushed the extra branch into Cathy. Immediately, the backlog of negative energies in me increased, but something else happened. When I put her wellbeing over my own, my heart chakra increased. More golden energy joined the reserves I drew on. It made a safe enclave that the polluted energies couldn't touch. The depression was still there, but I could see it for the lie it was. My thinking cleared, and I remembered I wasn't alone in a broader sense than the three of us in the room.

Lord Hapi, Prince of the Kingdom of the Gnomes, God of the fertile Nile silt, draw out this poison, let it dissolve and return to power new growth. So Mote It Be! I thought the prayer. The polluted energy flooded down the ground line into the earth below.

Carl kept talking. "I asked her if Linda put her up to it. Then it was like her eyes were glowing. She touched my chest and said, 'You are nothing, weak, pathetic. You hunger for other men. You live only to dominate women, degrade them so that you can pretend to be more than someone. You are guilty of every rape ever committed. You are every man who has struck a woman. You are a monster!'"

Carl opened his eyes, glanced at Cathy and cringed. She

still looked ready to kill someone, but as I grounded the energies, she was coming back to herself.

Carl's gaze turned to me. "I'm no saint, but I never hit a woman and no means no, always has, but I felt like it was all true. It hurt so much that I just had to end it. I took out my jack-knife and cut myself. Maryann seemed to glow."

"What colour was the glow?" I managed to ask through the energy fudge in my brain.

"It was violet. But it wasn't real. Then she said. 'Vengeance is mine. You won't hurt women anymore, Kerbä Tikkari.' What the hell does that even mean?"

"Kerbra Tikkari, I don't have a clue," I spoke the word to fix it in my mind for later.

"I must have passed out after that." Carl seemed to relax in his bed.

That was it. The wellspring of dark energies was exhausted. It took a moment for the ground to drain them out of Cathy and me. I focused my eyes on Cathy, who looked bewildered.

"I'm not really that bad, am I?" Carl's voice begged for reassurance.

Cathy shook her head and smiled at him. I could tell from her aura that what she said next was bullshit. "You've always been nice at the club."

"Thanks. I... All I can think is she slipped something into my drink." Carl sighed as Cathy and I removed our hands from his shoulders.

"That must be it. I didn't think to look for drugs."

I knew there would be no drugs, but the suggestion might just give the city the excuse they needed not to fire Carl. He could be a jerk, but I could handle him. That's always a good thing in a boss.

"No reason you should have. Thanks for saving me. The doctor said another five minutes and it would have been over and done with," Carl said.

"You okay now?" I asked.

"I just wish I knew where Maryann went. I mean, she

might have been a bitch, but she was fine. I couldn't think of a more perfect woman. No offence." He smiled at Cathy.

"None taken. Everybody has a type." Cathy smiled sweetly.

"We better go and let you get some rest. Is there anything you want?" I moved to Cathy's side. I felt depleted from the work we'd just done. Judging from her aura, so was she. The sooner we were away from the hospital and in an energy-rich area, the better.

Carl leered at Cathy. "A lap dance would be nice."

Cathy chuckled and traced her fingers provocatively over Carl's gowned chest before pulling away. "The nurses would probably object, but when you're better, come by the Gold."

Despite his blood loss, Carl's face turned rosy-red, and he smiled.

"Gotta go." I know what Cathy did for a living was an act, and I was mostly okay with it. Mostly.

Back in the entry area, I borrowed a pen from Jazzmen and jotted down 'Kerbra Tikkari' so that I could look it up later, then Cathy and I left the hospital and walked the little over a block to a trail that led up the Niagara escarpment. This steep slope formed a strip of wilderness ,effectively cutting Hamilton in half.

We followed the trail, breathing in the hot, humid air, both loving every moment of it. The trees rustled in the breeze as birds flittered from branch to branch. Our depleted auras sucked in the energies around us like squeezed out sponges, and it felt so good.

We were two-thirds of the way to the top when Cathy spoke. "You can say it now."

Slap. Blood from a particularly large mosquito stained my forearm. "What?"

"That it's not fair for me to pay attention to other guys when you're around."

I had to think for a moment because I was focused on Carl's situation. "The lap dance thing. That's your job. I've never sweated your work. Though I don't think it's a good idea to get Carl's blood pressure too high. He might start bleeding again."

"You are weird. You have no problem with me stripping, but I go on a date, you don't want to know anything about it." Cathy mopped sweat from her brow and wiped it on her shorts.

"Your job is like an actress kissing on screen. It's an act. A date is well, it's a date. Can we talk about something else?" We peaked the escarpment and by silent accord started towards Southam Park. The street separating the escarpment from the large, treed green-space was quiet.

"Maryann?" Cathy sounded concerned.

"That wasn't normal. I started to get depressed during the healing."

"I was ready to smother both of you with a pillow."

"And why would Maryann leave? Why would she say those things?"

"Your boss is a sleaze-ball. All the girls at the bar think so."

"You lied to him," I tried to sound surprised, but it was an act.

"It made him feel better. Blame it on being a psych major. I was watching his aura." Cathy's voice became serious for the last.

"Me too." We reached the park and sat on a bench under a shady tree.

"What do you think?" asked Cathy.

I leaned forward and rubbed my temples. Clearing a ghost is quick and easy, most times. Magic can be fun, I admit it. Going up against something powerful enough to do to Carl what had been done isn't fun. The difference was between playing with a house cat and wrestling an angry tiger. "There's something strange going on. I need to check out the pool. They aren't going to reopen today, so the residual energy should still be fresh."

Cathy rolled her eyes. "Of all the guys I could have fallen for, I have to pick one with a Lancelot complex."

"I'll be careful."

Cathy stroked my shoulders. I straightened so she could kiss me. "We'll be careful," she smiled. "I can't let you have all the fun, and with our different reactions to the energies, I think either of us alone will miss things."

"Thanks, you're the best. You ready to go down the escarpment stairs and get our bikes?"

She groaned theatrically. I didn't need theatrics. My bad knee was telling me what it thought of the idea.

– Chapter 3 –

A Punch Knows No Gender

CATHY AND I entered the pool office, being careful to touch as little as possible. We'd dressed in dark jeans and black T-shirts. I'd insisted we wear the same sandals we had the night before in case anybody got anal about an investigation. I uncovered the lit candle-lantern I carried from my apartment building. My code worked for the alarm system.

"Do you see anything," whispered Cathy.

I stared at her in the dim light that came from the candle. "Why are you whispering?"

"I… This is breaking and entering." She straightened up and stared at the pool.

"Technically, just entering. I have the key, but if we get caught, I will be canned for sure."

We stepped onto the pool deck and moved to the area where the night before we'd found Carl. We stopped and looked down in the candle's glow. There was still dried blood on the deck.

"They aren't in a hurry to clean up," remarked Cathy.

"They probably won't reopen. The repairs to the pump are scheduled for the end of the summer, and they're having staffing problems. They'll split up my team, shuffle us around the other pools and start the work early.

Did you bring the incense?"

Cathy held out a small, brass burner. I opened the Candle lantern's hatch and lit a wooden taper I'd brought. A moment later, the incense burnt. I doused the taper in the pool and returned it to my pocket.

"Ready?" asked Cathy.

"As I'm likely to be." We both sat on the floor in front of the incense burner.

I focused on the smoke, cleared my mind and spoke. "By Thoth God of wizardry and knowledge, I call for our eyes to see true what was and all mysteries to be revealed."

"By Nephthys who sees all in her sacred chalice, I call for our eyes to see true and all mysteries to be revealed," Cathy added.

Moments passed as we sat in the dim light breathing deeply. Shadows danced around us; the chlorine stench obliterated the smell of the incense. The smoke from the incense gathered, coalescing into an ugly cloud of violet, red, mustard-yellow and orange light. Faint lines of dirty colour reached from the cloud to Carl's dried blood. The repulsive cloud made my stomach churn, yet there was a sense of loss and pain about it.

"Sweet Lady Bast, how could anything hurt so much?" whispered Cathy.

"Don't let it get too close. This is just an echo but look at it. It was feeding. Sucking up the energy from Carl's dying."

I held up my hand and tried to get a better read on what I was seeing. The energies retreated. "I can't get anything else. It's like it's afraid of me."

"We have to help whatever left this. It needs to go to the other side. Nothing should suffer like that, nothing," Cathy sounded distraught with an undertone of anger.

"It's dangerous, Cath. It almost killed Carl. We'll help it if we can, but clearing it has to come first." My voice was firm. I couldn't let compassion get in the way of stopping a killer.

Cathy shook her head. "Typical male! If you don't understand it, shoot it!"

"Pardon?" I felt her words sting. Cathy could be a little feminazi sometimes, but we'd reached an understanding. She wouldn't treat me like a Neanderthal thug and I wouldn't act like one.

"I'm going to open my shields to it. Let it in. See what it needs to find peace." Cathy closed her eyes and took a deep breath.

"Let me anchor you first. I–" My warning came too late. The ugly light pervading the incense cloud dove into Cathy. I didn't have time to react before she was on her feet. I ducked a roundhouse kick aimed at the side of my head. I was lucky, with Cathy's training, I shouldn't have been able to avoid her attack.

"You sick son of a bitch!" Cathy screamed at the top of her lungs, and her aura was full of violet lightning bolts.

"Ra's beak, Cath! It's me." I scrambled back, gaining some distance and my feet, which is the only thing that saved me from several broken rips as Cathy's foot brushed the front of my shirt.

"Cath, let it go. Purge. Ground, damn it. Ground!" I was begging as much as one can as they back away from a wild cat hell-bent on their destruction

"Rapist! Murderer! Abuser! Man! I will have my revenge." Cathy kept up her tirade. The only luck I had was she was fighting angry. Her body had the skills that had earned her brown belt, but her mind wasn't directing them.

I gained a bit of space and pointed my hand at her in the symbol of the sacred bull.

"By Ra's great light–" A kick to the gut pointed out why one does not generally perform banishing's on the fly. I added the force of the next kick, that connected with my side, to a dive into the deep end of the pool. Sinking to the bottom, I removed my shoes and pants before I surfaced and assumed a reverse and ready position. Cathy prowled back and forth on the deck like an angry leopard. I took a moment to shake off the blows she had landed before I put my plan into action.

"Hey, woman, you didn't finish the job. Come on, come and get me. You know you want to. Come on."

Cathy stared at me from the pool deck.

I knew the next line would cost me, but I needed to get her into the water.

"Come on, you slut."

Cathy shrieked and dove at me. I caught her shoulder with my foot pushed away and dove under. A moment later, I came up behind her.

"Where are you? Where are you?" she screamed.

I took my chance. "By Khonsu, Banisher of Demons, by the Ennead of Heliopolis, I command you be gone oh darksome force of hate."

White light gathered around my hands. I rushed in and laid them against Cathy's head. The light poured into her, driving the ugly energies out into the water, where they dissipated.

"I… haa." She gasped then went limp.

Using a vice carry, I kept her head out of the water while using the eggbeater kick to bring her to the shallow end. I wanted her in the water in case the banishing wasn't completely successful.

"Oh, Goddess," Cathy half groaned, but otherwise she was limp.

I shifted position so I could cradle her in my arms.

Her eyes fluttered open.

"Are you okay?" So, I ask stupid questions.

Cathy threw her arms around me. I held her. At that moment, I knew I could hold her forever.

"Don't let go." She pleaded. "It was awful. It just got in. It was so angry. It took over."

She pulled a little away and gently touched the place where she'd kicked my ribs.

Now that I wasn't fighting for my life, I hissed. "Gentle. That one's gonna leave a mark."

"I'm sorry. I… Are you hurt badly?" There was a pleading

note in Cathy's voice.

"It'll heal. At least we know I was right about something." I smiled at her. She needed to know that I still cared.

"What's that?"

"Aquatic defence beats Karate in the pool."

Cathy snorted, then frowned and held me again.

"Lady Bast, Ray. There was so much hate. So much rage, but so much pain with it."

"Why'd it hate me?"

Cathy pushed away and, placing her hands on my shoulders, stood on the pool bottom. She didn't take her hands away when she was done. "Not you, Ray, all men. Everything male. It wants revenge for something."

"It's gone now." I smiled at her and moved her wet hair away from her eyes.

"Only the residual it left here. It splintered when it had to pull away from Carl while he was still alive. The main part is still out there. All that pain, all that rage. It's going to kill again."

I kissed her. It seemed like the right thing to do. "I'll stop it. It's what I'm good at."

Cathy rolled her eyes. "You read too many Jim Butcher books. Seriously, if a splinter could do that to me, I'm scared what the whole thing could do."

"You opened yourself to it without waiting for me to anchor you. If your shields were up, it never would have got in," I comforted.

Cathy shook her head. "Stupid beginner's mistake. From now on, I'll let you hold the rope when I jump off a cliff. I think it was having an effect before I opened to it. I… I didn't let you help me because I didn't trust you."

"I noticed." I pushed down on a surge of pain. The trust line had teeth.

"Ray." Cathy kissed me and made it better.

"I'm okay."

"Good, there's one other thing."

"What?"

Cathy grabbed my hair and pulled it just hard enough to hurt.

"Don't ever call me a slut! You know I hate that word." She let go of my hair and kissed me hard. "Now get your pants and shoes so we can get out. I want to reward the hero of the hour."

"Sounds good." I smiled and watched a wet Cathy clamber from the pool. Some things you just have to appreciate.

I did remember to sop up some of Carl's blood with a face cloth I'd brought in my pocket before I left. I doubted the smear in the dried blood puddle would attract attention.

– Chapter 4 –

Thunderbolts and Lightning

AN HOUR OR so later, I lay on my double bed with only the dim light from my window to see by. Light flashed, revealing my dresser and the Egyptian art prints covering the walls. A peal of thunder shook the room. An Egyptian cat statue the size of a very large housecat sat on the dresser top staring at me with its amethyst eyes. Wind whipped through the window, hot and humid, but with the first promise of cooler air. Cathy padded back from the bathroom and slipped in beside me. It was still too hot to cuddle, but she lay on her side and rested her hand on my chest. I didn't have the heart to tell her that she was touching where she'd almost broken my ribs, and it hurt.

"Want to ride the storm?" she asked.

"You'll have to give me an hour to recover, Hurricane Cathy." I grinned at her.

"Getting old?" Her fingers traced patterns on my skin.

"The downside of being male."

"Wouldn't have you any other way. Besides, that's not the storm I was referring to."

"You up to it? You've had a rough night. I'd intended to after you fell asleep."

"Try to keep up." She kissed me and then settled on her back.

With her hand removed, my bruised ribs settled down.

Some people will tell you that riding a storm is a good way to get hit by lightning, but honestly, in my apartment with lightning rods on the roof, I wasn't too concerned that the energy line connecting my body to my ethereal form would be the path of least resistance.

I breathed deeply, envisioning myself floating outside the window, not as myself but as energy, consciousness. I felt the storm envelop me. Power coursed around me. Water hurtled towards the ground. I laughed as the exhilaration of nature's might made me giddy. I looked to my right and saw a glowing sphere of purple, blue, green and orange energy. It was crystalline. Little flecks marred its perfection, but in its totality, it was breathtakingly beautiful. Lightning flashed across the sky and Thor threw his hammer. Energies that caused and were formed from a thousand human ills fled or were sucked up into the torrent. The Chinese believe that lightning is the Gods' way of disposing of vampires. In Norse mythology, it was Thor's hammer, Mjolnir, striking the frost giants. This wasn't the sandstorm of the Sahara my spiritual path dreaded. This storm was cleansing. It was life, raw and all-encompassing.

Whether I named the force Horus or Thor is of little import. Energy is energy. The names were applied by humans so we could conceptualise something greater than our minds could wrap themselves around. Call someone William, Will, Bill, or Billy; they can all be the same guy. Different cultures just have different business cards for the cosmic forces. That's why a wizard-priest can affect spiritual forces outside their own stream of faith. In the end, you are dealing with something that transcends and underlies all cultural differences. The trick is always to pick the right underlying force for your desired effect.

Riding the storm, I laughed, though there was no sound, allowing the vortex of power to suck me up and then careening down with the rain. I looked to my right. Cathy's form raced beside me. We moved close together and touched. Our energies mingled. The storm joined in, its energies flooding through us. It was a perfect ménage a trios. There was only power as the lines of self vanished. After a few seconds it was too much. Humans can only touch the Godhead for so long before the sheer glory of it will burn us out. I careened away, laughing and dancing with the winds. Was I Ray, or was I Cathy or something larger than both? In time my nature would reassert itself, but, for the moment, the definitions of self fell away. I was neither and both man and woman. I was neither and both human and God. Wonder took me as I played like a dolphin in the sea. This is magic. Not the useful tricks, they are the trappings that come as a side-effect of training and practice. The ability to, the privilege of, touching the life all around. To simply be in and of the world, that is what the path of the mystic is about. Being the storm, being the beloved, simply being. The mystic who doesn't take the time to do this has missed the point.

I looked down at the earth. The ethereal is an intermediate state between the astral plane and physical manifestation. It connects them, allowing communication between the two. Not so much a plane itself as a state of flux between two planes. When I looked down, I saw the glowing lines of force that crisscrossed the city and stretched out beyond. The escarpment, with its living forest, formed a band of green and brown light. A sense intruded from my physical form, and I swept towards it. The sensation became clearer. I saw the wards around my apartment and slipped past them. I lay beside Cathy, or did I lay beside Ray. I noticed that Cathy's form held her ethereal nature and surmised I was Ray. Either way, I reached out along the golden thread that connected me to my body and made myself swallow, clearing my airway.

That brief contact pushed a mortal thought into my energy form. When you're ethereal, or astral, a thought is all it takes. Immediately, my ethereal form floated inside my temple room. The bloody facecloth sat on the altar. Tendrils of energy, some glowing dimly and fading fast, others dark and menacing, came out of the bloody cloth. I ignored the ones that glowed, knowing they represented the fading connection to Carl and ethereally touched the dark tendril. I released the psychic equivalent of a gasp. My temple room vanished.

I floated in the corner of a bar I'd never been in. It was clean enough with bad lighting. I could sense the storm outside. Various minor spirits hovered around the room on the astral and ethereal levels. When I arrived, they found a reason to be elsewhere—spiritual tapeworms looking for a host who were just smart enough not to mess when a wizard showed up unexpectedly.

On the physical level, the black vinyl covering the chairs was cracked, and there was a general air of decrepitude and desperation. A chubby, middle-aged, balding man sat at the bar. Another stood behind it wearing an apron, looking tired and bored.

"Bottoms up, Will. I want to knock off." The bartender started to put the chairs on the tables.

"They're all bitches, you know," slurred the man seated at the bar. "My Ex-wife, my bloody boss, my girlfriend. They're all out to cut 'em off, just like a dog. Sometimes I think I should do the job for 'em, then they couldn't kick me around."

The bartender sighed. "Yeah, yeah, they're an alien species. We could never figure them out in a million years. I'm calling you a cab."

As I watched, a dark energy slid into the bar. I huddled back and made myself small. Whatever this thing was, it was to the spiritual tapeworms that ran from me what a T-rex would be to a sparrow. A small house sparrow. Only once had I faced something more powerful, and then I'd barely escaped with all the help I could muster.

The energy drifted towards Will and seemed to enfold him. His aura, already weakened by the alcohol, collapsed. The energy invaded him as I kept observing. The entity seemed to boil with ethereal power. I could see lines connecting it to earthly sources, a glowing thread of violet and red energy ascended into the astral. I followed that thread, elevating my vibration onto the astral level.

The astral is shaped by thought and reflects concepts in metaphor. I saw the line of red and violet energies entering a balloon-like bubble of hardened astral force as black as ink. I reached into that bubble with my emotions and felt the energies of rage and obsession inside it. It was as close to pure hate as I've ever seen. I heard whimpering coming from the bubble.

Focusing my will, I projected joy against the hate and madness. At the same time, I allowed my perceptions to penetrate the black shell. The astral form of a teenage girl appeared out of a fog of red and violet energies. Her energy nearly matched the environment around her. I'd have mistaken her for an energy construct except that there was a tracery of blue, brown and flecks of gold that distinguished her from the background forces. She was definitely an astral spirit, imprisoned in a pocket of hellish energies with nothing but hate to feed on.

"Go away," screeched the astral girl, and then in a whisper, "Help me. I don't want to."

"I'm here to help. Let's get you out of here." No sooner had I spoken than the flow of red and violet from the ethereal level increased, forming heavy chains that bound the girl. A headless swan flew in circles around us, making the bird song/flute sound."

The girl looked up and screamed, "Go away!"

The headless swan attacked me. Its wings pummelled me, tossing me away from the girl and beyond the black shell of the bubble. I almost slammed back into my body, would have, except instead of fighting the attack, I rode it back to the ethereal level where I found myself in the bar.

"'Course I can give you a ride, sweetness. Anywhere you want to go. What's your name?" Will still sat at the bar as the ethereal energies about him pulsed.

"Maryann. Pretty name for a pretty girl." Will stood up and held out his hand to nothing physical before staggering to the bar's exit.

"Wait for the cab," called the bartender.

I collected myself, grounded the rage energy from the astral attack then followed Will. I was nearly off my storm high. Thinking logically became easier. The downside was, as I became more attached to the physical, it became harder to stay in my ethereal form. It is always a trade-off when you travel in a spirit form.

Will made his way to a beat-up old car and stopped, seeming to caress the air. Judging from how his hands moved, I'd say his mental image of Maryann had a more than ample figure.

"You're a little hotty. Let's go, and you can prove you're a natural blond."

Will fumbled his keys. I did something distasteful. I tried entering Will, pushing my energies into him in a bid to displace the ethereal thing that was casting the illusion he was experiencing.

I saw what Will saw. A beautiful, blonde, twentyish woman, whose head came up to the bottom of Will's chin. She had a body that looked like it had been designed by a frustrated teenage boy with a blimp fixation. She stood beside him, running her hands over his chest and cooing nonsensically. A moment later, there was a growling sound. It felt like a massive paw swatted me away from Will. It wasn't an attack, unless a splinter considers being pulled out an attack. As I left, I managed to get his hand to spasm so that he dropped his keys.

I floated outside Will's car as he scrambled on the pavement with rain bucketing down on him. The rain served me. I allowed it to wash away the negative energies I'd found in Will. The predator took no further notice of me. Several of the lines that ran from the ethereal form to someplace on the earth-plane pulsed with power.

From the lack of a follow-up attack, I supposed that it wasn't structured to do more than displace things that came between it and its prey. I tried to re-enter Will but was repulsed by the entity.

Drifting back, I gathered my focus.

"By Khonsu banisher of demons, by Lady Sekhmet warrior Goddess, I command thee return to thy proper plane and place."

Maryann ignored me. There was a great deal of Earth-plane energy in the thing. If I'd been in my body, I'd have sighed with resignation.

There is a home-court advantage in a spell fight. If you belong on the plane of existence you're on, the natural energies of that level of existence will aid you. I didn't have that advantage against this nasty. With ties to the physical world, I couldn't banish it because it belonged here. This was something new to me. I hate it when the ghosties and ghoulies get clever!

Will found his keys and made great show of opening and closing the passenger side door before clambering behind the wheel. To anyone watching without the Sight, opening the passenger side door would have appeared nonsensical. He kissed the air beside him and groped somewhat lower.

Clearing my mind, I moved behind Will. Passing through the car's metal was unpleasant and grounded more of my ethereal energy. I found that I had taken on a roughly human appearance. Thus far, my form was asexual, but that wasn't going to last. It was also a sign that I'd be drawn back to my physical form soon. I tried to touch Will but was blocked by a shell of energy. I tried going to the astral vibration to try and reach Will's mind via his spiritual nature. Will's spirit was panicked, but it couldn't make itself felt through the ethereal static Maryann generated as well as the flood of alcohol. I could sense the prison encapsulating Maryann's astral level like a black bubble on a tether of red and violet, tying it to the ethereal energies. When I tried to approach the bubble, the headless swan appeared, driving me back. I returned to the ethereal level in the back of Will's car

Will started the car. In seconds, he was barrelling down the street. He careened towards a bus stop's rain shelter with shadowy figures within it. Desperate, I focused all my power and slammed into the glass of the driver's side door. There was a ka-thunk sound. Will jerked around to look for the noise pulling the wheel. The car jumped the curb, missing the bus shelter and its occupants. Will pulled onto the street before returning his attention to the invisible distraction in his passenger seat. In minutes, we were on Highway 403, careening along at nearly twice the limit with rain pummelling down and a drunk driver who thought he had a woman half his age and twice his class doing things you shouldn't do when you are driving in the first place.

I kept trying to break through to him but couldn't.

The temperature dropped.

I could hear Maryann's voice. It was harsh, cruel, venomous. "You let them all down. Your kids hate you because you're a loser. Your father thought you were a joke; that's why he sent you to boarding school. The older boys knew you were really a girl. They treated you right. You're nothing. No woman stays with you because you aren't worth staying with. You abuse everyone. You supported Afghanistan; no woman would support a war. You're a killer. A monster. Your boss knows how useless you are. She's better than you'll ever be. Any woman is better than you'll ever be, you drunk. The world is better off without you."

I couldn't stop it, and now the energy had noticed me. My ethereal body had almost mimicked my physical form. A sense of anger and hostility permeated the entity, but also hunger. It was about to feed. At least I knew how it became so powerful on the ethereal, but who anchored it? I was about to follow the energy trails that lead from it when Will floored the gas. The old car shook and rattled.

"You know what you have to do," spat Maryann's voice. The car shot off the road, over the ditch towards a tree. I let my ethereal form return to my body. There was nothing I could do, and I had a feeling that I would be next on the menu if I stayed.

I slammed back into my body. Cathy was gone. She didn't like sleeping at my place. Safe, my apartment's wards would keep the entity from following me, but alone to face my failure. I knew that the next day's news would report a story about a drunk driving fatality on the 403.

I told myself that I did all I could. I tried not to think of my greatest failure and failed at that. At times like these, my thoughts inevitably strayed to a brave man, his hair almost grey with a powerful body carrying a few extra pounds battling a beast of nightmare. I tried not to remember a final desperate spell by that champion. A spell that saved me. I tried not to think of the casket where they displayed my Grandfather's corpse, supposedly felled by a stroke. I tried not to remember that other time I did all I could, and it wasn't enough. I told myself I was only twelve, just a kid. My father should have been there, but it didn't help. It never did. The only thing that helped was the rage. The driving determination that it wouldn't happen again. A simple resolve that I would stand and somehow keep it from happening again. Victory brought peace. I knew at that moment I was on the hunt. With that realisation, exhaustion coupled with the cooler air allowed me to sleep.

— Chapter 5 —

It Lives In Us All

I AWOKE THE next morning to my landline's ring and picked up the receiver before the answering machine. Yes, the machine, I don't trust any corporation enough to hold my messages. Tracey, the Lifeguard one from Valley Park pool, was sick, read hung-over. They needed me to sub. Racing through my routine, I managed to get out the door and to the pool only ten minutes late. Lifeguarding, if you do it right, is hard work. Your eyes are constantly scanning; you're listening for what people say around you and for cries for help. If you're good, you don't do a lot of rescues because you prevent them. You hear the kids daring each other to go in the deep end and stop it before there is a problem. You see the old, fat guy going red in the face and quietly suggest he slow down before he has a heart attack.

Tracey's team did a lot of rescues, if they noticed that one needed to be done. Every time I turned my back, it was something. Guards reading on pool deck. Guarding with ear-buds and music blaring. Chatting up a patron instead of watching the pool. The list goes on. In a single day, they came to hate me and I them. Tracey's hand showed in her crew. I got home exhausted and just didn't have it in me to research. Cathy was at work and wouldn't be back until after bar closing. It was even odds that she'd be occupied with some 'friend' even then. I tried not to think about it. I collapsed in front of the TV with a Lean Cuisine and a bottle of beer.

The news reported the crash.

The next morning, there were no work calls, so I began my search. The internet was as useful as it normally is.

I started checking the word Kerbä Tikkari and got nothing. A few moments thought later, I started trying alternative spellings. Nothing. Repeating the word aloud, it sounded North American First Peoples to me. Again nothing. On a whim, I tried it putting on various bad accents. Scandinavian almost fit. Given its context, I guessed the word was an insult. Skimming several sites about various Northern European insults, I found Kyrpäyrjö. It was Finnish, and let's just say it was a less than polite way of saying ejaculate.

I moved on to checking up on suicide. Turns out that twice as many people in Hamilton committed suicide as died of traffic deaths and that suicide was grossly underreported. In other words, a dead-end, pardon the pun. Will's death would be recorded as drunk driving. How many swimming accidents weren't accidents? How many accidental overdoses were intentional? I realised there was an epidemic, but it didn't help with my hunt.

I tried checking the Hamilton obituaries, but there were too many, and I realised that this thing's hunting ground might not be restricted to the local area. Then again, people were creatures of habit. While this thing, whatever it was, wasn't human, it did have traits in common. It needed to feed to maintain its cohesiveness. I figured it used its victims' energies. Otherwise, it would drain the beings on the other end of the lines coming off it. That meant it had to hunt, and most predators had preferred hunting grounds.

Using the phone, I kept by my computer, I called Carl in the hospital.

"Hello." The voice on the line was solid and even.

I made my tone light. "Hey Carl, it's Ray. I wanted to see

how you were doing?"

Sekmara entered the room and, stretching up, sunk her claws into my thigh. I pushed back the office chair I sat on to make room for her. She leapt into my lap, butting the hand holding the phone. I started petting her. Purring, she settled.

"Better. Be glad to get out of here. They put a nurse on me that looks like Godzilla in drag." Carl sounded annoyed.

I ignored the fact that Godzilla was female, or at the least a hermaphrodite. My best girl proceeded to leave little red pinholes in the flesh of my legs. "I'm just curious which bar did you meet Maryann in?"

"It was the *Hungry Fox*. Wanted a sure thing and didn't want to have to work for it. You know what it's like." Carl's tone was almost brothers in arms.

"Right," I fought to keep my voice non-committal. I did mention that Carl was a sleaze. To be fair, he was a decent boss and kept it in his pants at work. People are rarely black and white.

"Man, just call Cat, you lucky pup. That woman is smoking. She ever dance for you?" Carl's voice implied that he wanted a story that would probably start with, 'I never believed the stories in your magazine until...'

I couldn't help it. I flashed back to my last birthday and smiled. And no, I won't give you details. "Cathy and I are complicated."

"Is she as good as advertised? I mean like, man."

I realised two things. One, that Carl was psychically recovered from his ordeal. Two, it had taught him nothing! "I'm glad you're feeling better. I'll keep an eye out for Maryann."

Sekmara shifted on my lap, picking a new section of thigh to knead. I scratched around her neck.

"Now that's another walking wet dream. I'd love to—"

"Goodbye, Carl." I hung up the phone. "Will he ever stop giving hetero guys a bad name?"

Sekmara stopped kneading, looked me straight in the eye and said, "Meow."

I smiled at her. "It was a rhetorical question."

My best girl went back to kneading the skin of my thigh.

Carl had given me a lead. The Hungry Fox was the likely hunting ground. But when? I wasn't into the bar scene, so staking it out would be a chore. Also, I wanted backup for that kind of on-the-ground work. Backup that could mystically take care of themselves and was preferably female, so that the creature would ignore them. Cathy was working the next few nights, and I really didn't like involving her any further than I had. Before, I hadn't known how powerful this thing was; now I did. I couldn't be sure she would be safe. I'm a condescending control freak with an aversion to putting people I love in harm's way. I've been told before!

I was stuck. The hamster on the wheel in my head kept running, getting nowhere.

Moving to my temple room, I checked the face cloth. The energy lines from it had snapped with my foe's last feeding. The phone rang. I went to the office side of my spare room to pick it up.

"Hello."

"Ray, it's Cathy."

"Hi, Cath. I—"

"I need to run. Feed Pakhetel for me. I'm going to be out of town for about a week."

"What? Sure, where?"

"I'm checking out some of the Toronto clubs. Shawn is putting me up, and he's got us invites to help with a booth at Fan Expo. I get to go free. Isn't that great? Thanks for looking after my cat. I've gotta go. Bye."

Click.

I hung up the phone.

"What happened to Fan Expo is too expensive for us to go?" I mentally pictured Shawn. He was tall and lean and taught at Cathy's dojo. A good-looking man, if you like guitar strings for muscle and more hair than an alpaca. I shook my head, swallowed my ire and convinced myself that hitting the wall was a bad idea. Retiring to my living room, I turned on the TV with the built-in power switch then slumped onto my couch.

The screen slowly came to life. A severely dressed woman with her hair in a harsh, unflattering style glowered out of the screen at me. "And we all know that domestic violence is just a euphemism for male violence."

I raced to find the remote and change the channel before my blood boiled. My father never hit my mother. Our issues aside, he deserved credit for that because the opposite wasn't true. Anything up to and including fireplace pokers had been used as weapons during her tirades. Since reaching adulthood, I'd prayed that he'd leave my mother.

I felt my anger mount as the silly twit on the tube prattled on about the evils of my gender, denying statistics, common sense and any sense of fairness. By the time I changed the channel, my buttons had been thoroughly pushed. How often do you tell a little boy that he is evil, guilty of all the worlds ills, responsible for every war, every murder, even if a woman committed it because a man must have pushed her to it? For how many years do you do that and not expect it to have an effect? After a while, that boy gets a belly full and decides that if he has the name, he may as well play the game, or, with the help of older evolved males, learns to refuse delivery of the lies, avoiding the hate mongers and their bigoted poison. He seeks out the truth that turns out to be there are good and bad people of both genders, and men and women are far more alike than not. He uses that truth as a shield and strives to reflect the positive masculinity demonstrated by the older evolved males recognising the false programming of man-haters for what it is.

The latest incidence of Cathy's use-me-when-convenient-and-toss-me-aside-when-she-wanted relationship made it hard to take the high road at that moment. Going to Fan Expo had been my suggestion. She'd talked about it, and while it wasn't really my thing, I didn't hate the idea. I knew it was something Cathy would love. It tied into other simmering resentments, like how I was sick of my sister and the self-serving way she used my parents when she wanted something from them, then vanished when she didn't. The way TV shows perpetually showed men as fools incapable of doing anything right without female supervision, and then social media, with its seeming inability to recognise the word 'some'. Say some men are abusive and you have an ally, say all men are abusive, and you are lying, and no, it is not implied that you are referring to a subset. It is not implied when making a statement about any other group, so why say men are too sensitive when we challenge a lie? Women, at that moment, I was sick and tired of the lot of them.

I pushed down on the thought. I'm a wizard, not a God. I have a full complement of human weakness and could be as much a bigot as anyone. Sometimes one slips off the high road. I'd trained myself to watch for catchphrases to stop the thoughts that made me less the being I strive to be. I took a deep breath.

Whenever you judge the individual based on the group's actions, you've become a bigot. Focusing my will inward, I turned back to the channel with the narrow-minded fool that spewed nonsense. Sadly, it was nonsense that had a ready audience. If all men are potential rapists, so are all women, because some women rape. History shows that women have the fortitude to go to war and can be more vicious than men. I listened to the fool's rant and deconstructed each argument. Sadly, no one on-screen did the same. It was obvious she hated my gender and would embrace any slander against us. That kind of hate ran deep, it was powerful, and I had to wonder what its seed was. Abuse, rape, both, or just a need to feel superior to someone. Vengeance and or ego. In the end, it was all hate, and I refused to let myself be a party to it on either end of the spectrum.

I kept watching as the 'documentary' put forward half-truths and outright lies coupled with an inaccurate and biased rendition of history.

It hit me while they were discussing the suffragette movement; ignoring the men that stood beside their sisters, wives and daughters in the fight to get the vote, that the venom the woman spewed had a familiar taste. The rage of my foe that I saw reflected in Cathy, the hate I felt towards myself. The male sleaziness of the targets and the way it ignored my ethereal form until I started taking on a male aspect.

"Men are the target; I already knew that, but what is the motivation," I muttered to myself as I shut off the TV. I hadn't focused on motive before. If I could understand the thing, maybe I could predict its actions. The ethereal aspect was overwhelming the astral with a steady diet of rage and madness. Still, motive normally took thought, and that was an astral force. At the least, some aspect of astral Maryann wanted men to die. It was a deep-seated emotion that the other lines into the beast could exploit by feeding it, so it eclipsed all other aspects of the personality.

The astral form was a prisoner in the dark pocket around Maryann. And to give it a physical allegory, her jailers were feeding food, air and water laced with the bath salts drug and PCP.

Why have an astral element at all? Flesh rots. As it decays, even the remnant of an ethereal pattern will break down. The astral had permanence. It was being used to refresh the pattern, like repeatedly photocopying from an original instead of making a copy of a copy of a copy.

The ethereal thing wasn't just killing men for food. It hated men. The energy lines linking it to the earth strongly implied a magical construct. It would have been programmed to hate men during its construction, and there was no doubt in that program. To do it, there had to be an element in the astral form for the hate to latch onto and a high degree of certainty on the part of the humans who did the spell work. The kind of certainty the thing displayed was rare in anybody.

Sekmara jumped onto the couch and nuzzled my hand. I absently petted her and looked at my cat. She lived with a being that could destroy her with ease or withhold the very necessities of life. She thrived or failed on my whim, yet she was fearless. She knew she had nothing to fear, so she gave and received love. "It fears men. Its hate is motivated by its fear. Its desire, aside from feeding, is vengeance. But vengeance for what?"

I stopped thinking of the thing as a creature and tried to put myself in its place. How would I make something like Maryann? How *could* I make something like Maryann?

"Rage, Mars, but Mars is too masculine a force for this construct. Sekhmet?" I muttered. Sekmara shot me a dirty look and stopped purring.

"I'm just thinking. She does fit with the rage, but I know she's no misandrist."

Sekmara started purring again and let me pet her. I tried to put together the pieces of a spell that could create an artificial elemental as powerful and perverse as what I'd encountered. I thought of the energies that could be tapped into. I considered Lilith, of the Mesopotamian mythic heritage, but she was driven by self-determination, not hate. The pattern of fear and hate, the hurt in the creature, was too raw for any archetype I knew of. I'm usually good with figuring out how to make spells work. How to shape energies to a purpose, even if the execution is beyond me, but this was too complex, the structure of the creature beyond what a human mind should be able to fathom. A good allegory would be like assembling a person out of amino acids without a blueprint.

Of course, they had a blueprint, the astral spirit. So, cloning was a better analogy, but it was still an incredible feat. Something about the spell eluded me, but now I had a starting point. The living anchors were, most likely, women. If one was a man, I would have pitied him to have such self-loathing. Women who had skill in the Art and a desire for vengeance against men that belied all reason.

I thought back to my foe. The lines binding it to the earth were strong, four of them too strong to be over a vast distance. So, there you had it, four mystically inclined women in the Hamilton area. The haystack shrank but became largely invisible. I didn't exactly have a standing invitation to the woman only groups, and Cathy had made no effort to befriend them. My head was starting to hurt, so I went to bed.

I pulled doubles at Victoria Park Pool for the next three days. The flu was going around, and half the city's lifeguard ones were down with it. Good crew, nice pool. It took a bad taste out of my mouth. On the fourth day, I worked only a half-day, leaving barely enough time to drive home and change into a dressy golf shirt and a pair of light slacks. The temperature was up again, but my preferred dress of a swimsuit just wasn't appropriate for a funeral.

I reached Woodlawn Cemetery and moved to the outskirts of the little group of people gathered about the grave of William Harris. An athletic middle-aged woman fidgeted and kept glancing at her watch. Two teenagers, a boy and a girl, stood side by side in dark clothing. The girl resembled how Maryann had manifested to Will, only less busty. The girl started to weep, and the boy hugged her. A chunky, middle-aged woman dressed in black moved to embrace the boy and the girl. If I took my memory of Maryann, added fifty pounds, a few imperfections, and twenty-five years, it would fit with the middle-aged woman.

"Everybody's got a type," Cathy's words echoed in my ears.

I stroked my chin as a thirty-something woman walked up to the woman and teens and said something. The newcomer looked like a cross between the teenage girl and the older woman. The older woman nodded and extended her hand. The woman shook it as they both wept.

There were a couple of other people at the funeral, but, all in all, the turnout was small. A pot had been set up to make donations to Mother's Against Drunk Driving instead of flowers. The hole in the ground looked barren.

A petite, old lady leaning on a walker beckoned me closer.

"Did you know my Willy?" she asked when I stood beside her.

"We met. I just thought I should pay my respects."

A trembling hand with skin like thin parchment touched

my bicep. "Thank you, that is very kind. He wasn't a bad man, you know. He just never found his place in the world."

"That's unfortunate." I sighed inside. I hate funerals. Whether the elderly can sense mediums because they are close to death and instinctively want to clear a path for future communication, or I just remind older folk of their favourite grandson, it always seems to happen to me. An elderly person would latch onto me and tell me their life's story. It would be sweet, except it is so irritating. Still, when someone is hurting, what can you do?

The funeral progressed, and I stood beside Will's mother. I did feel for her. I think she imagined she was standing with her Willy twenty years younger, with his life still ahead of him and hope for the future. Perhaps it brought her peace to recall a time when he wasn't broken.

On the strength of Will's mother's association, I met the family by the grave. The chunky blond was the ex-wife, the teens his kids, and the thirty-something the girlfriend. The woman with the watch was the boss. She left as soon as the dirt hit the coffin. The family all talked about Will in glowing terms. I had to wonder if he would have been so susceptible to the creature if they'd taken the time to say some of those things when he was still around to hear them.

I scanned the area around the grave for psychic links. There were none. Will had been drained dry. I visually searched the little group of mourners before scanning the area around the grave. A dark-skinned woman dressed in jeans and a blue T-shirt stood with a huge dog watching the funeral. I'd have looked at her twice anyway. She had the near-perfect proportions that have made some actresses a fortune. I'm not dead. I won't apologize for it, but something about her seemed off.

I slipped free of William's mother, leaving her with her grandchildren so they could truly morn. I managed to cross the distance to the woman without looking too conspicuous. Her dog seemed to get bigger as I approached. It probably weighed as much as I did and wasn't fat. Irish wolfhounds are, as a rule, friendly, playful, smart and intimidating as hell! The dog eyed me with suspicion.

Hello, child of Anubis. I am a friend to you and your person. I held the thought in my mind and visualized an image of me politely standing by the woman and petting the dog.

The dog continued to stare at me as I moved to the woman's side. "Were you a friend of Will's?" I asked.

The woman seemed to shake off a reverie and glowered at me. Her expression marred a truly beautiful face blending the best of African and European features. Her large, brown eyes smouldered with hate. She wore silver pentagram earrings, and her hair was curly and black as coal. Her perfume put me in mind of fresh-baked cookies.

"You always try to pick up women at funerals?" she snapped. I felt an empathic push against my shields. The dog growled and took a half-step towards me.

"You take a lot for granted from a polite introduction." I stood my ground. Never run from a predator, they see you as prey. I locked eyes with the dog. If I had to, I'd hurt it to ensure my safety, but I wanted to avoid that for two reasons. One, I like dogs, and two, rover was all claws and teeth. In a fight, attitude only goes so far.

"Stand down, child of Anubis." I kept my voice even and mentally envisioned my panther astral form. It wasn't an attack exactly, but a warning that the human was more than it might seem.

The dog stepped back, confused.

I pushed with my will and softly commanded. "Sit."

The dog sat with a surprised look on its face.

The woman startled and glared at me. Most men would be running for the hills by now. Her empathic push had been credible enough, for the bush leagues. Coupled with the dog's aggression, no one could fault any sane person for making themselves scarce. My shield had shrugged off the empathic push. As to my sanity, I was dating one of the most potent sorceresses in Canada, and I hunted monsters. I have no illusions as to my mental health.

"I…" She stumbled for words.

"Let's start again. I'm Ray, Ray McAndrues." Taking a little breath, I drew on my heart chakra and sent the energy to my hand, which I extended fingers folded to the dog. "I like your dog."

The wolfhound sniffed my fingers and tentatively licked my knuckles. I slowly moved to rub behind the ears of the enormous head. The dog's tail thumped as I poured more golden energy into my hand.

The woman looked at my hand. To someone without the sight, it would have just been someone petting her dog. To someone with the sight, the hand, and area being petted, glowed with golden light. She blinked, seemed to squint, then took a half step back and bit her lip. For the dog's part, she was thrilled to have made a new friend and panted happily.

"I'm not a friend of the deceased. I was visiting my sister and stopped to watch." The woman looked towards a nearby tombstone as she spoke. A pentagram had been carved into the rock.

"I'm sorry for your loss. Blessed be." I dipped my head and cautiously moved away from the woman and her dog.

Almost by reflex, the woman muttered, "Blessed be." That confirmed what I suspected. All groups have their ways, catchphrases, secret handshakes, identifiers that say, 'I'm in the in-crowd.' The mystery woman followed a mystic path, probably Pagan, most likely Wiccan.

With a concerned glance, she led the dog away. My new friend glanced back, gave a woof, and followed her Alpha. Blinking, I dialled up my second sight and saw the lines of force connecting woman to dog.

"Definitely a familiar," I muttered. I started walking towards the parking lot. I could feel the woman's eyes on me as I skirted around Will's funeral. Having only met the man as an ethereal form, it saddened me that I was the fourth to leave the funeral.

Chapter 6

Seeing Double

B Y THE TIME I got home, my shirt was sweat-soaked. Changing into my shorts helped a little, and then I went upstairs to feed Pakhetel. I figured she was going completely scatty from the thumping sounds coming through my ceiling. When I unlocked the door, I was surprised to find Cathy dressed in a t-shirt and track pants pounding on a sparing pole in the middle of her living room.

"Knock often?" she spat as she landed a savage round-house kick on the pole.

"Umm… Here to feed the cat." I involuntarily touched my sore ribs.

"Right." She punched into the post with all the power in her body. I was stronger than Cathy, she was more focused. At a physical level, I was trained to save lives; he was trained to kick ass.

"I can leave." I inched towards the door.

Cathy froze, looking at me. "I hate men!"

"Okay? Not something I have any intention of changing about myself."

"You ever cheat on a girlfriend. I mean, really cheat, where you told her one thing and did another?" Cathy eyed me. She knew the answer but evidently needed to hear it.

"Not really. I haven't always volunteered information, but never if things were getting serious."

"You're one of the few." She belted the pole, denting the rubber pad on its surface.

"What happened?"

"Shawn went back to his wife. He swore they were through, but all this time, he's been bouncing from my bed to hers." Cathy aimed a spinning kick onto the pole that could have ripped a man in half.

"Oh. But you weren't exclusive?"

"Oh, sure. He was all open, except it was his wife, and she didn't know about me." Cathy aimed a kick punch combination against the pole, and then half fell onto her couch. I moved to the end of her living room but didn't approach further. Facing an Irish wolfhound is far safer than dealing with a pissed-off redhead. I speak from experience.

"Goddess, Ray. You know my rule, honesty. Poly isn't cheating because it's honest. I should have known something was wrong, but Shawn just seemed so… I don't know. When he told me his marriage was over, we were on the phone. I couldn't see his aura. I was careless."

"You can't have your guard up all the time." I tried to send soothing energies into the convulsing mass of Cathy's aura. It didn't do any good. "Did you tell the wife that you were…"

"No. I'm pissed at Shawn, but I don't want to mess things up for him. I'll let him do that for himself. I never would have found out except she came to the booth to surprise him." Cathy stared at the floor as if she was going to sink into it.

I swallowed hard. I'd had similar, the only difference being Cathy never promised monogamy. Better to be hurt honestly than deceived.

"When he saw her, he treated me like kryptonite. I just handed in my pass and left. I didn't know what else to do. I feel like a home-wrecker. I'm just like Walter with my mum. At least Shawn doesn't have kids." Cathy shook her head and wrung her hands. This one was hitting her hard.

"He lied to you, Cath. All you're guilty of is trusting a creep." I took a step closer.

"But… I thought… well. Shawn wasn't just fun. He, well, he was like you, only less insecure. Someone I could really care about. At least I thought he was."

That sent an icy spear through me. I put up with Cathy's open relationship crap, but it wasn't insecurity that made me want monogamy. Then to find out that someone else was taking a place in her heart. It was a kind of betrayal. I didn't like drawing a line between sex and love. I could do it, but it never fit well. This was what scared me about open relationships, the potential area where the lines get blurred.

I thought of storming out. I thought of yelling at her. Telling her how fucked up she was, or being snide and mean, hurting her back. In the end, she was hurting, and I loved her, so I swallowed my own pain and listened. Later, I lay chaste beside her in her bed as she fell asleep.

Then I went for a walk, a long walk so no one could see how the moonlight stung my eyes and made them water. A man does what he must, but we're still human.

Sekmara thumped her tail on my face.

"What?" I said groggily.

Thump, thump-thump. Purrr purr purr.

"Do you want breakfast?" I rolled over in my bed and looked at the clock. 7:30AM.My normal wake up time.

"You could have let me sleep in."

Purr purr purr.

I rolled to a sitting position on the edge of my bed as the clock radio clicked on.

"From a halfway house in Hamilton's east end, police are saying that Jeffrey Johnson should be considered a dangerous sexual predator with a high risk of re-offending."

I released a sigh. "Is it wrong that I want to hang a dinner bell around this guy's neck and take the day off?"

Sekmara cleaned her whiskers.

The phone ringing pulled me out of the shower. It was Cathy checking to see if I'd been called in for a shift. A half-hour later, we sat on my couch, not talking about the elephant in the room. The last day's events stirred up a lot of issues for Cathy. I wanted to care, I wanted to support her, but I was almost happy that she was hurt for a change.

We chatted about anything but her relationships. I warned her about Jeffrey Johnson. It's a dangerous world, and sometimes being a little more on guard, particularly in Cathy's profession, was a good idea. Hours later, we parted ways. I gave my father his obligatory phone call then did the grocery shopping. The next day was my regular day off. I'd promised to drive down to my parents for a visit.

As usual, I came to regret my promise. My mother had arranged for her friend's recently divorced daughter to be there. The woman was obsessed with reality TV and thought science fiction was silly and didn't read. Parents!

That evening I hit the books before doing a divination. I started with the tarot, asking simply when and where Maryann would hunt again.

I shuffled the deck and pulled a card. The Moon: things creeping from the depths, the subconscious, but also more literally the moon. I got up and checked the calendar. Sure enough, Carl's attack had been on a lunar quarter. I couldn't be sure, but the moon is potent in magic and is a powerful female aspect in most cultures. It just might govern my foe's actions in some way. My gut told me that the next lunar quarter would be the time to hunt.

Why did Maryann hunt so quickly after her attack on Carl? I pulled the lightning struck Tower: plans disrupted; a break in the expected. I'd interrupted her feeding, so she'd not gone dormant. It made sense. If I missed dinner, I'd have a sandwich before bed to stave off the rumbles.

Where will Maryann hunt? The next card I flipped was the Four of Pentacles. A card of home and hearth. A card of the familiar. I was betting the *Hungry Fox*.

Seven days after the attack on Carl, Cathy and I hooked up, ready for the hunt. She wore a pale blue sundress that showed off her subtle curves. I wore a blue golf shirt and slacks. Looking at her, I wished we were really going on a date. We drove to the *Hungry Fox* and stopped in the parking lot of the decrepit looking bar.

I reached for the door handle, but Cath grabbed my shoulder.

"Ray, the idea is that you'll play bait, and we'll split up and both watch for the big bad, right?" Cathy looked me over with a serious expression.

"That's the plan."

"Then you better do something. You look about as bate-like as a great white. Your shields could stop photon torpedoes."

"Original or Next Generation?" I chuckled. You can't take the geek out of the girl. Closing my eyes and breathing deeply, I backed off the energy flowing around my body and partially activated my base chakra. I dropped it back to what I thought of my standard running shield

"Better. I like how you added orange to the aura. It makes you look more like a sleaze-ball. You need to go further. You still look like a tank."

"So long as you know the truth about the sleaze-ball thing. Keep an eye on me. I don't like taking off the armour."

"Do it in plate mail." Cathy smiled at me.

"Horrible movie. The knights should have been in woad or ox hide depending on if they were Celtic or Roman influence. I was reading an article…"

Cathy stared at me, sighed and shook her head.

"Right." I tapered further back on my shields. "Better?"

Cathy looked at me critically. "That will do, and boy, it does not suit you. We should go. If you get lucky, remember, wearing your rubbers can prevent colds and other nasty diseases."

"In this place?" I scanned the exterior of the rundown bar.

"I know your history, so don't you go telling me about you and big cats." Cathy fished an obsidian pendant out of her shirt and let it dangle in plain view over her dress.

I blushed. So, I've been known to date older women. It's not like her mom got to me first. "Let's go. I'm glad you brought the obsidian."

"One of us needs to be loaded for bear."

That expression seemed significant, but it wasn't the time to explore it. We exited my Hyundai Accent and walked over the asphalt to the bar's entrance.

Inside the bar, I moved to the chipped and grubby counter. The music was too loud, and the crowd mostly in their forties or up. Or at least they looked it. I perched on a cracking barstool and ordered a beer. Scanning the place, I couldn't see anything.

Cathy entered and was approached by a fifty-something man in a business suit before she could order a drink.

The life of the bar flowed around me. When I felt the aura of the place, it spoke of desperation, loneliness, and regret. The place was every mid-life crisis you could imagine rolled into one. If the bar was a man, it would be getting hair plugs and going into debt to buy a convertible.

"Hi, I haven't seen you here before." The raspy voice intruded into my thoughts.

"I… No, this is my first time." I turned to see a slightly overweight forty-something woman with dark brown hair and lovely green eyes standing beside me.

"It's normally busier than this. I'm Molly. My friends and I were wondering if you'd like to join us?"

I looked at the table she indicated. Three other middle-aged women sat at it all done to the nines. I shifted a little uncomfortably and smiled. "Thanks, but I am waiting for someone."

"Your loss." Molly went back to her friends.

"This isn't working. We should go." Cathy's voice came

from behind me. I turned to look into her eyes.

"Maybe a few more minutes. It isn't that late." I scanned the bar but had to agree. The 'sting' wasn't working.

Cathy looked at the floor. "I really need to talk with you. I..." She looked up. There were tears in her eyes.

"What's wrong?" I took her hand.

"Not here. Let's go to your place."

I let her lead me from the bar. Moments later, I pulled out of the parking lot. I thought I heard something, but over the sound of my rust bucket's loose muffler, I couldn't be sure.

"You sure you're okay?" I tried to get Cathy talking.

"I...I love you."

I was so startled I nearly missed my turn. My heart sped up. After all this time, was she about to meet me halfway?

"Cath, I'm so glad you said it. I love you too. But..."

Cathy traced her fingers over my shoulders and chest and reached lower. "I want you, only you."

I pulled into our building parking lot and stopped the car. I kissed her, and her hands were everywhere.

"Let's go." My voice cracked, and I swallowed hard to clear my throat. "Let's go in."

"Your place. I'm all yours," Cathy's voice was like warm honey.

Getting to the elevator and up to my floor was a blur. I'd known Cathy to be passionate, but this was beyond. My blood thundered in my ears, and I felt feverish. A small voice in the back of my head screamed a warning, but the rest of me wasn't listing. I was finally getting what I'd wanted for years. Cathy committed to me. Not just sex, but the whole package. I couldn't think. I desired her more than anything I'd ever known. Her lip-gloss tasted like strawberries. I wanted to devour her mouth. I unlocked my apartment door as her hands stroked over me and reached to undo my belt.

I entered my apartment. Cathy looked at me from the hall.

"What's wrong?" My pulse raced.

"Enjoying the view," flirted Cathy.

"Come in; I'll show you the rest."Cathy was inside my

apartment before I could realise my mistake. A home is a kind of sacred place. Add to that the wards that surrounded my apartment, not much got in without an invitation. The door closed behind me. Cathy pushed me towards the living room.

"You don't know what it means to me that you've agreed to commit," I whispered between kisses.

Cathy pulled away, her demeanour changing. Her beautiful features pulled into a glare of hate and disdain. My neighbours must have been cooking cabbage because the aroma filled the room.

"Fool, idiot, your mother should have cut it off. It would have saved any woman from having to bother with you," she snarled.

My mind was fuzzy. I could feel my higher-self screaming, but my emotions were a jumble. A clear part of me could see the danger, but it wasn't the part that could shield or banish.

"Cathy." I felt a sword of fire and ice cutting through my heart.

"I could never love you. You're not good enough for any woman. No woman could love you. No one could love you. You're not worthy. You're useless."

The thing that looked like Cathy poked over my heart, sending a searing bolt of dark energy into my chest. I tried to ground the attack. It only took the edge off it. The thing was inside my shields, playing with my doubts. Calling forth all the dark thoughts that plagued me on a sleepless night. Making the half-truths and outright lies we all tell ourselves in our weakest moments manifest. She made me hate my useless self. Unable to save my grandfather. Unable to earn Cathy's devotion. Unable to save my father from my abusive mother. A failure, a joke of a man. I began to sob.

"Women use you, and you deserve it. You're a convenience. You are nothing, a mewling puppy, a fraud, a sad joke. Your life is not worth living. You're a loser, a nothing. You should end it. Put us all out of your misery. Your existence is a mockery. You're an abuser, a rapist. Every time you touch a woman, it is abuse. You are evil! End it. Put yourself out of all our miseries."

My higher-self screamed inside my head, able to watch the body and mortal mind, but unable to influence anything. I walked to the sliding glass door of my fifth story balcony, slid it open, and stepped onto the platform. A moment later, I had one leg over the balcony railing. Some trace of the animal-self caused me to pause. Call it self-preservation. My primal will to live fought against the overwhelming wash of emotion as I teetered on the railing.

"It's the only way, you stupid, stupid boy," hissed the thing attacking me.

The beast had overplayed its hand. "Stupid!"

We all have things so hurtful and so deeply ingrained that they reach across all levels of our consciousness. "Stupid?" I shouted.

I had a stutter as a child. I grew out of it, but for years, teachers berated me because it made it hard for me to express myself. One had called me a "stupid, stupid boy." My Mother's casual cruelty every time I fell short of her view of perfection. The teasing and cruelty of the other children. It all combined to form a white-hot rage.

"I'm not stupid!" I bellowed as that rage burnt against the darksome energy of my foe. I wasn't yet in charge of my emotions, but neither was she. I teetered on my balcony railing, now leaning towards the safety of my apartment as the beast in Cathy's form backed away.

"You're useless. You're a rotten lay." The beast pressed its attack.

I heard my apartment door slam open, and Cathy raced into my living room. She was out of breath, and her pale skin was tinted red from exertion. The look of rage on her face would have made an Airborne Division Special Forces vet wet himself.

Lifting her hand in the symbol of the sacred bull, she pointed it at the false Cathy. "By Horus the warrior, by Bast healer of the mind, by all the sons and daughters of Atum's line, I banish thee back to the plane from whence thou came never to return. So mote it be!"

The energy in that banishing could have dropped an elephant. The problem was the creature had a tie to the earth plane. The force staggered it, but it couldn't be banished from where it belonged. Still in all, the energy blast forced the creature to give up the Cathy illusion.

With my spirit vision, I now saw the pretty, slender girl of maybe fifteen who'd been imprisoned in the astral bubble standing where the beast was. Here she was not composed of violet and red light. She had a dark completion indicating an African ancestry. There were tears in her large, brown eyes and an air of despair and desperation.

"They have to pay. Rapist. Abusers. Defilers. Betrayer. Men must pay," wailed the spirit.

Cathy stepped back as a wall of ethereal force slammed into her shield. She clutched at the obsidian around her neck as a portion of the energy disappeared into the rock, but it was like trying to bail out a ship with a thimble. My mind slowly cleared, but I could still do little more than lean towards my apartment door and away from the drop.

Cathy's shields were failing under the assault. I needed time. Precious seconds to regain my strength, but Cathy could only buy me so much. The sound of a hiss and a merrow that was a battle cry to set a thousand rodents to flight split the air. Sekmara streaked in from the hallway, leapt and sailed through the form of the ethereal, young woman. My cat hit the wall feet first and, without going to ground, pushed off again, sailing through her enemy to land on my couch and turn, fur on end, hissing at her foe. The beast staggered back from the force of having that much spirit and passion pass through it.

I raised a trembling hand and focused my will. "By Ra the All-father, By Isis Goddess of all sorcery, by Thoth, record keeper, God of Wizardry, I command thee, be gone from my home. All invitations, actual or implied, be revoked. By the Ennead of Heliopolis, I command thee, be gone!"

Gold, blue and purple light flowed from my fingers. The

ethereal image of the girl flickered.

Cathy straightened where she stood and raised her hand in a gesture of dismissal. "As she who stands as mistress of this home, I command thee to leave and never enter these premises again. All invitations, actual or implied, are revoked. By the Goddesses all, so mote it be."

The image of the girl clutched its hair and screeched, and then flew past me to dive off the balcony and vanish. The bird song flute sound echoed through the night.

A moment later, Cathy grasped my shoulder. "Come in, Ray."

I slid onto my balcony and let her lead me to sit on my couch. Sekmara climbed into my lap and head-butted me before she curled on my lap.

"Ray?" Cathy's voice was full of concern as she sat beside me.

"I'm… I'll be alright. I just need a few minutes."

"What happened? I ducked into the ladies' room to ditch a sleaze-ball who thinks he's Casanova. When I came out, you were gone. By the time I made it to the parking lot, all I could see was taillights. By the way, you owe me for a cab home."

"I'm good for it. Cath… I know what it does now. It feeds on despair. All your fears and doubts. Oh Gods, Cath, it's really you, right?"

"How many other redheads walk into your apartment and save your ass?" Cathy sounded almost teasing.

I smiled for a second, but I needed to hear the words. "You don't think I'm useless and a failure, do you?"

Cathy hugged me. "I don't sleep with losers. Trust me. It's your body I'm after. The rest is icing."

"It's gotta be you. No one else could say the right thing without even trying." I held her like I would never let go.

"Comes from loving you."

I moved enough away to look into her eyes.

Cathy kissed me. "Nothing's changed, but I figure you need to hear it. It's true, but nothing's changed."

I leaned back on the couch with my arm around her.

"What a pair we are."

"Yup, I'm right, and you're stubborn. It just goes to show you. I'm a woman; you're a man."

I closed my eyes leaned my head back, and let it pass.

"You can't go after whatever this is again until you recover." Cathy continued.

I nodded. "Agreed. I feel like my heart's been through a cheese grater."

"I couldn't see anything but an energy form. Was it… she, as hot as Carl described?" Cathy snuggled into me.

"Hotter, but nothing like he described."

"What did you see?"

"Perfection. Everything I could ever dream of in a woman. I think that's why I didn't spot her. She was what I wanted, that and I'd dropped most of my shields." I smiled as I felt Cathy stiffen against me.

"I guess you're ruined for us mere mortals then."

I opened my eyes and cupped her cheek. "She looked like you. Pretended to be you. That's why I left the bar."

Cathy kissed me long and hard. She understood as well as I that the creature would take on the form of its prey's perfect woman.

A long time later, Cathy sat up on my bed and started searching for her clothing in the glow of my bedside lamp.

"You could stay the night," I remarked.

Cathy smiled at me as she pulled on her shirt. "I sleep better in my own bed."

I was too tired to press a hopeless case. I closed my eyes and lay back.

"You don't have to be passive-aggressive about it!" snapped Cathy as she stood up to pull on her skirt.

I groaned inwardly. "I'm not anything about it. I'm tired. Can you blame me?"

Cathy looked at me and bit her lip. "What do you think this thing wants anyway? Why is it killing these men?"

"Feeding."

"That's only part of it. I sensed that much." Cathy sat on

the edge of the bed.

"It needs to kill to have any semblance of life on this plane. I think the astral form is being used to renew the base template for the ethereal form, but the astral form is being fed only negative energies that are reinforcing a very limited motivation base. If the ethereal form loses its connection to the earth plane, it will probably free the astral component to move to its proper plane and place, and the ethereal form will dissipate. I could feel it sucking energy out of me, like a straw in my guts when it attacked."

"That is the worst take on oral sex ever." Cathy grinned. "What do you think it will do now?"

"Hunt new prey. It could be anywhere. I don't know enough about it to predict its movements, and its energies are hard to pick out at a distance. They blend with the humans around it. I doubt it would go back to the bar we found it at. It's limited, not stupid... though?"

"Though?" echoed Cathy

"What did you get from it?"

"A headache."

"Seriously?" I leaned up on one elbow and scanned Cathy's aura. I'd been too battered at first to think of it, and then I'd been distracted. Now, I realised that she may have taken a hit. Her aura looked clean. I breathed a sigh of relief.

Cathy hugged herself. "Anger, sadness, revenge and... guilt. It was all jumbled up together with a lot of directed hate. I can't believe that anything that complex is an artificial elemental. Bast, there are dancers I work with that aren't as complex as this thing. I think you're right about the astral component providing structure."

"Could you get anything resembling likes, dislikes, desires?"

Cathy closed her eyes, and I went silent. "Strawberries, baking, daffodils. The spirit was probably human at some point. Why else would it like strawberries and daffodils?" Cathy shook her head. "Did you get anything like that?"

It was my turn to close my eyes and sift the memory of the

contact. "Cabbage, she hates cabbage not as much as she hates men, but defiantly hates it, and… sharks scare her, and cold. She doesn't like being cold." I rubbed my forehead and pulled away from the memory. "I can't right now. It's too close. I can feel it stirring my inner demons."

"Take some time. This thing isn't just rage and hate. There's individuality. Humans couldn't have made it. It is too alive." Cathy's fingers drummed against her arm the way they always did when she faced a puzzle.

"Maybe some construct of a dark God that did its job and never got turned off." I guessed, but I didn't really believe it. The idea felt wrong.

"It's not a splinter of the Sekhmet force. I would have felt that, and Sekhmet wouldn't cage a human spirit the way you describe."

"Agreed."

Sekmara chose that moment to leap onto the bed and give a merrow, adding her opinion to the discussion. I petted my cat, knowing I wouldn't be sleeping alone after all.

"I honestly don't know what this thing is, but I know I'm not going to work it out tonight. I'm toasted," I added.

"Goodnight, sweet prince." Cathy bent down and kissed me, then turned off my bedside lamp and left the room. I was asleep before I could hear my apartment's door close.

— Chapter 7 —

Seeing Double

THE SOUND OF my apartment door opening and footsteps woke me.

"Ray, you here?"

It was Kama. Since it wasn't her day to clean, I knew it had to be something important.

"In the bedroom. Just give me a–."I spoke as I sat on the edge of my bed.

"Nice view." Kama stepped into the room and let her eyes scan me as I scrambled for the sheet, which I'd left bunched at the bottom corner of the bed.

"Kama!" Embarrassment and annoyance shared equal measure in my voice. "You could let me put some clothes on."

She smiled sexily and swayed her hips. "That wouldn't be any fun."

I reminded myself of all the problems following my instincts with her would cause and pulled the sheet over my groin. "You're spending too much time with Cathy. She's rubbing off on you."

Kama smiled, but it didn't reach her eyes or her aura. "Fuck no, I respect you."

"What's up?" I asked.

65

Kama walked up beside me and put her arms around my neck. "You tell me."

I'm no saint. Ra's beak, my faith doesn't even view sexuality as an issue. Having a beautiful teen temptress that close sparked a variety of urges and thoughts that could very easily make me forget Kama's age and the mess it would make of three people's lives. I swallowed hard and settled on hugging her. We stayed like that for a long moment before she pulled away.

"We could, you know. It wouldn't hurt anybody."

I looked into that beautiful face and told my inner chimp to go for coffee. The chimp replied it didn't like coffee and continued to screech at me to take action. I ignored it.

"We both know you'd be on the outs with Cathy. Besides, Kuno might find out. I think it would bother him," I kept my voice even.

Kama shook her head sadly as her seductive manner fell away. "Fucking doubt it."

I swallowed in a dry mouth and let my heart slow. "I know you two aren't exclusive, but I'm his friend."

"We ain't nothing anymore." Kama sighed and sat on my bed. I sat beside her. The beautiful seductress collapsed into an insecure, young woman trying to put a harsh life behind her. After a long pause, she spoke again. "I'm sorry, Ray. I needed to remember there are some good ones left. You passed the fucking test." She released a mirthless chuckle. "Too bad. It would have been a fucking win either way."

I blinked. Kama could be as enigmatic as any sorceress. Then again, so could most women. She flipped from vulnerability to confidence like a switch.

"I got a letter. Kuno's dating someone." Kama sighed.

"Oh, I thought…"

"We aren't. The long-distance thing was fucked before it started, and like, I'm fucking sixteen. I'm not into the whole settling down and having the one point eight or nothing."

"I'm sorry." I knew there was more, but it would come in its own time.

"It's just…" Kama stared at the floor.

I waited.

"I've been with a lot of guys. I mean, a lot. My dad was a bastard, and most of the Johns were fucking jerks. It's easy for them to blur together. Like, learning that Kuno is seeing someone. We were done. I should be happy for him. Like, he's done more for me than pretty much anybody. I'd have been fucking Nukekubi kibble if it wasn't for the two of you. I really care about him, like as a person, but it still hurts. I know it's not fair or nothing, but it does. That makes me want to think that all guys will hurt me. I needed to show myself that you're not all Johns and bastards."

My blood pressure was back to normal. The thought that being the 'good guy' for Kama was a more important reason for not crossing that sexual line bubbled to the fore in my thoughts. I put a hand on her shoulder. "Give it time, you'll find a nice guy," I smirked a little. "Just look for the guy who can't get a date because he isn't exciting enough or doesn't know how to talk to girls."

Kama snorted. "Fucking voice of experience."

"Once upon a time."

"Explains a lot." Kama kissed my cheek, and then stood. "Pancakes, then you can help me with my chemistry homework."

I couldn't help but chuckle as she half bounded from the room. "How did my life get so complicated?"

I swear I could hear distant laughter coming from the picture of Ra that hung over my bed. I picked my robe up off the floor and went to take a shower.

Hours later, Kama left my apartment, chemistry book in hand. I settled in front of my computer and checked my e-mail. The Nigerian prince was still having trouble getting his money out of the country. Checking Facebook, I skimmed the start of a post by a man who followed some perverted form of Norse Paganism that endorsed bigotry. He was ranting about how all Muslims were terrorists. I stopped reading.

Later, I got the official word that my pool wouldn't reopen

for two months. I was then offered a guard shift under Tracy. I declined, much to the annoyance of my temporary boss, who didn't want to accept personality conflict as a legitimate excuse. After a brief tirade about how I wouldn't work under an incompetent, uppity, spoiled child that was more concerned about her hair than bather safety, they decided that they could find someone else to cover the shift.

Alone in my apartment, I lay on my couch, stilling my mind. I dropped my shields and gave myself over to feeling. In memory, I retraced the battle of the night before. Somewhere the memory tied to the residual energies in the room. I could sense an echo of my prey. She, it definitely was a she, was filled with rage, hate, and vengeance. This I already knew. I reached deeper and felt sorrow, regret, and shame.

I thought of beginnings. The energies obliged. The visions came as jumbled images. Black and red flickering candles. Women in black robes. A drumbeat, slow and steady. I felt cold inside. Pain shot through me. Branches sporting brown leaves that rubbed in the wind like aged hands. A searing heat that tore through the cold but didn't banish it. Sorrow, the smell of henbane and mandrake smoke. Dimming coals spark into flame. Rage!

A chant, a name repeated over and over, *Loviatar*, until it seemed to fill the world.

The taste of bitter herbs in wine. Blood drips from a wrist. A swan, its head is cut away, blood pours on the ground, energy sparks. Darkness surrounds me like living tar. A small dot of light in eternal night. The swan's headless body on the grass wings outspread.

My body jerked. I gasped. I hungered, I mourned, my pain floods back. No escape, no peace. Betrayal, confusion, why? Hunger. They caused this!

A foggy image before me. A face, it is male, Caucasian, teen, sneering, dark hair. The stench of foul breath, two others follow similar but individual, pain. A wave of rage and fear then…

I opened my eyes. The energies were played out. There

was nothing left to draw on. Sitting up, I grabbed a pad and scribbled some notes.

"Definitely a ritual, shamanistic elements on a Wiccan base." I closed my eyes. The dead leaves not yet fallen. It had been autumn. But which autumn? This thing could have been hunting for years… Lifetimes? I pondered that. The ties to the earth plane reflected a living link, an anchor. So not lifetimes, unless it was linked to a family line and magic like that is tricky.

I went to my computer and scanned some of the more aggressive Goddesses. I had a name but wanted context. Sekhmet, I knew well. She is a lovely Goddess, just don't piss her off. Lilith, I was aware of. Judaic, supposedly Adam's first wife who refused to be subservient to him. Called the Mother of Monsters, and more recently reclaimed as a force of female empowerment. Kali, the Hindu Goddess of Destruction. I'd never worked with her, but, like with most of the forces, I'd been told she wasn't as bad as some made her out to be. Personally, I viewed her as another face of the Sekhmet force. Loviatar I only knew from playing D&D. My Finnish mythology was weak. It's an hours in a day thing. The Kalevala, a Finnish epic poem, says it better than I can.

The blind daughter of Tuoni,
Old and wicked witch, Lowyatar
Worst of all the Death-land women,
Ugliest of Mana's children,
Source of all the host of evils,
All the ills and plagues of Northland,
Black in heart, and soul, and visage,
Evil genius of Lappala,
Made her couch along the wayside,
On the fields of sin and sorrow;
Turned her back upon the East-wind,
To the source of stormy weather,
To the chilling winds of morning.

Not someone you want to take to the prom. Though I did have a buddy once, his ex-wife came close.

The picture in the D&D: *Deities and Demigods* notwithstanding, she was supposed to be hideous. Her virgin offspring are the plagues that trouble mankind. A dark Goddess that would fit with what was created by the ritual, but why? The Gods are busy dealing with God stuff, keeping the fusion rate of the sun stable, riding herd on the earth's magma, so the volcanoes don't all pop at once. It's a big job that some humans call natural process. I won't argue with them because we're both right.

Whatever made the thing I hunted, it had a personal stake, and that didn't fit with a Godforce. Humans had to tap the power and shape it. Which brought me back to the incredible complexity?

My head was starting to hurt, so I checked out a couple of cat videos and opened a tin of soup.

I passed out on the couch and awoke just in time for the late news. Turning on the TV, I was assaulted by the image of a muscular, bald man with tattoos on his scalp and arms waving a knife at a uniformed police officer in what looked like a seedy motel room shot from outside its open door. The sound was awful. I turned up the volume to the point where I could make out the words.

"I did them all. I don't deserve to live. I'm a monster." The man with the knife bellowed.

"Drop the knife!" ordered the cop, who held his gun levelled at the other man.

"I'm a monster!" The bald man seemed to pause as if listening. "I did, I did. You're right."

The news anchor's voice blasted out of my television. "This just in: The man in the armed standoff with police has been positively identified as Jeffrey Johnson, recently missing from a Hamilton halfway detention facility. Mister Johnson is a repeat sexual offender."

I sat up on my couch and started breathing deeply. If I could get astral, I could maybe do something. Maybe..."

"You're right." Jeffrey sobbed into the air.

"Drop the knife. We can talk about this."

Jeffrey reached with one hand and undid his belt dropping his trousers around his knees.

"I'm a monster." There were tears in his eyes.

"No! Stop!" called the cop.

Some tech digitised the lower part of the screen. Screaming, Jeffrey emasculated himself and threw the severed organs to the side of the room. I knew the digitised red arc on the screen was blood. Jeffrey spun around, and splotches of red painted the room. The cameraman kept recording, obviously using a zoom to give the illusion of proximity. Jeffrey dropped the knife and sprawled on the floor. Paramedics rushed up and pushed the camera to the side.

"We repeat: these are live images of the apprehension of Jeffrey Johnson. These images may be too graphic for some viewers," said the announcer's voice.

The camera returned to the doorway. Jeffrey lay on his back, jets of blood rising from his mutilated groin. A paramedic rushed to apply a pressure dressing against the gaping wound where Jeffrey's genitals had been. The cop stood covering Jeffrey with his gun while the other ambulance attendant scrambled to retrieve the severed organs.

"I'm sorry, Suzy. So sorry," Jeffrey's last words barely sounded over my television before he lost consciousness.

"Shut it down," ordered the cop.

"But," objected a man's voice.

"Get me some ice for this." The ambulance attendant's voice came from outside the frame of the shot.

"Right. Why…" the feed was cut and the newsroom appeared. The anchors sitting behind the news desk looked like matched Ken and Barbie dolls, except their completions were as pale as a sheet. The man cringed as his arms disappeared behind the desk, suggesting a defensive posture. Looking down ,I could see I was cupping myself with both hands. The woman looked pale.

"Why would…" she began.

The man shook his head.

"What..." the woman looked off-screen. "Right." She wet her lips. "This has been a live news feed of the capture of Jeffrey Johnson, known sex offender who vanished from a half-way house two days ago. Our tip line received notice of Mister Johnson's whereabouts earlier this evening. As is our policy, we shared the information with the police. The..." The woman swallowed hard. "Go to commercial."

"We..." began a voice from off-screen.

"Just do it, Frank. My God, just do it," ordered the male anchor.

A commercial for feminine hygiene products started to play.

I sat back on my couch. I had no doubts about what had happened to Johnson. I tried to feel something, but really, was it such a loss? I still needed to stop whatever this was, but I found it hard to care in this case. What I did care about was that my foe had fed. When I faced it, there would be no wounds from our last encounter to weaken it.

On TV, a commercial for tape played where a woman declared her superiority to her husband by fixing a dozen things to his one.

The news anchors appeared.

"Ladies and gentlemen. We will keep you apprised of the capture of known sex offender Jeffrey Johnson as details become available. Now to Jamie Walters and sports." The male anchor's voice sounded solemn.

I turned off the TV and got ready for bed.

I awoke to the creaking of bedsprings and opened my blurry eyes. Cathy sat on the edge of my mattress. It was full night. My first thought was that too many people had the key to my apartment. My second was that Cathy was trembling. Then came the third thought.

"I need the bathroom." Maybe not the most romantic thing to say when you wake up to find a beautiful woman in your bed, but I'm only human.

"I'll wait." Cathy sounded stressed.

"Minutes later, I was back in my room. Cathy's dark silhouette on the edge of the bed staring at her hands like Lady Macbeth.

"Shawn again?" I sat beside her.

"Did you hear about the sexual predator that emasculated himself on the news?" Cathy's voice was small and almost a monotone.

"I saw the broadcast. Did he make it?"

"No. The radio said he was Dead On Arrival. I… I knew him. He was a regular at the club. I didn't know he was a sicko until you told me about the news broadcast about him."Cathy turned to look at me, but the darkness hid her features. "I only danced for him once or twice. I don't think I was his type. He liked the broken girls. The ones with issues or drug habits."

"I'm glad you're a confidant, empowered woman then." I could sense her upset, but I was at a loss to what it was about.

"He came in tonight. Ivan, the DJ, did time with him and heard about him pulling a run-up on the news. He told me some guys just don't belong on the street, so he called the cops. Jeffery didn't stay long enough for the cops to show, and I couldn't just let a serial rapist get away. I…" she looked at the floor.

I sighed. "What did you do?" The thing about magic is it lets you strike out in ways human law doesn't acknowledge. This wouldn't be the first time Cathy did something without thinking first.

"My obsidian pendant was still full of energy from last night's fight. I brought it to the club to try and purge some of it. There is a lot of Yang energy floating around a strip joint. I was hoping to maybe balance the twisted yin and—"

"I get it. Good thought. So, you had the obsidian with you."

Cathy sighed. "I purged the stone into his aura. I couldn't just let him run away. He was a menace. I figured since it attacks with guilt…"

"That you could make him feel remorse, so he'd turn himself in." I rubbed my forehead. I didn't have a quick answer.

"It worked too well. I killed him. Drove him to suicide, just like MaryAnn. I'm a monster!"

"He had it coming. Besides, I'm pretty sure that what you dumped on him couldn't have caused his reaction. From the news, it sounded like remorse was not one of this guy's strong suits."

"Pretty cold, Ray."

I remembered back to a night long ago when a dear friend sobbed in my arms. I was powerless to change what had happened. In a better time and place, a man's blood would have stained my blade for that night's work. "Some monsters just look human. You didn't kill him."

"What?" There was hope and disbelief in Cathy's tone.

"Turn on the bedside light." Opening a wooden box on my nightstand, I pulled out a quartz crystal on a thin, purple, silk ribbon and held the ribbon looped over my fingers, letting the crystal dangle. The bedside lamp gave enough illumination to see the pendulum clearly.

"I call on thee oh spirit guide by the power and wisdom of the Ennead of Heliopolis to answer truly." I picked my words carefully, mindful of Cathy's feelings and the need to be accurate. "Was the felon that died by his own hand this night a victim of the creature known as Maryann that I have faced in combat?"

The pendulum scribed a circle. A year ago I would have used a water glass and let the pendulum strike it, but people grow, and this was easier. I still couldn't divine with a map to save my life. I think my guide has a lousy sense of direction and won't admit it.

"Did Cathy's action against the felon in and of itself cause his death?" I kept my voice neutral so as not to influence the answer.

The pendulum swung from right to left in a straight line. "No."

A thought formed as the fog of sleep cleared. "Did the

energies act like a beacon causing the beast to target the felon over other potential prey?"

The pendulum went back to scribing a circle.

"Thank you, my guide and good spirits, all." I stilled the pendant's swing and tucked it back into its box. "See. All you did was direct Maryann away from an innocent to a sleaze-ball who deserved what he got. The energies acted like a homing beacon."

"That's still awful. Like hanging a stake around someone's neck and dropping them in a tank of sharks." Cathy looked at me with pleading eyes.

I hugged her and spoke with quiet assurance, stating a fact. "Ask the women he doesn't rape how they feel about it. We do what we can. Sometimes there is no right answer. Maryann would have fed anyway. This way, there is one less evil bastard in the world. I think Lady Ma'at would be inclined to agree."

"But to cut off his own junk. I…" Cathy took a shuddering breath and seemed to consider. "Thanks, Ray. I came right over after work. I don't want to be alone. Why don't you throw on a robe and come up to my place?"

"You could stay here," I remarked.

"Please." She patted my shoulder. I put on my robe and grabbed my keys.

Chapter 8

Links In A Chain

THE NEXT MORNING, I woke up in time to go home and find a message from work. They needed me to cover a shift at *Jimmy Thompson Pool*. The morning passed in a rush, and then the day began. I wish parents would realise that water wings are ridiculous. If one deflates, the child is held up by one arm with their head under the water. If both deflate, they sink, and they prevent the use of the arms, so they don't help the kid learn how to swim. I went home that evening with two more checks in the lives saved column and a twisted knee from slipping on the pool deck while I ran to make the second rescue.

Cathy left a note on my kitchen table along with her obsidian pendant enclosed in a wooden box.

The note told me she was at work and said I could do what I needed to with the pendant. I closed my eyes, opened the box and let my hand hover over the black stone. It felt warm. The energy it had taken in had only partially purged. I knew it would come in handy, eventually. For now, it was like having a bare electrical wire plugged into an outlet. I closed the lid and sat thinking.

The ritual I'd caught glimpses of clairvoyantly was

complex. The symbolism, very dark. Red and black for the candles spoke to death magic… mandrake and henbane also. And a blood rite, as was shown by the cut wrist. Why a swan for the sacrifice? Yes, there were many of them around Coot's Paradise and Hamilton Harbour, which bordered the grave-yard, but there were more geese, and the geese would be easier to catch.

For the next two days, I spent my free time delving into my library and scouring the internet. The more I looked, the more frustrated I became. In searching animal sacrifice, I did come across one news piece from last November. A headless swan was found on a grave in *Woodlawn Cemetery*. There were 'other trappings of 'satanic rituals' surrounding the grave. The article was full of misconceptions and a Christian bias born of either ignorance, bigotry or both. Still, it fit what I'd seen and the timeline.

I spent time searching the internet for swan myths. After ploughing through Greek, Roman, Celtic, Hindu, Norse, American first peoples, I was about to give up when I stumbled on the fact that the whooper swan is the national bird of Finland. I followed my nose and found YouTube videos that told me that in Finnish mythology, the swan was able to move freely between the world of the dead and the living. It was believed when the swan ducked its head underwater it looked into the land of the dead.

Symbolism is vital in magic. It ties to the astral 'temples' energy, and it also directs the subconscious and spiritual levels of the self that communicate in whole concepts and symbols. Often in ritual, you use metaphor to get the point across. The metaphor of a headless swan fit with caging the astral spirit, keeping it from seeing the astral plain around it. It was a sick, sad and evil thing to do. A break in the natural cycle that caused suffering beyond the grave, but the symbolism fit. Loviatar and a headless swan. It looked like I'd be boning up on my Finnish magical practices.

After work on the third day, I picked up my falcon-headed cane, in deference to my wrenched knee, put on every defensive charm I could find, turned my shield up to twelve and went to *Woodlawn Cemetery*. The article hadn't listed a grave, but I felt confident that if Maryann was there, I'd sense her.

I paused at William's grave. Fresh turf had been laid over it. Cracking open a sample bottle of whisky I'd brought, I took a swallow then emptied it onto the soil. "Sorry I couldn't do more."

The grave was cold. Even the trace ethereal energies you expect to be there were gone devoured by a thing driven by hunger and… Hate was part of it, but only part. I set the thought aside and moved on.

A loud woof caught my attention, and I saw a mass of grey, shaggy hair bounding towards me.

Suppressing my instinctive reaction to run, I braced myself. My new doggy friend slammed into me, tail wagging and a doggy grin on her face. I petted her, rubbing around her neck.

"Morgana, you get back here! Bad girl." The lovely, dark-skinned woman I'd seen at William's funeral raced between the graves towards us.

I smiled and kept petting the dog. "We meet again."

"I'm so sorry. I let her off the lead. She always comes back when I call, but this time…"

"I'm fond of the children of Anubis. Morgana's no trouble." I let the woman know a little about myself in hopes that she'd reciprocate. Two meetings were pushing coincidence.

"I…" A smile touched her lips, quickly hidden by a scowl. "You're lucky she didn't bite you."

I scratched between the dog's ears. "Why would she hurt a friend?"

Morgana gave a soft, "woof," of confirmation.

The woman smiled despite herself. "Ray, wasn't it?"

"Good memory." I smiled back and added just a touch of come hither to my voice.

The woman shrugged. "Katelin."

I held out my hand, and we shook. I felt a familiar tug. I'd become accustomed to long-past friends and associates showing up in my life. For whatever reason, I seemed to be dealing with a lot of karma in this incarnation.

"Are you visiting your friend?" Katelin nervously fingered the leash she carried.

"In part. With the day being so clear, I wanted to stretch my legs, and this seemed as good a place as any."

"It is peaceful here," Katelin's voice was soft as if peace was a rare thing in her life.

"Have you tried the Royal Botanical Gardens trails? They're a bit much with this heat, but when it's cooler, they are lovely." I kept my body language open and inviting but passive. An invitation, not a request.

"I like it here. I can visit my sister." Her eyes strayed towards the grave with the pentagram on the stone.

"May she be joyful in the A'aru."

"The what?" Katelin stared at me.

"The Summer Lands." I bet that Katelin knew her own tradition well enough but wasn't overly eclectic.

"Oh. It's only coming up on a year. It's nice to feel her close. She'd only just moved to Burlington when she died. It's been lonely. I... I'm sorry. You don't need to hear my life story. I don't know that many people around here and..."Katelin trailed off and bit her lip nervously.

"I understand." I pulled out my wallet, extracted a business card and held it out to her. "If you'd be interested, there are open circles in Hamilton. The community isn't perfect, but there are good people in it, and it's a great way to network if you're looking for a group or tradition that you might be interested in. Give me a call, and I'll get a schedule for you."

Katelin looked at the card like a child offered candy by a stranger.

Tentatively, she took the card. "My wife is expecting me."

She watched for my reaction. Would I freak out, come on hard, blush, I understand it. It's something everyone in an invisible minority runs into. Gay, Trans, Pagan, doesn't matter.

If the person passes the test, friendship is possible, not assured but possible. If they don't, you move on. In this case, I was also the litmus test for the local Pagan community.

I smiled and pitched my voice to just friendly, dropping the come-hither inflexions. "I won't keep you then. I don't know if your wife would be interested, but she'd be welcome at the open circle as well."

Katelin bit her lip. "Thank you, Ray. I might just call about that schedule." She clipped the lead to Morgana's collar and walked away.

I watched Katelin for several moments before moving to her sister's grave.

"Maryann Walker." I read the tombstone, then closed my eyes and extended my senses. The first few centimetres of dirt were normal enough. Below that the ground seethed with ethereal energy. Sunlight forced it to stay in the darkness, but it reacted to my probe reaching up towards me. I mentally retreated, and it fell away.

I glanced the way that Katelin had walked and shook my head. "Why can't anything be straightforward?"

Sweat dripped off me as I paced the ground around the grave, focusing my will through my cane. I'd completed the work on the cane since it saved my bacon nearly a year before. Representations of the elements were carved into the shaft under the falcon head, and gemstones representing the charkas dotted its length. All in all, it was nice work, if I say so myself. More important, only someone who knew something about the art would recognise it as anything but a grandiose walking stick.

I cast a circle around Maryann's grave, feeling thirteen lines of energy as I walked its perimeter. Twelve lines bound the ethereal energy to the earth and one reached to a trapped spirit on the astral. The circle cast, I started with the weakest of the binding lines. I followed it until it cut off. All I could tell was it headed northwest. The line represented a person who had lent their energy to Maryann but had since ritually broken the connection. I followed two more lines with the same result. The fifth and sixths strongest lines stretched northeast, but they snapped as I mentally touched them, unable to take the strain of even a gentle probe. Those linked to these lines were separated from the spell, possibly by distance, more likely by just moving on with their lives. In either case, there wasn't enough of a tie to track. The ethereal energies writhed up towards me each time I probed a line then fell back when they hit the light of the sun.

Coming to the seventh strongest connection, I got a flash of memory. A woman, girl really, teens, bone-thin, jet-black hair with blond roots, and dressed in a tattered black dress. Black lipstick with a pentagram the size of a hubcap hung around her neck. Pure punk-rock Goth showing off how much of a rebel she was by doing exactly what the rest of her group were doing. I didn't know her, but I had seen her. The line was moderately strong and flowed with a mix of energies. It stretched into Hamilton.

I paused in thought. I would have most likely seen her at a public ritual. A lot of teens go through a stage as what I call a switch, shock witch, playing a role for effect. Most drift away from the old ways. Some evolve into a deeper understanding of the Craft. The wise let the children play and maybe grow up.

I thought about the memory of the public circle. There had been a cold draft coming into the temple area, a decrepit, empty room over a local cafe, and there were wet boots lining the wall behind the girl. That placed it at Imbolc, February eve, a celebration of the lengthening days and the hope of spring they represented. The ritual had been okay, except for the teens who were there to show off. I tried to remember more, but there wasn't anything. The girl was unremarkable to me at the time.

Mentally filing the impressions, I moved on. The next line was thin but persistent. Rage energy and a sense of unfinished business seemed to stretch out to the Northwest. I got a mental image of mountains and a sense of betrayal. I bet whoever it connected to was separated by distance, not conviction. The line fought me. I felt a flood of red energy lash out as I tried to break it. My circle took the hit, sending the energy into the ground. Maryann attacked out, but the sun dissipated most of the ethereal force. For me, it was still like being caught in a vice. I slammed down on the line with my cane, directing a bolt of heart chakra energy into the malice, hate and rage. Red and black energies spilt over the ground. I took a deep breath and slammed down on the line again. This time it snapped, the severed ends writhing apart. The line vanished before I could trace it. I'm sure someone, somewhere, had a migraine from the backlash.

I took a deep breath. Four lines plus the one reaching to the astral remained. It was a start. The problem was the four lines were far more robust than the last one I broke. Thus far, my efforts had weakened my foe and narrowed her options, but she was still a dangerous adversary.

I probed the lines. One was red with rage and black with hate; the next was heavy on rage and hate but covered a mottled mix of other energies as well. There was something odd about it, but it repelled my probes. The strongest line filled me with a sense of sorrow. It was the gold of love tarnished with the muddy brown of regret and loss. I could guess its source. I grieved for Katelin, she had loved her sister, but loss didn't excuse releasing a hungry beast on the world. The next line appeared greenish brown like rotting vegetation. These lines pinned the ethereal energies to the earth, but they were too simple to have established its pattern. The pattern came from the trapped astral form. How was still a mystery to me.

I was feeling maudlin, which meant fatigue was setting in. In addition, I was losing the light. I'm not Van Helsing from a bad movie to tackle the baddy that can't face the sun at night. I fight to win, and Maryann was bigger than me if I played in her sandbox. I was going to take any advantage I could get. Besides, the simple way had done as much as it could. The remaining lines were too robust to snap with my cane and the improvised ritual space I had erected. Opening my circle, I hobbled to my car as my knee spoke of how little love there was between us.

At my apartment, I took a cool shower and had a bite. Sekmara made great show of walking all over me. She's a cat, what else is new? At least she didn't try to deny that she did it, like most of the females in my life.

When the sun set, I drove to the *Hungry Fox*. Entering the bar, I scanned it. The mystical tapeworms were conspicuous by their absence. I figure they didn't want to be caught in the crossfire. Even metaphysical scum have a sense of self-preservation. I ordered a beer before taking a seat in a booth. I pulled my aura in tight while projecting an obscuring glamour around myself. Sipping my beer, I waited. An hour passed. I ordered fish and chips with another beer. All appearances to the contrary, the food was good. I made a mental note to ask if they did take out.

People came and went. A couple of people with parasites in their aura walked in. I dropped my cloaking field long enough to be noticed. The parasites found someplace else to be. We do what we can. After the second hour, I decided I was wasting my time.

The next morning, I had another shift at work. When I got home, I checked the online news and found nothing. I went back to examining the evidence.

Maryann couldn't have been hurt enough by my breaking the links as to be out of the running. Could it be her tie to the lunar cycle? Did she have other hunting grounds? What was I missing? The phone rang. I decided to let the machine get it.

"Hello. You have reached Ray's Lifeguarding and Pool Safety Services. Please leave your name and number after the beep, and we will get back to you."

"Hello, It's Katelin. We spoke about a schedule for the public rituals. I—"

I dove for the phone and picked it up. "Katelin, sorry about that, it's Ray."

"Oh, hi. I. I wanted to take you up on your offer."

"Sure thing. Just let me go to the other line."

"Thanks."

I couldn't be sure, but something sounded off about her. "Are you okay?"

"Fine, just. Maybe this was a bad idea." She sounded hesitant.

"What? Getting a few dates." I focused on the superficial. Something was wrong, but if I pressed this stranger for information, it would spook her. "I'll be right back."

Setting down the phone, I raced to my computer room/temple and picked up the line.

"Just let me pull out the flier." I opened my desk drawer and sorted through a stack of papers, pulling out a tri-fold flyer with a pentagram on its front.

"I really appreciate this," said Kaitlin. "It's been two years since Elly and I moved here, and I hardly know anybody. I guess I'm not that great at making friends. Elly went to Mohawk years ago and was active in the LGBT community. She has friends from those days, but I haven't really clicked with any of them."

"Well, things are turning around because you just made a friend," I replied with friendly enthusiasm. "Do you have a pen?"

"Yes."

"Good. The circles are held on the first Friday evening on or after the major sabbats and the first Saturday evening on or after the full moon. They're supposed to start at seven, but you're probably good to seven-thirty. You know, Pagan Standard Time. There's a potluck feast after the sabbat circles, and the circles are dry except for the ritual wine or beer. Street legal clothing is required. Ritual robes are optional."

"Got it. Ray?"

"Yes."

"It's silly."

"Go ahead."

"I love my wife. I need you to know that, so you don't get the wrong idea."

"Okay?" I'd had calls like this before. The idea had been a

no-strings weekend while her husband, my friend, was out of town. I'd declined the offer and lost two friends anyway. Go figure.

"I… I need someone to talk to, and you seem nice. Are you free to meet?" Katelin's voice was pleading.

I took a deep breath. This would probably forward my hunt, but was it fair to meet just to do that? To pretend friendship? Then again, was it pretending? Katelin seemed nice, and she was socially isolated. I knew what it was like to be lonely and how easily it could eat away at someone. If she was desperate enough to reach out to a stranger, what else could desperation drive her two? Lancelot came riding in on his big, bloody horse and trampled common sense. When will I learn?

"Sure, my girlfriend–" I know. It sounds better than occasional sex partner that I am in love with. I didn't want to look totally pathetic. "—is busy tonight."

"Great, can you meet me at the *Garden Restaurant*? It's on Plains Road just across from the Rose Garden Parking Lot."

"I'll be there in half an hour." I kept my voice friendly but neutral.

"Thanks. I…Thanks." There was relief in her voice, and then she hung up.

I shook my head and, with a sense of dread, got dressed and rushed to my car.

The *Garden Restaurant* had once been a really nice place. You could see it in the quality tables and wood trim, but the years had been less than kind with dings in the furniture and walls. Still, it was safe and clean and, thankfully, air-conditioned.

I walked in and immediately spotted Katelin in a booth close to the door. Not waiting for the hostess, I approached her and said, "Hi."

Katelin looked at me and smiled. The smile was lovely, the split lip and purpling bruise around her left eye, not so much.

"What happened?" I asked.

"I walked into a door." Katelin gestured towards the bench

-style seat opposite her.

I slid into the stall, trying not to let my incredulity show. My dad wore long pants, even in summer, to hide the bruises from my mother kicking him. She'd throw a punch at his face, where it would show, forcing him to catch her wrists to preserve his dignity, then proceed to kick him in the shins until he was black and blue.

"The door had no right to do that to you," I commented.

Katelin stared at the table and bit her lip. "I really don't know why I called you. I…"

I reached across the table and squeezed her hand. "Hate to eat alone. So do I. Nothing worse than choking down an instant dinner in front of the TV watching a Next Generation rerun hoping that they'll finely reveal that Wesley is a Borg spy."

Katelin snorted. "You're too buff to be a geek."

"And I'm a macho lifeguard, go figure. I left my one ring on the dresser." This brought a smile.

"At least you don't wear a cowboy hat."

A middle-aged waitress in a white blouse and black skirt uniform came up and took our orders. Her brown eyes and tone of voice reflected disapproval about something, but she held her tongue. Her issue was her issue. As long as she didn't make it my problem, I had bigger fish to fry.

Katelin and I chatted about geeky things through the meal. I liked her. For one thing, she agreed that Babylon5 was the best TV science fiction made to date. We also both had crushes on Muri Furlan, Claudia Black, Alyson Hannigan and Jessica Alba. It is a little surreal when you realise the beautiful woman you're eating with has the same taste in women as you.

After finishing the food, we sat with ice teas. The mood at the table was companionable.

"I've missed this," Katelin commented.

"Eating over-cooked hamburgers and sipping too-sweet iced tea?" I raised an eyebrow, Spock-like, and smirked.

Her smile widened. "Talking, having a friend. I haven't had many since I left Calgary."

"Did you grow up there?" I couldn't help but think that Calgary was northwest, but I kept it to myself.

"No. I grew up in a little place called Kakêpâcihtwâwin. About two hours north of Calgary. Famous for its annual stampede and soccer teams." Katelin sneered at the mention of soccer. "I did my undergrad at the University of Calgary."

"Did you meet your wife there?" I kept my voice conversational. I would have asked the same thing if it had been a husband.

Katelin blushed a little. "I found myself there. I mean, back home everything was so repressed. I think I knew I liked girls, but I never really admitted it to myself. I mean, I fooled around with a couple of girls behind my boyfriend's back, but nothing serious. University was so different. There I could be myself and not have to worry about my mom finding out."

"Parents are always fun to deal with. My mom keeps calling my girlfriend a prostitute."

"My mom hates Elly. It's part of why we moved to Ontario. That and… well… other reasons. Mom freaked out when Maryann came to live with us. She blames me for Maryann committing sui… I'm sorry. Here I am, I hardly know you, and I'm telling you my tale of woe." Katelin's voice held worlds of hurt.

"It's okay. I'm sorry about your sister. If you ever need to talk, two shoulders, no waiting."

"Thanks. Elly got me through that. She's wonderful." A note in Katelin's voice and red shading her aura implied qualifiers beyond what she said. "She's always saving me. When we first met, it was my second year. I was on a date with this really, 'I'm such a rebel I sleep with girls' type."

I snorted. "My sister went through that faze. It lasted until my dad tried to set her up with the daughter of a friend of his. Once she knew he was that accepting, she went back to dating guys and looked for something else to rebel about."

"Some people are like that, not most."

"True enough. It's just human foibles are funny, and my sister, well, you'd have to know her." It's likely a trace of exasperation entered my tone. My sister tends to bring that out in me.

Katelin smiled at me. "In any case, a couple of rednecks saw us holding hands and started harassing us."

"Jack asses!"

"No shortage of them. Anyway, it started getting rough. Ellen was campus security. A boot to the back of the leg and a few harsh words later, and the two guys were on the run. Ellen walked us back to my place, and I got her number. I mean, she's older sure, but she is hot, and there is something about a woman in uniform. She proposed a year later. When I wasn't accepted into law school, she got a job offer in Hamilton, so we moved out here.

"I mean, I can do the Law in Humanities program at McMaster, and that will look great when I re-apply. I really love Elly. I just wish she got SF and fantasy. She likes murder mysteries and lesbian romances."

"How about a murder mystery, lesbian romance set on a spaceship?"

"With green dancing girls."

"And Captain Jane Tamara Kirk."

"I think it's called fanfic."Katelin giggled into her iced tea. She winced as she patted her swollen lip with her napkin, then glanced at her watch."I have to go. Elly will be home any minute, and I have to walk Morgana." Katelin glanced around, looking for the waitress.

I sighed. I'm a wizard, not a councillor. I knew in my heart what was going on, but if I couldn't save my own father, what could I do here? "I'll get the bill. You just go. I hope we can do this again soon. It was fun."

Katelin stared at me. "I couldn't stick you with the bill, that would be like a date, and this wasn't, you know that, don't you?"

"It was a dinner of friends. You pay next time. Give Morgana a dog treat for me."

"You're a lifesaver." Katelin got out of the booth and kissed my cheek before she ran out the door.

I touched my cheek where Katelin had kissed it. There was the warmth of an act of affection. That brought a smile to my face. People fail to realise that friendship is a type of love, and Katelin and I were friends. We probably had been for several lifetimes. The easy camaraderie with someone I'd just met indicated that, as did just how much emotion a pec on the cheek triggered. Often the heart remembered far more than the head when skipping from life to life. I'd poke at it later. Under the warmth, there was a layer of fear, a pain that was woven into the core of Katelin in this incarnation. A wound probably from childhood that her spirit had a hope I might help with. Her soul was looking for a lifeline before it was too late. Probably why we were steered together.

I paid the bill, shorting the tip for the rudeness the waitress had shown us, and then I stepped into the night.

— Chapter 9 —

The Left Brain's Contribution

I AWOKE AROUND three AM to Cathy slipping into my bed. Much later, I got back to sleep. Later still, we sat at my battered kitchen table in two of my bathrobes, sipping coffee and eating toast with jam, like a real couple.

"Kama told me that Kunio has a girlfriend," remarked Cathy.

I shrugged. "Had to happen sometime. A lesser good that is surrendered to a greater good."

"That's mean. Kama is great." Cathy glowered at me, and I could see the protective aspect of her nature. Cathy is a true daughter of Bast. If she considered you part of her pride, woe betide anyone that harms you. Part of what kept me around was that fierce loyalty. Problem was, I was thinking about why I did stick around more and more, reminding myself of her virtues to balance her faults. When does it become too much work to convince yourself?

"Kama is great, but for Kunio." I shook my head. "They were good for each other at a time and place, but for a lifetime? It's not a comment about either of them, just how things are." I felt a dull ache in my chest. The conversation skirted too close to home.

Cathy stared at me across the table. "All right then. Anything new on Maryann?"

I nodded as my voice became serious. "A group ritual brought her into being. I just can't figure out how or why. The ethereal form is as nuanced and complex as a person. If the astral component wasn't trapped, I'd say vengeful ghost. But the mortal links to the ethereal aspect are calling the shots. I found a grave that is the focus of the energy and broke some of the links that ground her to the earth plane, for all the good it will do."

"It's a start. How old is the grave?" Cathy took a long swallow of coffee.

"About a year. That's another thing I don't get." My puzzlement showed in my voice."If Maryann has been active for a year, why are we just noticing her now? Something that powerful dropping a trail of bodies should have set off alarms all through the local community."

Cathy looked at the table and took a deep breath. "People hide suicide. I had a cousin. We pretended that it was an accidental over dose. We all knew it wasn't."

I took Cathy's hand and squeezed her fingers. "I'm sorry."

Cathy sighed and squeezed my fingers back. For that moment, my doubts disappeared.

"He was a really nice kid, just confused. Billy loved to paint, dreamed of being an artist. My aunt made a virtual gallery as a memorial to him. You have to love the internet. People from all around the world can see his art," Cathy's tone was sad.

" 'Speak his name for when a man's name is spoken, he lives'," I quoted from the *Book of Coming into the Light*.

"I need to work on my thesis, and then get some sleep." Cathy stood up and kissed me before heading for her clothes in the bedroom.

Moving to my computer, I typed Maryann Walker's name into the search engine. Facebook yielded a plethora of possibilities. I added Kakêpâcihtwâw in Google and came up with an old fluff piece about a grade eight graduation. After that, things seemed to go blank. No team photos, nothing to do with Maryann. I'd have expected something. I tried Katelin's name, and there was a smattering of mentions. She'd been a member of a girl's softball team. A picture of her acting as a booth girl for a ranch supply firm. I paused to look at that twice.

Rage, shame, pain. I closed my eyes, a sick feeling welling up in my stomach. I typed in Kakêpâcihtwâwin and rape. A series of news articles popped up. I shook my head and started sorting through them. By the time I finished, I had a good idea of how this mess had started and a name for what Maryann had become—revenant. A very general term for one risen from the grave, often for the purpose of vengeance. The term was more general than I liked, but vampire didn't fit without blood as an allegory for the life force, and the force's active manifestation was ethereal. At least with the name, I could search the lore. Magic is a living science; things change and evolve, so sometimes, you just go with the best match you can get.

The stories I found covered a range, with many of them focusing on an evil man in life who returned from the grave to continue his wicked ways after death. Others closely paralleled those of Maryann.

Such as the man who took a younger woman to wife. From all reports, they were happy, but it didn't last. The man soon suspected that his wife was cockling him with a young man from the village.

One day the husband calmed to be going to inspect his fields but hid amidst the rafters of his house instead. Sure enough, his wife's paramour came calling and soon they were defiling the oaths of marriage she had sworn.

This enraged the husband so that he bellowed, revealing himself. The wife's lover leapt from the bed. Grabbing a broom, he pummelled the husband, who fell from the rafters, breaking his neck.

The young lover dressed and fled the house while the widow concocted a story of how her husband was inspecting the roof and accidentally fell to his death.

And so, the husband was buried in hallowed ground.

But that was not the end of the matter. Days later, the wife awoke to the sound of banging on her house's walls. Looking out the window, she saw her husband, gaunt and decayed but still recognisable, circling the dwelling, throwing things against the wall.

In terror, the widow closed the shutters and huddled in her bed. Three nights later, she sickened and died.

Soon after, her lover succumbed to an illness after seeing the husband he had murdered.

Next came the death of the widow's friend, who had carried messages between the lovers.

Finally, the people of the village dug up the husband's remains, finding them to be bloated with blood and in a state of decay. They cut off the corpse's head, burnt it, and then sprinkled the ashes on holy ground. They then sprinkled salt on the corpse and drove an oak wood stake through the heart before burning the body and scattering the ashes. After that, the visitations of the husband ceased.

The legends were typical attempts to explain material manifestation blended with mystical ones. They formed a hodgepodge of superstition with a trace of actual mystical practice to be gleaned by those in the know. I didn't personally believe in physically reanimated corpses, walk-ins, where a spirit inhabits a fresh body immediately after its first inhabitant departs, being a notable exception. However, the spirit using a corpse as an anchor or gateway to the material world could certainly happen. And a spirit could be perceived as a physical manifestation that could be deadly.

I went back to investigating the goings-on in Kakêpâcihtwâwin.

Several articles spoke of a minor girl and three boys who gang-raped her in the back of a car. They were all under eighteen, so the names were withheld. The girl had pressed charges. A year later, the case ended in a plea bargain that saw the boys charged as minors to a years' probation each.

The article from the local newspaper was written in a 'boys will be boys' manner and spoke as much about how the boys were part of the soccer team as the case. References to the girl noted a questionable reputation and implied that she shouldn't have been in the car in the first place. The article disgusted me, but information is where you find it.

"Poor Maryann. To go through all that and have it come to nothing." I rubbed my face. Some more digging and I found the name of the judge, Tomas J. Hoffman, circuit court judge.

I put the name into the search engine, and an obituary came up dated December.

Some more digging revealed the prosecutor and the defence attorney. Both had obituaries dated in December.

I back peddled my search and found five obituaries from Kakêpâcihtwâwinin November. Two were older people, but three were in their late teens. I now had a sense of what I was looking for. A few minutes with an online almanac revealed that the first death had been on the dark of the moon. The second death had occurred on the waxing quarter, the third on the full moon, the fourth on the waning quarter and then back to dark, and so on. I was now certain that Maryann fed on the quarter moons. The revenant was made by women to reflect a woman's revenge, using a woman as a template. The moon is usually seen as feminine, though there are exceptions. Still, the moon is tied to the aspects of the universe generally viewed as under women's domain.

Some more searching pulled up the pictures. Judge Hoffmann was Caucasian; late middle age. The prosecutor was an Asian man in his mid-thirties. The defence attorney was Caucasian, maybe thirty. The three teens were all Caucasian, athletic and generally in poses that reflected a smug arrogance. In most of the photos, they were dressed in soccer uniforms.

I looked at the pictures on my computer screen. People were seldom one thing, and I knew I was unfairly judgmental, but I was sick of a system that let such things happen. Three thugs abuse another person in one of the most intrusive ways possible and because they can kick a ball around the people, who are supposed to stop such things, let them skate with a slap on the wrist. Or was it that they didn't want to ruin three boys' lives for a single mistake, but what of the girl, what of Maryann's life?

I was tempted to give it all up as a bad idea. Maybe a revenant was what the world needed. Vengeance and justice are cousins, but then I thought of William's grandmother. William, not such a bad guy whose only fault was thinking he could hold onto a little joy when it was dumped in his otherwise miserable life. For that matter, Carl, while admittedly an embarrassment to all men, never took that which was not freely given from a woman. And lest we forget, Maryann attacked me. I sighed. It wasn't as simple as man bad woman good. Men and women are people, and all of us are shades of grey. There is a long gradient in sleazy. I've said it before; there is reason in all things.

I checked for other obituaries in Kakêpâcihtwâwin on the lunar quarters. There were two in January: A farmer who threw himself into an automatic hay bailer and a minister who emasculated himself after leaving a confession about how he abused several girls in his youth group. Some more digging showed that the farmer had coached a girls' soccer team for several years, then stopped for unstated reasons. I thought of the ritually broken lines.

It made sense. The women in the group had come together to create a weapon they could use to extract what they saw as justice. Most, when their personal justice had been served, stepped away from the working, broke the link, and moved on with their lives.

I shifted my search to Calgary and found January obits for two rapists who got off on technicalities. Both were on lunar quarters. I also found an obituary for the defence attorney who had represented them on the first lunar quarter in February. That left a gap in the cycle, but Maryann could have been out of province for that feeding. I looked for obits in Toronto that matched the quarters. There were too many to choose from, besides I had what I needed.

I was convinced that Maryann chose hunting grounds proximal to those linked to her. Furthermore, at least for the early kills, she was directed by one of the women who participated in the ritual that created her. Their rage at the injustice, either to themselves or a loved one, was the targeting mechanism, at least at the start. When had it changed, going from rapist abusers and their enablers to all men? When had vengeance become obsessive misandry?

In any case, as more and more of those that created Maryann achieved their goals and broke the lines that tied them to the spell, she found herself with fewer and fewer hunting grounds, fewer defined targets. Thus, each area would be hunted more heavily to supply her needs, making her actions more obvious and... That was it!

Her needs.

Her hunger.

A shudder ran down my back. The longer Maryann stayed active, the stronger her existence. She had to feed to continue, and she wanted to continue. Bound by the nature of her creation, she had become self-actualised within those limitations. I bit my lip. There was something more. The feeding schedule changed for some reason. Admittedly, I'd interrupted Maryann's meals several times, but not so severely that she should have forsaken the lunar quarters' schedule.

I took a deep breath and fell back on lessons learned in a journalism class I'd taken as a bird course. I matched it with a stream of conscious technique and sought my answers.

Who: Maryann Walker, a teen rape victim who died shortly after her attackers were let off with a slap on the wrist. Did MaryAnn die by her own hand? Katelin thought so, but was she right? Was Maryann's motivation murder? According to the myths, Revenants were driven by the will to avenge their own deaths. Could the incident that motivated a suicide be considered a murder weapon? If the women who empowered Maryann's rising saw it that way, then why not?

What: I was still working on it. An ethereal, artificial

elemental with more juice than most true spirits, and a pattern as complex as many living souls drawn from an imprisoned astral form. Revenant, I know, but a name doesn't give you all the details.

Where: A radius around one of four earthbound entities, one I knew for sure, one I suspected and would be close to the first, and two I had no clue about. The last two nagged at me, but I had to shelve them for later.

When: How often did she hunger? Lunar quarters, and if interrupted, just after.

Why was she created? To avenge rapes and the injustice that followed. To bring some sense to an evil that should never have been. It was a blind unbalanced justice, but at its core, it was a form of justice.

The answers were piling up. But so were new questions.

How did Maryann die? Katelin thought suicide, but was that really the case?

Who were the remaining energy lines attached to?

The sun was setting, and Sekmara reminded me that it was time to fill her food bowl.

Chapter 10

Links In A Chain

THE NEXT MORNING found me standing on the back patio of my parent's house, my hands pressed against a willow tree that had been planted years before I was born. The bungalow behind me was made of scrap ends my father had salvaged from the dump over the course of years. The new vinyl siding did a good job of masking its appearance, as did the new wallboard and cosmetic trappings on the inside, until you realised that no two floors were on the same level. Still and all, it was where I grew up. The yard was huge by today's standards.

The willow tree towered over the patio of concrete slabs laid around it. The tree had a try-form trunk large enough that I could reach just under halfway around it.

I focused my thoughts and sent my mind questing into my leafy friend. It seemed like I'd spent half my childhood in its branches.

"I'm sorry, but the danger is too great. With the rot in your trunk, the wind and ice could topple you into the house," I spoke softly.

"That's stupid. It's just a tree. It can't hear you." I glanced at my mother, who sat on a reclining chair on the patio. She was in her mid-fifties, medium boned with dark hair marred by grey roots. She wore a colourful blouse and shorts.

"This tree is my friend. It lives and has spirit. So, if you want me to risk breaking my neck to cut it down, I'll do it my way, and I'm not going to listen to any complaints about it!" I may not have been pleasant, but subtle didn't work with my mum.

My mother snorted and buried her face in a romance book.

"Mom, you're going to have to move. A branch could fall on you."

"Why you can't come back another day, I don't know. It's not like your father and I are horrible people." Her tone was querulous, as usual.

"I have to do this around my work schedule, and I need dad around. It's not a one-man job." I kept my voice even though the Gods know it was a strain.

My mother snorted and stomped off, disappearing into the house.

As if on cue, my dad emerged from the tool shed at the back of his property, carrying a block and tackle and an electric chainsaw. He added these to the pile of rope he'd already placed on the patio.

"I really need to tidy it up in there. We should have a cup of tea," remarked my dad.

I sighed. It was early enough that the day hadn't reached its full temperature, and already sweat dripped off me. "Dad, why don't we wait and use the cooler temperature to do the work. We can take a break when it's hotter."

He gave me a look like I'd just kicked his cat. "I'll get the extension cord."

Minutes later, I was up the tree with a makeshift safety rope looped around it and my waste. The small chainsaw whirred to life, and I started on the first of the upper branches. Soon wood chips mixed with sweat covered my face. My dear friend shuddered with pain, but what could I do? Sometimes you had to do harm to do good.

The branch released, and the ropes I'd tied to it took its weight. Supporting the chainsaw on a secured branch, I pulled off my safety goggles and whipped off the haze of sawdust that blinded me. With the block and tackle, I lowered the load. I'd trim the leafy shoots later and plant them. The essence of my friend would live on. The ethereal pattern would draw strength from the ground, and a new existence would take place. The astral form of the tree would move on to a new life as the shoots formed astral forms of their own. It was the way of some plants, starfish and worms. I didn't know of any more evolved life forms that functioned that way. Usually, once separated from the astral form, the ethereal pattern dissipated. Trees and 'simple' life forms could draw on the general energy of the world. 'Advanced forms' required specialised energies to subsist.

My father would dry and burn the wood from the tree, reducing his winter heating bill. Being useful wasn't the worst of ends. Maryann was useful to the women that sought what they saw as justice. Evidently, she'd fulfilled that purpose for most of them. Why not all? Was it time? The seemingly random nature of the attacks of late was confusing. How could someone generate the emotion required to drive Maryann from just a general bigotry against men? Did the women who created the ethereal form know they also imprisoned the astral form?

I was about to retrieve the ropes that my father untied from the now grounded branch when it came to me. I closed my eyes and thought back to when I broke the lines to Maryann. The four that remained were so strong and... The flow. I kicked myself. Sometimes I'm not the sharpest tool in the box. I couldn't be sure. But was one of the lines flowing out from Maryann? If someone was using Maryann to garner power to themselves, that would explain the increase in feeding. I've mentioned spiritual tapeworms. Was a human parasitizing Maryann? Why?

"It's ready to go," My father called up. I dripped sweat as I hauled up the ropes and shifted my improvised safety line.

"You're an old woman, Ray. It will take all day with you fiddling with that blasted belt," scolded my father.

I gritted my teeth and looked at the patio. For years I'd been my father's personal slave. Case in point, the patio blocks had yow-yow-ed from the front of the house to the back several times, and I'd carried every one. Those suckers are heavy! Finally, I'd decided if I was going to do jobs for him, I was going to do them my way, and he could just live with it. I tied myself off and started on the next branch.

The next time I paused, waiting for my father to untie the lines, I thought of Katelin and her clean aura. That wouldn't be the case if she was absorbing energy from the deaths. Was it possible that she wasn't even aware that Maryann was still hunting men? But what about the three other lines?

By the time the third branch came down, I was convinced that Katelin was only an anchor for Maryann, a focus that kept the energies from dissipating. How much the quality of her legs played into this assessment, I'm not going to dignify with an answer. Really, I'm not. Okay, she did have great legs.

The other lines could be a different matter. Who were they to Maryann or Maryann to them that they should weep for her?

Shifting position, I dropped lower on the tree, almost falling as I did so until my safety line caught me up.

"You okay up there," called my dad.

"Slipped a little."

"You should come down. I don't like you being up there. Victor, why didn't you hire a cherry picker," complained my mother from the back door to the house.

"I told you. They couldn't get one in around the house and other trees. Ray doesn't mind helping out, do you, son?" My dad's voice held the weary note of the perpetually henpecked.

"I'm up a tree with a chainsaw and a winch. I think that answers the question, dad."

"You don't have to be like that," snapped my mother.

"Do you want me to thank you for this wonderful opportunity to break my neck? Gods, mum, isn't the fact that I'm doing it validation enough for you? Should I paint myself blue and sing a happy song? I'm not a bloody Smurf!"

"He's like this because of you." My mother stalked back into the house.

"Sure you don't want to stop for a cup of tea?" My dad looked up hopefully.

My t-shirt and shorts were sweat-drenched, wood chips covered my face, hair and arms, and I felt like I was being slow-roasted. It was only ten-ish, so the day was still relatively cool. "Just tie a bottle of water onto the cord I lower. I'll come down when I need the bathroom."

"I'll get your water." My dad shuffled into the house. I noticed he'd found the bow-saw in the tool shed. A shudder ran up my spine as I remembered hours spent doing work that could have been done in minutes with a chain saw. The things you do for family. I loved my parents; I keep telling myself that.

By mid-afternoon, the tree was limbed out, leaving only the main trunks. I was getting dizzy and knew I was in the early stages of heat exhaustion, so I climbed down from my perch.

"So, should I put the kettle on?" asked my father.

I stared at him blurrily. "I'll have juice or water, thanks." To give Dad his due, he'd trimmed off a large bundle of the fallen branches with a pair of garden shears and had the shoots sitting in a bucket ready for me to take.

Dad gripped my woodchip and sweat-covered shoulder and smiled at me. "Son, I really appreciate this. Your mother does, too. It was only luck that the tree didn't come down with last year's ice storm."

Suddenly, I didn't mind the work so much.

My mother emerged from the house. "You're not coming in like that. Hose yourself off. I'll not have sawdust all over my carpets. Now hurry, I've made lunch. It's too hot to bake, but I did up a pie for dessert last night when it was cooler. It's blueberry."

Blueberry has always been my favourite. In her own way, my mother just said the same as my father. Family.

It was too dangerous to work on the trunk in the afternoon heat, so I focused on trimming the felled limbs. My dad and I agreed that even if we didn't get to it that year, the trunk was safe for another winter with the overburden removed.

After dinner, mercifully prepared by my father on the brick barbeque I'd helped him build years before, topped by the last of my mother's pie, I headed home with the trimmed shoots wrapped in a damp towel covered by a plastic garbage bag crossing my back seat.

The pattern of life from my old friend would persist and be spread wherever the shoots took. That made me smile. I might not be able to create the spark of life, but I could breathe on that spark and make it grow. I could revitalise a pattern that was fading. How often do we overlook our own greatest powers? Our own spark of divinity manifesting in our actions? I…Then I saw the parallel.

Maryann's complexity, the strongly ethereal nature of her being, I remembered the line from Saturday Night Fever, "When is killing yourself not killing yourself?"

Even a dead body holds a trace of the ethereal pattern. Strongest when life has newly fled, stronger still if the person fought to hold onto life. If someone had enough power… If you threw kindling on ashes, sometimes hot coals under the surface will ignite it.

I took a deep breath. I'd gone on the assumption that Maryann had committed suicide. But if she'd been sacrificed. Would Katelin have permitted it? Then again, if the sacrifice had been made to look like a suicide…

Light can only exist in contrast to darkness. The power to cure is the power to kill, and empathic projection is not a hard skill to gain. There are ways to kill with magic. I could do it, build up charges of negative emotion, depression, despair and feed them into a vulnerable victim's aura. In effect, enhancing the anguish over some real event and poisoning them to the point that they can't recover. Can't heal the emotional wound, bleeding out all the positive energy.

I took a deep breath and concentrated on my driving. Fortunately, the Queen Elisabeth Way was slow that evening.

At that point, I needed to talk to Cathy. I needed another brain on this, and I needed to remember that there was good in the world. If I was right, this tragedy ran deeper than even Katelin knew.

I got home and took a bath in deference to not having water pounding against my sunburned arms and legs. I lay in the cool water, closed my eyes and dozed off.

I woke up to having one of my un-sunburnt regions receiving unexpected attention. I opened my eyes.

"I saw your car and figured you'd be in," Cathy remarked before I'd finished processing her presence. Okay, it isn't always a bad thing that other people have a key to my apartment.

"Cath, Gods." I reached up and tried to pull her in for a kiss, but my arm was like fire as soon as I touched her. I hissed with pain.

Cath leaned down and kissed me. "Let's get some aloe on those burns. Gods, haven't you heard of sunscreen?"

Much later, we spooned on my bed, aloe slathered over my burns and a fan blowing cooler outside air in from the window. The heat wave had broken, and the nights were comfortable.

"It makes sense. They pumped up the ethereal remnant and turned it into a weapon." Cathy echoed my thoughts. "The astral form was still close to the physical, so they bound it to stabilize and refresh the ethereal pattern while surrounding it with rage and hate so that its autonomy was curtailed. It explains the complexity. Maryann is really a next-generation variant on making an artificial elemental. Impressive, but understandable when you realise most of the heavy lifting was done by piggybacking on the pre-existent ethereal and astral forms."

"Then, with each kill, the ethereal form absorbed more energy until it took on self-awareness," I added.

"And, of course, instead of shutting it down when its work was done, the people that made it just broke their connections and left it up to the rest of the group to dissipate it. Irresponsible! Careless!" Cathy shook her head.

"They shouldn't have made it in the first place. I just hope that the karma for the ethereal construct isn't echoing out into Maryann's spiritual essence." I tried not to move in deference to my sunburn.

"I understand why they made it. At the start, all the male victims deserved to be punished."

"The judge and lawyers?" I gently questioned.

"Perpetuated the problem with an attitude of male entitlement. Ray, not all guys are like you. You're too naive." Cathy took on a long-suffering tone.

I let it go, though I could have made some comments about women. "Whatever, the problem remains. We need to shut her down."

"We need more details about the spell that made her. It is still a God's load of energy to pull it off. Could you ask this Katelin woman?"

"I think she'd just block me."

"Turn on the charm." Cathy smiled, "You hussy."

I chuckled. "I think she's immune. Besides, her wife might object."

Cathy chuckled as she turned and stroked her fingers over my chest. "Don't be so sure. A lot of people are more flexible in that department than you might guess."

"Speaking from experience?" there was a trace of surprise in my voice.

Cathy rolled her eyes. "Please! Once, sort of, to see what all the fuss was about. I laughed so hard she got offended and stormed out. I lost a friend over it." Cathy's voice became sad at the last. "Point is, a lot of people straddle the fence. You shouldn't make assumptions."

"Maybe, but she's still married and I won't go against that.

If you don't live up to something, you live down to everything. Though I think I will invite her and her wife to the next open circle. That is innocent enough."

Cathy snorted. "You're not Lancelot. You're Galahad."

"Galahad is not my thing. I'm too Pagan to be celibate."

"Good, I hate to waste resources. So, what's the next move?" Cathy became serious for the last.

"The girl I saw clairvoyantly. We need to find her. I want to check out her aura to be sure she's clean."

"Grandma probably knows her. She's pretty up on the local community."

I closed my eyes and smiled. Beth, Grandma, was a High Priestess and Elder of the Hamilton community. A sweet lady, a master at scrying, and an incurable busy body and gossip. She and my grandfather were 'friends' before he met my grandmother. She kept telling me how much I looked like him. Having seen a couple of old pictures of Beth, I had to appreciate my Granddad's taste.

"I'll call her in the morning." I closed my eyes as sleep covered me like a tide.

"We'll go see her tomorrow. I've got to drop off some gemstone essence I've made to help with her arthritis anyway," was the last I heard that night.

Chapter 11

An Elder's Words

THE NEXT DAY started with a panicked phone call, followed by me filling in teaching school groups. Summer was officially over, though the daytime heat didn't know it, and the business of the schools was in full swing. The regular instructor had been in a traffic accident. Long and short, I made my rent for that month. It was late afternoon before I had a chance to see Beth. Cathy was already at work, so I took the gemstone elixirs over for her.

Beth's house was a small bungalow with a front yard divided into planter boxes. I tend to be a book in one hand herbalist, and a casual glance at what grew in those boxes made me nervous. They were pretty, but if you didn't know what you were doing, deadly as Tartarus. I went to the heavy, wooden door with the stained-glass window in the form of a warding. Mistletoe grew in a hanging basket under the porch eaves.

I knocked and waited. The door was opened by a grey-haired, heavy-set man with a military bearing. "Ray, good to see you."

"Hi Dan, is Beth about?"

"She's in the back garden."

"Permission to enter?" I said it half kidding. Dan had been a Master Sergeant and still carried an air of authority. We got on well because we treated each other as equals. I had a standing invitation to join Beth's coven that I'd never take up for that reason. If Dan ever saw me as subordinate, that would end a friendship I valued. I also asked because entering Granny's house uninvited could bring down, literally, the wrath of the Gods.

"Granted, just go through." Dan stepped aside.

I walked down a hall bedecked with pictures of God forms and stone circles. The back door was custom built like the front with a stained glass insert that was another warding. The house felt safe, like being held in a lover's arms. In fact, it was a mystical fortress that would stop the dangers of the world.

I exited onto a wooden deck. A greenhouse fronted by a vegetable garden filled the end of the lot. A large oak tree grew to one side, shading the house and deck. Beth sat on a little stool amongst a cluster of tomato plants, turning something from a bag into the soil with a garden trowel.

"Hello, Ray," she greeted me as I approached her.

"Hi, Beth," I replied. She was all of five feet with a wiry build and grey hair. Her face was wizened with laugh wrinkles and eyes as green as new leaves.

She cupped the wilted branch of a tomato plant with her hand. "Will you look at this? It's that idiot next door with his chemical fertilisers. He's dumping so much nitrogen into the soil that it's burning my poor tomato's roots."

"Bummer, I knelt beside her."

"I'll just have to dig in a clay barrier to stop the runoff. He'll cry foul when his backyard turns into a puddle, but I've told him before."

"Sounds fair enough. Beth, I need to track someone down. A wanna-be Goth girl that was at the Imbolc circle in the last two years."

"Pick up a trowel and start turning some of this sand into the soil, would you? I'm trying to get something inert in to blend out the dam chemicals. I'll need a bit more information.

There are a lot of switches at the circles, you know." Beth went back to adding sand to her soil.

I picked up the tool and started working the dirt. You did what granny wanted; it was the way of things."Teen, blond, died-black hair, skinny, tattered black dress. Pentagram the size of a hubcap. Probably on a hate man kick."

Beth nodded as she worked. "Penelope. Why a parent would give that name to a child, I don't know, but she owned it. Refused to respond to Penny. Sad really, so much anger. She thought Goddess spirituality was about hating men. Parents were some sort of born-again types. She was in full rebellion. They'd tossed her out of the house for her 'devil's ways' when she showed up with a girlfriend. Worried what the neighbours might think."

Beth stopped working the soil and looked at me as she continued."Stupid, if only her parents had eyes to see past their bigotry and hate. She never stopped eyeing up the men at the circles. I bet she ends up in a house in the suburbs with the standard one point eight children. If you could listen past her foul mouth, she wasn't stupid. Confused and opinionated, but that's just being young."

Beth returned to her work. "She stopped coming to the public circles. I heard that some independent group recruited her, and then something they did scared her off. I just hope they didn't do any permanent harm. Some of these independents can be more than a little wacky."

Beth smiled, looked at me and chuckled."Look who I'm telling. Back in the day, your grandfather and I dealt with more than our share of overly talented, novice twits who got themselves into trouble. That's how he met Susan. Your grandmother was such a pretty girl, and some men don't like taking no for an answer. This one fool—"

"I've heard the story, Beth. I need to talk to Penelope." I kept turning sand into the soil.

"Got herself into trouble, has she?" Beth leaned back and looked serious.

"Maybe. Do you know where she is?"

Beth bit her lip. "Well, last I heard, she was working as a cashier at the No Frills on Main Street. I don't think she would have gone back to her parents. Too much resentment there. I really hope she can let it go for her own sake. I…"

I put down the trawl and dusted off my hands. "Thanks, Beth, I—"

Beth smiled at me and said, "Just like your grandfather. Always racing off to the rescue."

I looked into the elderly features and, for a second, saw a young woman looking out at me. She had a pixy-like beauty and the gentle gaze that only came from loving someone. Granddad had loved my grandmother, but there was a time when he had other options.

Beth continued in motherly tones. "Tell Cathy from me that she better shit or get off the pot. You can't wait forever, Ray, nor should you! I learned that the hard way with your grandfather. Though it worked out with Dan, and Susan was a dear. Live for yourself a little. Even heroes deserve some joy."

I smiled. The old woman saw my Granddad in me. He was a hero. Me; I do what I have to. "Thanks, Beth. I better run." Standing, I brushed the dirt off my legs and made for the door into the house.

"Take care of that knee. Your limp is getting worse." Beth called behind me.

I drove to the No Frills on Main. Stepping into the air-conditioning was like diving into cold water. I took a saunter down the frozen foods section as a special treat. By the time I was done, goosebumps had covered my arms. Picking up milk, bread and OJ, I walked the line of cashers. Penelope was at a checkout. She'd stopped dying her hair. The first two inches was blond, then black to her shoulders. She'd also removed several of her facial piercings since I'd last seen her. The hubcap hanging around her neck was now a two centimetre across pentagram with semi-precious stones at each of the points. All in all, it was an improvement. Her clothing was the store's uniform, so I couldn't judge anything from that. I scanned her aura. It was pulled in tight, but the colours were clean. There was a trace of a shield and the dim image of a raven.

I made sure my Hirakata pendant showed, sauntered up to her cash, and waited in line while mentally projecting an image of a long line behind me. When I reached the register, no other customers were waiting.

"Hi, did you find everything you were looking for?" Penelope shot me a glassy smile.

"I think I have. Penelope, I need to speak with you." I pushed empathically. The girl's shields held for a second. Not great, but better than your average mundane. She was practising. The image of the raven stirred but was discerning enough not to activate to energies of trust and friendliness. Someone had talent and a desire to protect this girl.

Penelope bit her lip as the energies I projected at her did their work.

"I… Who are you?" she half-whispered.

"Ray, Ray McAndrews." I smiled reassuringly.

"I… you go to the public circles?"

"Sometimes."

She looked down. "I… I'm not interested in going out to them. I… It's embarrassing. I was such a poser. I'm not that person anymore. At least, I'm trying not to be."

"Work in progress, aye." I kept smiling and pitched my voice to be friendly.

"Ya… Something like that." Penelope looked up then slowly started moving my items over the scanner. "The head cashier hates me."

"Got you. I'll forget my pin. That will give us a minute. I'm not into judging, and I'm not trying to get you to come to circle. I just need some information about the other group you joined."

The sickly mustard yellow of fear cascaded through her aura.

"I don't want to talk about it." Her voice shook.

"I'm trying to fix it." My words were pitched to be soothing, and then I took a gamble. "I may be able to stop the nightmares."

Penelope nearly dropped the orange juice she was scanning and looked at me with mixed incredulity and hope. Her voice dropped. "Really?"

"Really. When do you get off work? I'll treat you to some Tim's." I kept my voice low so her supervisor wouldn't over-hear.

Penelope eyed me over. "Andrew, my boyfriend, is picking me up."

"He can join us as long as you don't mind talking in front of him."

"I get off in half an hour. We'll meet you out front." Hope and incredulity warred in her tone.

"Sounds good."

Stowing my purchases in a cooler bag, I went out to my car and waited.

Penelope exited the store with a tall, lanky youth with short blond hair and a scraggly beard. Norse runes were tattooed up and down his arms, and he wore a Mjolnir pendant. There was no mistaking the kid's affiliation. He looked at Penelope. A wave of clean yellow energy flowed out of him to wash over her. The raven in Penelope's aura glowed brighter. He was a student of the Norse Runes and perhaps more. I guessed, just starting on his journey. More importantly, he loved Penelope. You could see it in how his aura brightened when he looked at her. I liked him for that. I'm a romantic.

I moved to intercept the couple. Minutes later, we sat at a plastic table in a nondescript coffee shop sipping cold drinks and sharing a jumbo box of doughnut holes.

"Penelope says you can help with her nightmares." Andrew eyed me sceptically.

"I may be able to. That's why I'm here." I looked Andrew in the eyes. In two or three years, we could be friends. At that time, he saw other males as rivals and wanted to place them in the hierarchy. You can take the chimp out of the jungle, but you can't take the jungle out of the chimp. Most of us outgrow it.

"Why should we trust you?" he challenged.

"Because, while your raven is nice work, it's not up to the job." I kept it matter of fact.

Penelope grabbed Andrew's arm and looked startled.

"Really." Andrew traced the tattooed rune Tyr on his forearm.

I sighed, reached with my mind and drew a grounding line up through the table, dissipating the energies he was building.

"If it helps, I'll swear by Mjolnir, the Spear of Lugh and the scales of Ma'at that I have Penelope's best interests at heart." That, the way Penelope gripped his arm and the fact that I'd blocked his shot without breaking a sweat, stopped him cold.

Andrew nodded. "Go ahead, honey."

"What do you want to know?" asked Penelope.

"The ritual in the graveyard where you killed the swan. I need more details." I kept my voice steady and tried to add a comforting note.

"You know about that? I… I didn't know they were going to do that. Katelin seemed so nice. I'd only done a couple of rituals with the coven. I'd never seen most of the other women at that one, they came from all over, and boy, were they aggressive. I mean, yea, some guys are jerks, and I had a big hate on for men back then. I…" Penelope closed her eyes. "I had a good reason, or at least I thought I did."

Andrew hugged her around the shoulders. "It's past. That bastard can't hurt you again."

Penelope rested in that embrace. After a while, she nodded and took a deep breath, then continued. "The coven had been nice up until then. You see, I was, well…"

"Dating a girl and a community that understood was pleasant," I filled in the line to leapfrog us to something useful to me.

"How did you know that? It was a phase." She sounded desperate not to be pigeonholed.

Andrew squeezed her hand.

I smiled. "Probably, and it doesn't matter so long as you're happy with who you're with."

"She's the one that brought me into the group. Last I heard, she was living in North York someplace," said Penelope.

"Tell me about the ritual?" I encouraged.

"It was scary. Cecilia was High Priestess. I never liked her. She seemed angry all the time and never smiled. Not even at Ellen."

"Ellen, Katelin's wife?"

Penelope nodded. "Yea. Cecilia is Ellen's mum. In real life, not just in circle. I always got the feeling she didn't like Katelin. I think it was the racial thing. You know that bullshit that peoples of the north shouldn't mix with others. It was stupid. Even if it wasn't bullshit, like lesbians, how are they going to mix bloodlines?"

"I hate it when people use northern religions to draw lines like that. The wisdom of Odin is for all." Andrew shook his head sadly.

I smiled at him. The kid seemed to have found a good path for himself.

"Did they tell you to pick a man to be punished?" I kept my voice soft and pushed warm, supportive energy towards the girl. Penelope was young and not just in years. The young needed to be protected. I could understand her attraction to Andrew. He needed to protect. He was a guardian, a hero in an age without heroes. Left without an outlet, that heroic nature could become twisted. For the moment, they were good for each other. For the future, who knows?

Penelope stared at the table. "I picked… It doesn't matter. He just vanished, and I don't care if they ever find him." She looked into my eyes as if expecting judgment.

"Ma'at's feather will weigh what it weighs. It's not my place to check the scales." I shrugged.

"All right." She gave me a sad smile. "I picked my dad too."

A bolt of worry shot through me at that.

"He… The hypocrite cheated on my mom. All his bullshit about 'the way' and he does that." Penelope's cheeks reddened in anger.

"Is he alright?" I kept my voice even.

"My mom forgave him, so I kinda had to. I don't see them much, but, you know, they're still my parents."

I sighed with relief. Penelope's distance from the spell and forgiveness must have moved her father down the target list to inconsequentiality. I still made a mental note to follow up if Maryann wasn't quickly dealt with. "When the quarters were called, which aspects were used?"

We talked until the doughnut holes were devoured, and the waitress started giving us the stink eye. What I learned was frightening. The ritual was dark. When Tiamat wants nothing to do with a rite, that should tell you something. I used some of the time that Penelope spoke to closely review her aura. The connection point from where I'd broken the link to Maryann was still raw. In a mystical sense, it was like something had stung her and left the stinger behind. In time her energy systems would expel the foreign negativity, but it would cause problems until then. And I had promised to help with the nightmares. I invited the couple back to my apartment, where I could safely purge the last of the Maryann energies.

When Andrew stepped into my temple room, his eyes darted from my arcane library to the altar and back so fast, I thought they would pop out of their sockets. I felt him touch my standard wards, and he looked on the border of peeing himself. To his credit, he moved unconsciously between Penelope and me. The kid had guts, at least as far as she was concerned.

Penelope stared at the statuary with a surprised expression. "Egyptian, right?" she asked.

"Primarily, but I'm pretty eclectic. You know the Horus of the Egyptians is the Lugh of the Celts and all that jazz." I kept my voice soothing. "Let's see about those nightmares." Moving to my altar, I opened a drawer and pulled out a small piece of obsidian. "May I?" Penelope nodded. I touched the stone to the area over her heart chakra.

She nodded. Andrew stepped to the side and watched cautiously.

I focussed and reached with my will, finding the energy left from the dark ritual and her connection with Maryann. I had been right. It can happen, but don't tell Cathy. She won't believe you.

Even with the connection broken, the spell traces were powerful. Activating my heart chakra, I sent bands of power into Penelope and pulled the Maryann energies up and into the obsidian, like a poultice drawing poison from a wound. It was delicate, low-intensity work, not my best suit, but it was straightforward with the link broken. When I was done, Penelope was clean, and the dark ritual could now take its place in her past as a lesson learned.

Andrew scanned her aura nodded and took her hand. "Thank you."

"Any time. If you ever need a hand, keep my number. We're all in this together."

Getting them out of my apartment took only moments, then I was back to work on the revenant. Holding the obsidian in one hand, I traced the spines of my books with the other. Three called to me. I took them off the self.

One contained an English translation of the Kalevala, big surprise. The next was on shamanic practices of the Finns, and the third on creating artificial elementals. The books joined Sekmara and me in my bed. I awoke the next morning to my alarm with the texts still beside me.

After work, I hit the books again then sat quietly in front of my altar. I'd cast the circle and lit the altar candles. A fan droned in the window, covering the sounds from the street. Cathy was at the bar, and I'd turned off the ringtone on my phone. I'd told Kama I was not to be disturbed for anything short of a threat to life, limb or vital organ. Kama knew I was serious, so she'd give me space. Funny, for things like that, Kama respected me more than pretty much anybody else in my life. My parents knew better than to drive up unannounced.

"Lord Thoth, God of wizardry, Lady Aset, Goddess of sorcery, Lady Nephthys, lady of divination. I pray thee, open my inner eye. Let me see clearly that which I must so as to face this darkness that has taken the form of Maryann." I spoke the words that would help channel my thoughts and focused on the items I'd collected thus far that had traces of the revenant's energy.

My breath caught as a feeling like someone staring at me with malignant intent crept up my back and made my fingers twitch. I pushed past it. "Reveal yourself!"

My eyes closed as lights flashed against the backs of my eyelids. I kept my mind empty. Slowly, the lights coalesced. I saw a youthful man's face distorted in pain, blood spurting from a wound in his groin. There was a warm wash of power. Sluggishly, an independent thought formed in what had before been nothing more than an imperative to perform an act.

A simple, primal thought. 'Hungry.'

This was the kill when the ethereal Maryann had accumulated enough energy to evolve beyond being a magical robot. The revenant's first bit of self-determination. The feeding I was witnessing in my vision was the point where the women that forged her from a young girl's ethereal remnant lost control.

Kill after kill followed. The proto awareness grew more independent with each death. The motivation became more complex as more of the pattern was drawn from the astral. Hunger, vengeance, anger, rage, then, as the connection to the astral template strengthened remorse and curiosity. The parts of Maryann that were not used to make the weapon started to push into the ethereal form. Then came a kill, but the warm wash barely touched Maryann before it was pulled away.

I could feel the revenant's rage. Like an animal being offered food only to have it snatched away. She reared up. The tie that had stolen the energy flashed with power. The revenant was forced back as if whipped. Maryann had responded like any hungry animal denied its kill. She'd hunted again.

I pondered what I 'saw'. Maryann, the etheric entity, had become more complete with each feeding. She had taken on aspects of selfhood far beyond an artificial elemental and was connected to an astral pattern. That connection meant that something like consciousness leaking through wasn't surprising. The traces of her trapped in the objects around me were still connected enough to the main entity for me to sense her pattern. A disturbing thought came to me.

Where is the line drawn between a revenant and a demon? With each feeding, Maryann became more independent of the spell that made her. Would there come a point that she broke free of the lunar schedule that had been part of her creation? Broke free of the modicum of control the spell forced on her? Would the constant bombardment of hate and anger around the astral form eradicate the gentler parts of that spiritual pattern bringing about a full union with the twisted ethereal form?

Another thought. One of her creators was powerful enough to still exercise some control over the revenant. Would she want Maryann able to hunt at will? If she stole the energies of the kills, she probably would.

I shook my head. Long and short, I couldn't rely on the cycle of lunar quarters to know when my foe would hunt. Especially if she was being used as someone's personal attack dog. That made me think of Morgana, Katelin's familiar. I felt sorry for the pooch being tangled up with this mess.

"I'll have to set some kind of alarm on Maryann's grave," I muttered.

Opening a drawer in my altar, I rummaged through a collection of jars and loose paraphernalia, finally extracting a glass jar of iron nails I'd bought at a blacksmithing demonstration. Materials in hand, I got to work.

Chapter 12

Love Long Past

T WAS THE following evening before I could get out to Maryann's grave. I paced its perimeter, sensing the energies beneath the surface. Taking an iron nail, I pulled my camping compass from my pocket and located east. Focusing my will, I thrust the nail I'd enchanted into the ground. "By the citizens of Duamutef, she may not pass east, save that they shall tell me."

I moved to the south and repeated the action with another nail. "By the citizens of Imseti, she may not pass south, save that they shall tell me."

I stepped to the west, and a third nail followed. "By the citizens of Qebehsenuf, she may not pass west save that they shall tell me."

I moved to the north, inserting the last nail into the ground. "By the citizens of Hapi, she may not pass north, save that they shall tell me."

I strode to the location of the first nail and brushed the earth with my fingers. "By the lords of the elements four, the sons of Horus, the avenging son of his father, the lord of those gone before, let not this restless being journey forth save that I shall know her passing."

Okay, I can get a bit pompous when I do incantations.

I walked to the shade of a nearby tree and commenced with the second part of my reason for being in that particular graveyard. People, and dogs, are creatures of habit. I closed my eyes and thought of Morgana, the dog, not the Goddess. I pictured her running up to me. I imagined myself giving her the dog treat I had in my pocket, then I mentally pushed that image out into the world. To call it a summoning gives it too much credit. An invitation would be a better description. Twenty minutes later, I heard a bark and opened my eyes to see a shaggy brown behemoth bounding across the grass towards me with Katelin in hot pursuit.

I'd gained my feet before Morgana reached me. The force of her welcome almost put me back on the ground.

"Morgana! Bad girl! I… Ray." Katelin stood breathing hard, staring at me.

I petted the massive canine head and slipped her the dog treat from my pocket.

"Hi, Katelin. Good to see you."

"You too. I'm sorry about Morgana."

"She must have caught my scent and wanted to say hi."

"Were you visiting your friend?" Katlin's voice became comforting.

"Just out for a walk." I kept my tone light.

"Oh."

"Company?" I smiled.

Katelin smiled back. "Why not? It won't be a long walk. I have to get back and put on dinner for Elly and her mom."

I heard the drop in tone when Katelin mentioned her mother-in-law. There was hostility there to burn. "That's okay. I need to get home soon anyway. Cathy's coming for dinner."

"That's nice. So, how are things?"

We sauntered among the tombstones.

"Better now that the city pools are on fall schedule. A lot of the guards are students, so they have spotty availability. If I'm willing to pool hop, I can get hours easy. It will steady out when the rest of the school groups start swim lessons. Same thing every year. I've had some freelance work doing safety assessments for backyard pools and some private swim lessons." I kept it conversational, just the day-to-day minutiae of life.

"It must be nice working with kids."

"It buys the cat food. You know, the important stuff," I grinned.

Morgana gave a woof and waged her tail.

Katelin smiled. "Morgana seems to agree."

A low thrumming sound filled the air. We both scanned the sky.

"There," Katelin pointed.

The silhouette was unmistakable. The Lancaster bomber flew to the south of us, the noise of its four engines nearly shaking the trees.

"Beautiful old bird. It's one of the last two flying," I observed.

"I love the air museum. They have a spitfire as well. Elly and I went there just after we moved here."

"My granddad was bomber command. He loved Lancasters." I paused in thought, then sang, off-key and shaky. It doesn't matter because I'm a little tone-deaf anyways.

"Comin' in on a wing and a prayer
"Comin' in on a wing and a prayer
"With our one motor gone
"We can still carry on."

Katelin joined me. Her voice was considerably better than mine.

"Comin' in on a wing and a prayer
"What a show, what a fight
"Boys, we really hit our target for tonight
"How we sing as we limp through the air
"Look below, there's our field over there

"With our one motor gone
"We can still carry on
"Comin' in on a wing and a prayer
"Comin' in on a wing and a prayer
"Comin' in on a wing and a prayer
"With our full crew on board
"And our trust in the Lord
"We're comin' in on a wing and a prayer."

Katelin smiled at me. "It was a dark time, but you have to admire the courage and selflessness."

"Politicians and big business make wars. The rest of us endure them. We'll have to go to the air museum sometime." I let my tone lighten for the last.

"I'd like that. I…" Katelin looked at me. It was one of those charged moments. We both knew what we wanted, and we both knew it was wrong for so many reasons. I could smell her, a spicy aroma that made my heart pound.

"I better get home." Katelin broke the moment.

"Me too. You have my number. Maybe you, Ellen, Cathy and I could double sometime."

"Maybe. Bye," The mixed emotions added a strained quality to her voice.

I waved and watched her walk away. It was a surprisingly good view.

I got home to find that Cathy had left me a message. "Something" had come up. She cancelled our dinner. I was betting from the BMW I'd seen in the guest parking that her pilot friend was in town.

I'd have to cook the stakes I had marinating over the next couple of days. The potatoes would keep, as would the pie I'd bought for dessert. I put the candles back into storage and put the good dishes, wine glasses and tablecloth away. The stake was extraordinary, but it turned to bile in my belly because of the circumstance.

My evening was shot, so I retired to the temple room after dinner, set my wards, and invoked Thoth, the record keeper of the Egyptian Gods.

Slipping into meditation, I visualised a long table with hats from various time periods. I walked its length, and then picked up a British officer's cap from WWII. I'd touched that life before. I'd been twenty-one, a spitfire pilot in the Battle of Brittan. What I remembered most was an image of a cockpit in flames and the ocean coming up fast. I'd had six kills to my official tally. I also remembered a rosy-cheeked, blond woman in a polka-dot maternity dress waving as a truck full of other pilots took me away. Past lives are like that. Fragments that you pieced together to get what you needed. What lived on was the important stuff, courage, love, compassion, kindness, the essence that makes up your personality. Details cling like flotsam to the core. Tonight, I needed more than that. If I could understand the connection between Katelin and me, it might show me how to break her link to Maryann. I was betting without Katelin's link, the revenant would begin to dissolve into the background either. In the meditation, I could feel the connection to Katelin most strongly from the officer's cap, though there were traces of it in some of the others. This one was the closest in time and issues dealt with.

In the meditation, I put on the cap and let Ray slip away. I was in fighter command during the Battle of Britain.

The visions that came were like living the experience in present time. I was who I had been, and the events were happening in the now. Later I would have perspective, but for the duration of the regression, that was how it was for me.

I clutch the control stick. The rest of the squadron are down, but my rudder is sluggish. I can see the ground through a hole by my feet, and part of my canopy is blown out. "That one almost had my bloody number on it." The stink of fuel is thick in my nostrils, and my engine is spewing smoke.

"Hold together, girl. Get us down, and they'll patch you up right as rain." My accent is British, middle class, nothing special.

The engine coughs as if my spitfire heard me. I manage to get her nose up. There's a jolt from the right, followed by one from the left. I'm on the ground. I kill throttle and let the tail drop. The spit slows, and then stops. I pop the hood, release my harness, and bolt out of the cockpit. I stop running when I'm twenty paces away, just in case that fuel leak catches.

A moment passes.

"You glorious bastard!" I feel a blow to my back as relief courses through me. I turn to see a handsome, pale face with a cap of black hair. The man is dressed as an airman. My heart lets go of a fear that has clutched it since I lost track of him during the dog fight.

Another airman strides up and slaps me on the shoulder. "That were five and six for you. Would 'av been seven 'sept that Gerry ducked out of the clouds."

"Five and six." I'm not as proud of that achievement as I should be. Six families to grieve. I swallow it down. We didn't ask old Adolf to send his bombers over, but sure as hell, we weren't going to lie down for it either.

"Come on, first rounds on me. Let the boys in maintenance patch up our birds." The first man grabs my arm and pulls me away.

There's a time break.

We're in a pub. I feel pleasantly numb.

"Ricky, time for bed." The first man to speak to me, the special one, takes my arm and guides me up a staircase.

Break.

The door to a simply appointed bedroom closes. The man is in my arms, holding me, kissing me passionately.

"I thought I'd lost you when that bloody Nazi shot out your tail," says my handsome paramour.

There is humour in my voice. "Keith, you know you're the only tail gunner that will ever get a shot in with me."

Keith gives a short laugh and holds me close. "I love you."

I pull away enough to lift his chin with my finger and kiss him. "And I love you."

The vision skips. I'm naked on the bed with Keith.

"When are you going to tell her?" asked Keith.

I feel a pang of guilt. I'm torn in two. "It isn't that simple."

"You said it wasn't just school boy hi-jinks."

"It isn't. Keith, I love you, but she is my wife, and she's carrying my child. Then there's the law. What if she decides to turn us in?"

"So, you just keep living a lie?"

"No. I'll tell her when the time is right. When we can go someplace safe, but really, with the war, either one of us could buy it any day. Then what good would it have done to hurt her like that or to take that kind of risk? And if the air force finds out, you know what they'd do."

"No fairy squadron."

"Bloody right! Dumb as it is. Love, for today, isn't it more important we do our bit. After that, I'll tell her."

"Promise?"

I cup his cheek. He cannot know what I feel, how much he means to me. Rose had been a mistake, something expected of me. Then he had come, and it was like my heart came alive. "I know who I love. I promise, when the war is over, I will give you all of me." I kiss him. He responds in kind.

Time Break.

The siren sounds. I run to my plane. The boys worked through the night, and she's as right as rain. I rush through the pre-flight, and then shoot Keith a thumbs up. Wingman, beloved. I had something to come home to, even if it was just a room for let above McCleary's Pub.

The roar of engines. The dance of man and machine, then the jolt, the dive, the fire, the water, and blackness.

The trance left me feeling disoriented with an intense need to reaffirm my sexuality. I open the circle and stagger out to find it's just shy eleven pm. Biting my lip, I moved to my computer side phone and called Cathy. The worst she could do was say no, and she did stand me up. She answered on the second ring. I can hear a man snoring in the background. I don't need to say how that made me feel.

"What?" Cathy sounded peeved.

"Cath, it's Ray. I know it's late, but I need you. Can you come down?"

"Ray… Oh, why not. I can't stay the night. Give me a minute to shower."

I hung up, hating myself. How little self-respect did I have? At least she was showering.

Fifteen minutes later, I opened the door. Cathy stepped in, wearing a housecoat, with her still wet hair loose.

"So, what do you need?" she asked.

I closed the door and pushed her against the wall, kissing her. She responded in kind as my hands explored. The effect touching her had on me drove away a thousand insecurities. I needed this after the regression. I'm a hetero man, and having my self-image challenged by a past life wasn't pleasant. There was a good reason I hadn't accessed the particulars of that life before now. I don't knock others for their orientation, but I still need to be me.

Over an hour later, Cathy kissed me and left my bed.

"You saved my evening," remarked Cathy as she pulled on her robe.

I leaned on one elbow. "Really?"

"Let's just say, Tom, is only good for short flights." Cathy shot me a saucy wink.

I could have lived without the reminder.

She kissed me again, and then left the room.

I leaned back and thought about the connection to Katelin.

The next evening, I opened my circle, having prepared myself for battle. It was the lunar quarter. I knew Maryann would be hunting for sure. I also had a good sense of the general area that she would be in. She was still bound by her links, and the mortal links all lived in the area around the Royal Botanical Gardens main garden. I also had a plan on how to lure the beast.

A half-hour later, I parked at the back entrance to the

Grindstone Marshes Trail. I opened my car's trunk and pulled out the duffle containing my ritual tools. If I had the time, Maryann, and her puppeteer, were going to get a harsh lesson in what a wizard could do with a little preparation.

I followed the trail by the river that wound up a wooded valley following the raised platform walk that made up much of the path to the wooded area beyond. Finding a relatively flat piece of ground that was shielded from view, I opened my kit, pulled out my crook and flail and paced a circle. Setting a simple altar and summoning the elements took a few moments more. I then spread out a towel I kept in my kit for wiping up spills and sat on it.

The calliope of nature closed in. Bats flew after insects as mosquitoes swarmed. I broke down under the onslaught of bugs and lit some incense sticks that I thrust into the moist ground. The smell of sandalwood permeated the forest. It's possible that some of the mosquitoes were dissuaded, though I doubt it. Obnoxious little vampires. My respect for life has limits.

I felt something like being doused with cold water. My alarm around Maryann's grave had been triggered.

I closed my eyes, took deep breaths, and set my lure. I thought of Katelin. She was a beautiful woman. Her lack of interest in my gender didn't alter my interest in her. I filled my mind with the thought of her. What it would be like to touch her, caress her, kiss her. In my fantasy, she responded in kind. In my imagination, things progressed. I projected the energy of my fantasy out of my circle. I was less than a kilometre from Maryann's grave and as close to Katelin's and Ellen's residence. I taunted the ethereal beast, doing the mystical equivalent of chumming shark-infested waters.

Energy slammed into my circle. The effect was like being in a tent during a windstorm. Ethereal energies raced around the protective orb, which flexed, spreading the force of the blows. I slowly stood, picking up my crook and flail.

"Gnomes, I invoke thee spirits of the earth, citizens of Lord Hapi, son of Horus the warrior. Bind the force that seeks my end. Tie it to the living world and drain its power." I made a striking motion with the flail. An arc of green energy lashed out into the reds and blacks of the revenant.

The attacking force was driven into the ground as a scream that only I could hear split the night. The energy pulled away. I focused on the spell, keeping my concentration on my foe. Words mean nothing. The controlled will is all. Incantations and actions distract the conscious mind and help translate the intent into the language of the spirit. A true master needs do no more than sit and concentrate. I use incantations and actions. I'm not self-deluding.

Maryann pulled away until my grounding spell faded, and then she was back. This time I was treated to the mental image of me embracing Katelin and the sound of a scream. In the vision, I watched as I was torn in two, and my head went flying away from my body parts. Emotional energy filled the area around my circle: despair, regret, shame, rage.

There was a sense of betrayal. Maryann was a being of energy. She couldn't tell the difference between the fantasy I projected and reality. In her limited perspective, I had persuaded the one she loved in the very pattern of her being to join the enemy camp. I felt the emotion as if it were my own. It resonated with the pain Cathy's running around caused me. It clawed at that wound and made me want to weep in joint sympathy with Maryann, but that would mean letting her in, and I knew the danger of that.

The mood changed. In a fury, the revenant slammed against my circle. The life of the forest responded by fleeing the area in a mad rush of rustling leaves and swaying branches, giving the two crazy predators plenty of space. My warding shook. I directed my energy into the circle.

There was a pause, then the sound of distant sobbing. The energies before me coalesced into the form of a pretty Black woman, in her early teens, with a sad expression. Maryann as she had been in life. The emotions changed to despair and crushing fear. I wanted to comfort her. This attack pulled at a deep core of masculinity that called me to defend, to heal. I knew it for a deception. Maryann couldn't conceptualise positive masculinity. What mind she had couldn't think of men as anything but evil.

Taking a breath to steady myself, I projected my perceptions into my foe. The four lines remained. I realised that energy flowed in both directions along each. One of the lines pulsed with tarnished gold light. One with red rage and one black, waiting to draw away the energies it expected Maryann to acquire for it. The green one trickled along. The third was the most daunting of the lines. Even dormant, there was a frightening power. She who was linked by it was a master of her Craft.

Maryann slashed at my probe, sending a bolt of energy along its length. My knees buckled, and I hit the ground, barely managing to direct the attack into the earth. After a few moments of resting in the protection of my circle, which was being bombarded with an ethereal tornado, I picked up my crook and flail and rose shakily to my feet.

"I adjure thee, child of Loviatar, born of pain, fed on despair."

The tornado stopped. The name of Loviatar held power over my foe, but not a power that would do me any good. I got the sense of a stalking komodo dragon mixed with a feted swamp when I touched that archetype.

"By the flail that commands and the crook that guides. By the powers of Khonsu, banisher of demons, and Aset, Goddess of Sorcery. By Sekhmet, warrior Goddess of two faces, I command thee be bound to your grave. Your time is past. Sleep in the earth. Trouble the world of the living no more. Return your energies to those who made you. Lay quiet at your rest."

Purple, gold and red swept from my tools. I visualised chains wrapping around Maryann's arms and legs, dragging her back to her grave. I saw her energies flow up the links, feeding the living emotions that bound her to the earth back from whence they came. There was a psychic wail as the energies retreated, and then stillness.

I took a half step before sinking to sit on my towel. I doubted that I'd bound her for good. I'd check her grave later, but, for the moment, she was chained. That night, no man would die because of Maryann, and that was good.

Rising, I thanked the Gods, opened my circle and made my way home, scratching at a myriad of bites and cursing mosquitoes. I was running on fumes, and half the night was shot by the time I hit the sheets.

— Chapter 13 —

An Ugly Situation

MANAGED TO get to work only five minutes late. A special needs man defecated in the pool, forcing us to super chlorinate the water, meaning that all the other programming for the morning had to be cancelled. It would be bad enough if this had been the first time this had happened, but I knew this character and his handler from last year when the same thing happened. After a day of being yelled at because of policies that respect the rights of the few to the detriment of the many, all I wanted to do was sleep. Instead, I got home to my phone ringing. I let the machine get it.

"Ray, it's Katelin. I need help. I—" Her voice sounded stressed.

Dropping my gym bag, I raced to pick up the line.

"Katelin, it's me. I just got in from work."

"Ray. I… I know you don't know me that well, but I need help."

Sir Galahad charged up on his bloody big horse and trampled common sense. When will I learn not to be a sucker for a damsel in distress?

"How can I help?" How much trouble have those words gotten me into?

"I'm at St. Josephs' Hospital. Can you pick me up? I... I really need a friend. You said we were friends." The memories from the regression were fresh in my head. What could I say? Love doesn't die. Evolves, changes, yes. Dies, no.

"I'll be there in fifteen minutes." I pumped all the reassurance into my voice I could.

I raced to my car and was at the hospital in ten minutes. Katelin sat out in front of the main entrance. At first glance, she looked alright, and then she moved, revealing bruises on her arms. She limped to my car and took my passenger side seat.

"Walked into a door, fell down a flight of steps, got hit by a car," I listed off the usual suspects. My dad had used them all at one point or another.

"She pushed me down the stairs." Katelin's lip trembled. Soon she was sobbing. I stopped on a side street and put my arms around her. She collapsed into the embrace. After what seemed a long time, she pulled away. "Thank you."

"Do you want to go to my place and talk?" I offered.

"Please. I know you hardly know me, but..."

Lancelot had joined Galahad, and they had commonsense on the ropes.

"Whatever you need." I made my voice soft.

The drive to my place was conducted in silence.

When we reached my door, I had a thought, *A good thing about being an eclectic archetype is you have a lot of defence options.*

I opened the door and motioned Katelin in while saying in a formal tone, "Be welcome if thou would be bound by the law of mistletoe."

"I. We're just friends. I don't..." Katelin looked confused and a little scared.

"It means a peace bond. You will take no actions to harm me, nor will you invite anyone or thing in that may do me harm. That's all. I guess you haven't studied the Celtic mysteries."

"Sorry, all I know about mistletoe is you kiss under it."

Katelin blushed.

"The tradition is more involved. It invokes the druidic laws of hospitality. Short-form, we both promise to be decent to each other."

"I like the Celtic version." Katelin stepped through my doorway, passing under the sprig of herb I kept on the sill. In minutes, we sat on my couch with cups of Camomile tea. Sekmara snuggled in Katelin's lap, receiving an absent-minded petting and purring to beat the band. Have I mentioned that I love my familiar?

"I like your place. It's… uncluttered." Katelin sipped her tea.

"Less to dust." I kept to a light tone. She'd talk when she was ready.

Katelin gave a sad smile. "I don't know what I'm going to do. I've got no place to go. My mom's out west and we don't get on. I really don't have any friends here, and I don't know if the women's shelters would take me. I mean because, well… you know."

"The great lie that women somehow aren't people, so they couldn't possibly abuse someone." I nodded, agreeing with my own assessment of too many things in my culture.

Katelin bit her lip and nodded. "I guess you figured out the truth about my black eye."

"I figured. Why did you put up with it?"

"It wasn't always like this. I… What I said about university was true. It was good before Cecilia, Elly's mom, moved in and… My sister dying hit me hard before that. At first, after Maryann's death, Elly was so sweet and supportive. I guess it got to her after a while. It's my fault. It can't be easy to live with someone who's always depressed. Maybe if I promise to be better, she'll take me back? I—"

I shook my head and spoke with gentle firmness. "So next time she can stab you with a kitchen knife? Or maybe beat you with a fireplace poker?"

Katelin looked at me with a shocked expression.

"I've heard this crap before." A weary resolve entered my

voice. It's hard to watch someone you love being hurt. My father's situation left me with little tolerance or understanding of domestic violence. "I'll tell you the same thing I told my father. Ellen's actions are her own responsibility. She chose to hit you, and no matter what it was like before, you are living in the now. She is hurting you in the now, and if she really loved you, she wouldn't do that." I felt a little chime going off in the back of my own mind, but, as I'd done all too often, I chose to ignore it. Maybe I was a little more like my father than I wanted to think.

"Your father." Katelin paused in stroking Sekmara.

"Dysfunctional families are a dime a dozen. Point is, it isn't your fault, and when you realise that, you can start to make things right."

Katelin resumed petting Sekmara, who purred. "Maybe you're right. My mom always told me I wasn't that great, and I'd be lucky to get a man to look after me."

I snorted. "You don't need a man, or a woman, for that matter. You're smart, funny and have looks that could stop a truck."

She sighed. "Thanks. Now, if I wasn't homeless."

"Use the couch tonight. We'll pick up an air mattress to-morrow. We can find you something more permanent over the next couple of weeks."

"I couldn't." Katelin's voice blended surprise and tentative hope. My guess was she hadn't known a lot of simple kindness in her life.

"Just don't leave hand-washing hanging up on the shower-curtain rod. Cathy does that, and it drives me nuts. Bath-rooms are for cleaning people, not pantyhose." I kept my voice light.

"Are you sure? Won't it bother… your girlfriend?"

"One, there is nothing for her to be bothered about." Being two-timed in one night still irked me no matter that I'd invited her to do it. "Two, she insists on casual, so she has no right to be bothered. Three, she'd never refuse help to some-one who needs it. You have a place to stay until we can get you settled."

Sekmara leapt down while Katelin threw her arms around me in a hug. "Thank you."

"We'll go to your place tomorrow so you can get your things. By the way, what was Ellen's excuse last night?" I had a suspicion I wouldn't like the answer.

"I don't know. For some reason, I started thinking about Maryann, and Elly started getting angry. I used to think it was something to do with her cycle. For nearly a year, like clock-work, every seven days, she'd fly off the handle. Anyway, Cecilia got on my case about me not hanging up the laundry. Elly joined in, complaining that I was a slob and never did the housework. She got madder and madder. I went to get the laundry basket, and Elly pushed me down the stairs. When I came to, the ambulance guys were checking me over. They took me to the hospital for observation." Katelin looked at the floor sadly.

And, of course, I was to blame. Well, maybe in part. I'd driven the emotional energies back from the revenant up the binding lines. Ellen got a hit of rage. Then again, from what Katelin said, that must have happened whenever the revenant hunted. Probably, with fewer links taking the load, the hit was harder, and I'd put it over the top. Still, being angry doesn't mean you have to act on it. No, on this one, I put my guilt away. You don't hit people you supposedly love. A slap on the wrist to stop a toddler from sticking things in a light socket is one thing. Pushing someone down the stairs in a fit of pique is another.

We talked a little more, and then I made up the couch. The next day was going to be trying. The last thing I did be-fore going to bed was to hang my robe on the bedroom door-knob to remind me to use it in the middle of the night.

The next morning, I drew the line when the special needs man showed up in a swimsuit. I insisted on a water-safe adult diaper. The handler flew off the handle. Three of the other patrons saw what went down and thanked me. I asked them to pre-emptively call the city and fill in my bosses on the situation. Guards had been fired for not allowing 'special needs' people to ruin the pool for everyone else, and I needed my job. That day everyone else got to enjoy the pool.

I got home to find Katelin and Kama sitting at my kitchen table over tea.

"Hi, Ray. I came to do the cleaning, and Katelin was here. I can't wait to tell Cathy." Kama smiled at me from her seat.

"Katelin is just staying for a few days. We're not—"

"I know, but Cathy doesn't need to know that. It will serve her right. You can help me with my homework next week. I know you have things to do. You should call Precious Paws. They might be able to help find Morgana a place to stay for a few days." Kama got up and kissed me on the cheek, then whispered in my ear, "Don't go all noble. It's about fucking time Cathy stopped treating you like a doormat," before she waltzed out the door.

"How many women do you have in your life?" asked Katelin.

"Kama is like a kid sister," I explained.

"You may think so." Katelin snorted.

I shrugged. "Ready to go?"

Katelin nodded. "I'm hoping Elly will still be at work. Cecilia will probably be there. I wish she hadn't moved in. We've never got along, but what could I say? She's ill: cancer. The doctor gave her six months, but that was nearly a year ago. Elly wanted to look after her mom."

I sighed. Family was something I had no business commenting on, but it was another piece of the puzzle falling into place. People do horrible things to cling to life. The turning wheel blocks our view ahead and lends fear to us all.

The drive to Katelin's semi-detached house was quiet. A quick stop at the liquor store provided us with boxes that filled my back seat and trunk. I knew they wouldn't be enough, but the essentials would probably fit. Her brown, brick house was identical to every other unit on the street with a postage stamp for a front yard. An apple tree grew in the yard's centre, surrounded by a circular planter of various low growing herbs. Concrete steps led up to the front door. The front window was adorned with a press on mock stained-glass bear. I walked with Katelin to the entrance. She produced a key from under a fake rock on the porch.

"First thing, I get my purse." She opened the door to reveal a long corridor that opened to a living/dining room on one side and a staircase on the other. I could glimpse a refrigerator through a door at the hall's end. There was a large picture of an elk hanging up in the hall, as well as a pentacle made up of vines and sticks hanging on the front door.

"Elinore, is that you?" A harsh voice called from the far end of the hall. A woman who looked like she was made of piano wire stretched over a frame of broomsticks and covered with age-spotted skin walked into the hall. She wore a heavy, black dress.

"You! I hope you're happy with all the trouble you caused. We had the police here. All because of your foolishness." The old hag came up. I could almost see the venom she spat.

"Cecilia, just go back to the kitchen." Katelin stood her ground, but I could feel her emotions wavering. I projected confidence towards her as I wrapped my shields around both of us and boosted them.

"You mind your manners, girl!" Red energy blasted towards Katelin, but my shield deflected the attack. The old woman snarled at me. "What is that doing in my house? Leave immediately!" She flicked her wrist at me, sending a wave of energy towards me.

I instinctively grounded the attack and reinforced my shields. Katelin was competent, but as I said, bush-league. It didn't surprise me that her mother-in-law could will-dominate her. The woman was, to continue the analogy, Babe Ruth at bat. The empathic thrust was nearly undeniable. Nearly.

"We're just here to get Katelin's things. There is no need for this to get unpleasant." I took a deep breath and thought an invocation to Horus. My aura filled with golden light. I met the old hag's gaze.

"She's not going anywhere!" Cecilia held my eyes and

spoke with a voice like rusty iron. This was pure. Two trained wills locked one against the other. In the course of a few seconds, battles were fought. Strategies made and discarded. I saw inside her. She hated me, hated my gender, hated that I was foiling her plans. She couldn't help but sense that I was the one that had been thwarting Maryann. Seconds ticked by as I felt her fear. Death courted her. It hounded every second of her day and invaded her dreams at night. This hag stole the lives of others, feeding on energies through Maryann to extend her time and give herself a false vitality at another's expense.

Still, I had to give her credit. She was a master of her art. Her will thrust against mine, trying to break my self-image. Trying to make me view myself as a villain so that I'd drop my guard and accept her punishment. I had a secret ace. After being raised by a mother who told me that every evil of humanity was the fault of men, I'd had to cast off those teachings to have any kind of positive self-image. My resistance to what Cecilia peddled was pretty high.

I countered with pure will, pushing in with my energy like a battering ram. Her shields gave way. In the physical world, she stumbled back a step.

"You would attack an old woman in her home?" the hag pleaded pitifully. I knew it was a ploy. I'd won round one, but she still had cards to play.

"It's Katelin's home. I am her invited guest. I came in peace, and, if permitted, I will leave in peace," I countered.

Cecilia sneered. "This one will destroy you, Katelin. You can't trust men."

"Come on, Ray. Let's get my things." Katelin's voice was conciliatory as she glanced from me to Cecilia and back.

"Go, *Myrrysmies*, and pray we do not meet again." Cecilia shot me a look of pure malice then swept into the kitchen.

"She backed down." Katelin sounded surprised.

"For now." I started up the stairs. Katelin followed.

Packing the boxes and getting them out to my car took over an hour.

I was closing my trunk when a Mazda Miata pulled into the driveway behind me. An athletic, mid-thirties blond woman in a McMaster campus security uniform got out from behind the wheel. She could have been attractive if she did something to soften her appearance, but, as she was, she was all angles and harsh lines.

"Kate, thank Goddess, you're here! The hospital wouldn't tell me where you were." The blond rushed up and embraced Katelin.

Katelin bit her lip and looked torn. I looked her in the eye and waited. People have to want to be saved.

"Elly, let go." Katelin pushed away from her wife.

"Kate—" Ellen looked stricken.

"You could have killed me. And it's not the first time. I'm not a punching bag! I'll be back for the rest of my things." Tears flowed out of Katelin's beautiful, brown eyes. I wanted to hug her, tell her everything was going to be alright, but I couldn't. It wasn't time, and it would have been a lie.

"I'm sorry, Kate. You just made me so angry. You—" Ellen stepped towards Katelin, who backed up, keeping her distance.

"Did I push myself down the stairs? Did I punch myself in the eye? Did I hit myself with a hammer? I need to get away. Maybe if you get some help, we can talk. I'm done being a punching bag for you and your mother." Katelin's voice was harsh as she fought back tears.

Ellen's face went red. "Leave my mother out of this."

"I wish you would! Ray, let's go. Elly, move your car so we can pull out."Katelin stepped towards my car.

"You've taken up with one of them. You slut!" Ellen grabbed Katelin's arm, stopping her progress and pulling her around.

Katelin slapped Ellen across the face, anger replacing despair. "Don't ever call me names again!" Katelin jerked out of Ellen's grip and strode to my passenger side door.

"If you would, please move your car. I'll drive over the lawn if I have to." I kept my voice even despite the hate I saw in Ellen's eyes.

"You'll regret this," snapped Ellen.

"I believe, not as much as you." I got into my car and backed out over the corner of the lawn.

I began a silent count down. By the time we were driving past the Hamilton Cemetery, Katelin met my expectations.

"Am I making a mistake? Elly and I have a lot of history. I love her, and maybe we can work things out. Maybe I should—"

"You left her that option. You told her if she got therapy, she could have a second chance. More like a seventh or eighth from what you've told me. You put the ball in her court. Leave it there."

"I…Thanks for all this."

"No charge."

We offloaded the boxes into my apartment. By the time we finished, it was too late to pick up the air mattress. Subs made up a late dinner. Later still, we sat on my couch as Katelin talked, confirming much of what I suspected or knew.

"After that idiot judge let those rapists walk, Maryann collapsed in on herself. The whole town was against her. I brought her out to live with me. For a while, she seemed to be getting better. Then she got depressed. She must have stolen the pain pills out of Cecilia's purse when she visited us. I came home, and it was too late." Weariness and pain married Katelin's beautiful features as she spoke.

"I'm sorry." I squeezed her hand, trying to convey support.

"I tried so hard. After that, Cecilia moved in, and she said it was the fault of those boys. Elly and her mom wanted to take revenge. I got swept up in it. Elly had friends in the community. Some of them knew people. We put together a coven and did a ritual. It scared me, but Cecilia insisted that I owed it to Maryann. It did make me feel, I don't know, closer to her. I miss her so much." Katelin took a couple of deep breaths, calming herself.

I nodded sagely. Knowing when to shut up and listen is one of the powers of a good friend, forget wizard.

"The coven didn't last. Everyone went their own way. Anyway, after the ritual, things changed with Ellen. It wasn't much at first. I thought it was just the stress of having her mum around, but that's when it started getting bad." Katelin hugged herself.

"People react differently to stress. Add magic, and things can go completely sideways." I pitched my voice to be reassuring and allowed my aura to blend with hers, flooding the shared energies with golden heart energies, making in effect a blanket of love and compassion for her to wrap herself in.

"Ray, what am I going to do? I haven't been single since second-year university, I was never very good at it. Elly is only the third woman I've slept with. Part of me hopes she calls." Katelin's eyes were pleading.

She was vulnerable, and every instinct in me wanted to make it alright. "Katelin, I'm no expert on love, and Gods know I'm even less of an expert on the gay community, but I can say anyone would be lucky to have you. You are the full package."

Katelin hugged me. Past lives, present attractions, the need to feel positive about myself, her need to do the same. It happened. A platonic hug pulled back and became a tentative kiss. Time passed as the tentative kiss became more. Later, Katelin and I lay together in my bed, her warm skin pressed against mine.

She looked at me and smiled. "That was better than I remembered."

I kissed her. "Experience teaches, the difference between boys and men."

She snuggled in close. "I didn't intend this."

"I know."

"I'm still gay."

"I know."

"I'm still going to get my own place."

"Good."

"Just so you know."

I bent to kiss her. "Friends first, whatever you need."

The next day, I picked Katelin up after work, and we drove to get Morgana. We found Katelin's possessions thrown out on the front lawn. Fortunately, it hadn't rained. Collecting them took less time than packing the car the first time. All the while, Cecilia glared at us through the front window. We then walked Morgana, who had been chained in the backyard. The food and water bowls had been filled, which put my opinion of Ellen up a couple of notches.

I took the opportunity to check the binding on Maryann's grave, giving Katelin some alone time with Morgana as they wandered the cemetery. The binding was there, but the energies were already degrading. By the next lunar quarter, Maryann would be free to hunt again, and she would be even more desperate.

A dragonfly skimmed over the graveyard and came to rest on the headstone.

"Hello, little friend," I greeted the tiny beast. Its wings sparkled with a tracery of transparent cartilage, and its body glowed in iridescent metallic blues.

The insect slowly moved its wings. I opened my mind and reached out to it. Something had compelled it to come to me, but I got nothing more. I like dragonflies; they're pretty and have never done me harm. The bug watched me while I finished my work then flew off.

Back at my apartment, Katelin and I didn't bother to get an air mattress. It seemed redundant after the previous night. Dinner and the first three episodes of Red Dwarf, which Katelin hadn't seen, filled the evening, along with other activities.

— Chapter 14 —

The Inevitable

I WOKE UP to Cathy's voice. "What in the name of Set is this?"

"Who?" breathed Katelin.

"Cathy." I sat up in bed.

"I… I… I'll go." Cathy stormed out of my bedroom.

"Ray," whispered Katelin.

I took a deep breath. "Fuck it!"

"Shouldn't you go after her?"

Part of me wanted to. Part of me wanted to make a point. Part of me was aware of the beautiful, naked woman in my bed that I didn't have to chase after and grovel to.

"She didn't when worse happened to me. Maybe Kama is right. Maybe it is time she got a taste of her own medicine." Getting out of bed, I started for the door.

"Where?" asked Katelin.

"Bathroom." I smiled, though it was lost in the dark. "Then we'll see."

It was early evening the next day before Cathy knocked on my door. Katelin was at school and was going to bus it back to my place. I opened my door. Cathy looked like she was about to step into Caligula's party room.

"Hi, Cath, what's up?" I decided on casual.

"Is that all you have to say to me?" She glared at me.

"Pretty much. Do you want to come in?"

"Is she here?"

"Katelin's still at school, if that's who you mean?"

Cathy pushed into my apartment and glowered at me. "Pretty fast shacking up with some women you barely know." Cathy led the way to my living room and sat in my armchair. I sat on the couch.

"She's escaping an abuse situation and has no place else to go."

The dull red haze of anger parted in Cathy's aura. "Abuse?"

"Katelin's wife has been beating her. Katelin finally had enough, and I was the only one she could turn to."

"Wife, Ray. Goddess, when I told you not to pigeonhole people and to turn on the charm, I wasn't saying you should James Bond her!" Cathy sounded exasperated.

"It's not like that. It just sorta happened, and there is a past-life connection. I care about her." I kept my voice firm but neutral, refusing to be put on the defensive for something that needed no defending.

"Oh, so it's just casual." Cathy dug her fingers into the arms of my chair. Her expression wasn't happy, but the anger haze continued to dissipate.

"For now, it's casual. What happens next, I don't know. I care about Katelin, and we have a lot in common."

The red flared in Cathy's aura as her posture became aggressive.

"What about the revenant. Are you just going to let it keep killing because you got a piece of strange?" Cathy went back to glaring at me.

"Of course not! You know me better than that, and I don't appreciate the insult!" Now there was heat in my voice.

"So, you'll work on it when you have the time?"

"Cath!" My tone held a warning.

Cathy must have guessed how thin the ice she was skating on was because she changed gears to something she thought she could beat me on.

"How do you think it made me feel when I walked in on that?"

"You could have joined us. Katelin would have loved it."

Cathy's expression went from pissed to shocked and appalled, back to pissed again so fast anyone who didn't know her well would have missed it. "Not funny, Ray."

"You seemed to think it was when the same thing happened to me. And I'll remind you, your comment was about the same."

Cathy's face went as red as her hair. "That was different!"

"Why?" My tone was ice. I didn't want this to go the way it was going. I loved her too much for that. Problem was. I realised that unless I wanted to be in the same situation twenty years from now, we had to have this out. We were stuck in a loop. One way or another, the cycle had to be broken.

Cathy shook her head. "I'm just looking out for you. She won't change. In a while, she'll find a woman, and you'll be hurt."

"Possibly. I've come to realise that people don't change unless they want to, unless they care enough about something to change. Being hurt is the risk you take. I've known plenty of hurt over the years."

Cathy's lips formed a hard, thin line. The anger spoiled her beauty. "I'm warning you."

"About what? Cath, you're the one who insists on an open relationship. You're the one who gets in the way anytime I start getting close to someone. You like casual sex, but for me, the person has to be at least a friend. That's worked out great for you because I let it. No more! I like Katelin, and there may be room for something to grow. You can just suck it up, the way I have for years." I started pacing the room. The conversation was long overdue. I'd tried to have it before but let

Cathy deflect it one way or another.

"That's not fair. Just because you're so insecure, you insist on owning me. I—" Cathy almost spat the words.

I turned on her, raising my voice. All the times I'd swallowed my pride, swallowed my hurt, was at the surface. Every emotional wound her catting around had caused me. "I'm not insecure. I never have been. I never freaked about your dancing or minded you having male friends." I emphasized the last word drawing a distinction between friends and boy-toys with my tone. "Most men would have drawn the line long ago. I'm tired of you tossing that in my face. Damn it, woman! I love you, and no, I will not not say it because you have some weird hang up. Your parents cheated, and it put you through hell. I lived in the hell my parents created. The only stability I had was that they were faithful to each other. I've waited for years for you to realise there can be advantages to the stability and depth of commitment fidelity brings. I've been shown day after day that I was a convenience. Someone to call when you want furniture moved or your date for the night falls through. Do you think it was fair to me to cancel a dinner I planned and went out of my way for, so you could take up with your flyboy? Dammit, I suggested Fan Expo because I knew you'd like it, and you said no. Then Shawn snaps his fingers, and off you go. And that's just two times out of dozens. You say you love me. You have a damn funny way of showing it. I'm sick of being your doormat. You don't get to comment on Katelin and me. You want an open relationship, well honey, you got it, with all its downsides intact."

"I—" Cathy glowered at me. "If it's so awful, why have you stuck around?"

"Maybe I kept hoping you'd wake up." I let the heat slip from my voice. The next words were soft and sad. "Cathy, I love you, but I've come to realise that I love myself a little bit more. I've waited, hoping you'd grow in my direction. Maybe I waited too long. Now things have to change. Katelin is going to get her own place in a month or two, and we're not committed. You have a little time to think, but I won't continue to be your convenience man."

Cathy stood up. There were tears in her eyes. I wanted to hug her, to make it all right, but it wasn't all right. We both knew it. I'd spoken truths that couldn't be unspoken.

"Goodbye, Ray. I hope your dyke makes you happy, until she doesn't need you for a place to live anymore. I'll need my key."

I nodded. "If that's your choice, I'll need mine as well."

Cathy pulled my key out of her shorts pocket. I fetched hers from the hook in my kitchen.

Seconds later, I watched her walk out my door. It felt like a fist of ice around my heart, and my stomach churned. An era had ended, and there was no telling what the next era held. For more reasons than I could count and for reasons unbeknownst, tears trickled from my eyes.

If Katelin wondered at my mood that evening, she didn't ask. We had a quick dinner before we drove out to walk Morgana. This time Ellen and Cecilia glowered at us through the window. More of Katelin's possessions were carelessly boxed up and left in the garage. I felt an empathic thrust against my shield as I packed the car. Turning, I saw Cecilia staring at me through the window. She slowly beat an oval drum with symbols on its surface, which I couldn't hear through the glass. My skin started to prickle, and I felt nauseous.

"I can't believe Elly just threw my track trophy in a box like that. It's a miracle it didn't break." Katelin emerged from the garage carrying a box. "What's wrong?" She put down her load and rushed to me.

My mind was filled with the fight I'd just had with Cathy. All the regret, all the self-recrimination.

"Take Morgana and go. I'll meet you at the Grindstone Marsh Trail parking." My voice was strained with emotion and from the effort of boosting my shields.

"Ray…" Katelin glanced at the window where Cecilia looked out with an expression of predatory glee as she beat her hand drum.

"Go. I can look after myself."

"Ray, I…"

"Please." I could probably deal with Cecilia. Protecting Katelin at the same time would be too much. Yes, Katelin was a mystic, but we weren't accustomed to working together, and she wasn't skilled in battle magic. So, it's a name out of a Role Playing Game; what else are you going to call it?

"Go, I'll be all right." I had my doubts. Cecilia had gotten the drop on me, and I was already vulnerable from the fight with Cathy.

Katelin gave me a concerned look then went to get Morgana.

I turned to face Cecilia. The old woman stared at me with malignant glee.

I closed my eyes, visualizing a mirrored, parabolic dish between me and the hag. At the same time, I took deep, even breaths. With each exhalation, I saw crimson light leaving my body. The pain that my breakup with Cathy had left rode that wave out of me. My heart skipped. Cathy and I had broken up. The pain got worse, and it became hard to concentrate. I pushed through the emotional haze, knowing it was what Cecilia's spell was trying to do. She was locked onto my pain, dragging it forward to distract me. Making it a weakness she could exploit.

I mentally held the parabolic mirror shield in place. A common blind spot is that many magicians ignore science. Energy is energy. The domed shield collected the wave of despair and emotional triggers Cecilia directed at me and focused them to a fine point as they reflected back at her. Her personal shield would have taken the hit from a straight reflective defence, whereas the energies focused to a fine point burned through a spot in her shields.

I kept breathing out the pain of my breakup. I'd have to really deal with it later, but not in the middle of a magical fire-fight.

Cecilia must have sensed the effect of the reflected

energies because the attack stopped. Seconds later, my emotional turmoil was expelled. I was pissed off, but anger is a useful emotion if channelled by thought. The old hag stood waiting, undoubtedly bracing herself for my counterattack. I considered taking a shot at her, but she was in her own home where her defences would be strongest.

"It's better to not fight at all, but if you have to fight, fight to win. That means picking your battleground. Never face an opponent in their place of power if you can help it." I almost heard my grandfather's voice when he told me how to deal with the bullies at school.

I smiled, tipped my head to Cecilia and finished packing the boxes in my car. The old woman's smile slid away as she went red in the face.

At one point, I felt energies building. I paused, looking at Cecilia through the window, and then I waved my finger back and forth in a dismissive way. Let her think I was so above her that I viewed her best shot as a child's tantrum. In magic, attitude can be as useful as real power and skill. If she thought I was a hotshot, it gave me an advantage.

Truth was Cecilia had decades more time to hone her art than I had, and power wise, I suspected we were a match. She didn't need to know that. When I got the last box from the garage, I paused by the front door. Invoking the Sight, I examined the tracery of energy lines woven over the space between the screen door and the door proper. They led to a small bear statue set in the gap between the doors. Bands went out from the bear circling the house. I could guess what would have hit me had I pressed an attack against Cecilia. In the Finnish tradition, the bear was a powerful totem.

Minutes later, I met Katelin. We took the Grindstone Marshes Trail, avoiding the graveyard. Morgana was thrilled to be on a new walk. It wasn't long before Katelin was laughing. The sound was a balm to my emotions, and, for a moment, I forgot all the odds against us.

The sun was setting when we got back to the Grindstone Marshes Trail parking lot. I opened my rear door. Morgana hopped in and lay across my back seat. Katelin and I climbed into the front seats.

Katelin paused and stared out the window. "You know, this is the first day since Maryann passed I haven't visited her grave."

"I could stop on the way up." I may not have sounded too enthusiastic, but I offered.

"No… I…" Katelin bit her lip and took my hand. "I think it's a good thing. I… Can I tell you something without you thinking I'm crazy?

"Of course."

"Sometimes, I think Maryann is with me. I mean, I can feel her like she was in the room, almost hear her voice. That's silly, I know…"

My mind whirred. Was Katelin sensing the revenant?

"What's it like when she visits?"

"Sad and angry, like she was towards the end. Or scary, like when she threw a tantrum. I hated when that happened. I don't deal well with anger. I think it's because my mother would throw fits. I just tend to withdraw. There were times with Maryann after those thugs raped her I didn't know what to do or say. It's like that now when I think I sense her. In a way, I lost my sister when those bastards raped her. Am I awful that I'm glad they're dead?"Katelin's question begged for comfort, pleaded for me to tell her that she was still the good person she thought of herself as.

"Not awful. Human," I comforted. I had a sense of things now. The revenant was visiting Katelin, but Katelin was blinded by denial and the love she bore her sister from seeing the abomination she'd been turned into. The revenant bled out its pain and rage on Katelin and Ellen. I could only hope that the astral Maryann's karma wasn't taking a hit because of what had been done to her.

"Though I don't think Maryann would want you dwelling on it. From the little you've told me, she seemed like a sweet kid," I said aloud.

"She was. The rape, then having those sons' of bitches get

off with a slap on the wrist, changed her. She went from sweet and loving to angry and depressed. I hoped getting her out of that backwards town would help, but she only got worse after she moved in with us." Katelin's voice blended anger and despair.

A resolve to help the astral spirit hardened in me.

Morgana barked, and it near shook the windows.

"Oh, no." Katelin hung her head.

I looked up and saw Ellen walking down the steeply sloping street towards us.

"I could drive away," I remarked.

"No! She's still my wife, at least under the law." Katelin opened the door and got out of the car.

"Kate," Ellen slowed her pace and looked nervous.

"Ellen. I'm not coming home."

Ellen stepped closer with my car between them.

"I know. I… I wanted to apologize for the things I said yesterday. I was wrong. Hitting you was wrong. Mother, it's hard, and I get so frustrated. The stupid thing is I don't even know why I got so angry. I love you."

From my seat, I couldn't see either woman's face. A dragonfly came to rest on the hood of my car and seemed to watch me.

Morgana stood up on my back seat and gave a small woof.

"I hear you, girl. We'll just have to wait and see," I whispered.

"I love you, too," replied Katelin, "but I think we need time. I know I do, and I can't live with your mother. She brings out a side in you I just don't want to see."

"Don't make me choose! That's not fair!" Ellen put one hand on my car's rear window as she leaned in. Her torso shifted about oddly. At the time, I didn't think anything of it.

"No, it isn't, to either of us. You know my terms. Counseling and your mother not living with us, then we can see what happens. I love the woman I married. When she comes back, we can talk," said Katelin. I was glad to hear firmness in her tone.

The door opened, and Katelin got in. "Drive, Ray. We can drop off Morgana while Elly is walking back."

Ellen took her hand off my car and forlornly stared at us as I drove away.

Morgana was safely ensconced in the backyard with full water and kibble bowls in minutes. Katelin watched Ellen as we drove past her on the street.

Katelin turned to me. "I love her... Does that bother you?"

I thought about it. Oddly, it didn't. "Not really. I like you, a lot. I also could see something growing, but, for the moment, I can wait and see what happens. I mean, the sex is fun, and I feel close to you when we, 'make love', but its early days. If she suits your tastes better than me, that's just how we're wired."

Katelin smiled at me. "You would have made a great lesbian."

"I'll take that in the spirit it is meant. Do— Ra's beak!" I swerved, barely missing a pickup truck that had ignored the lane ends markings to the last second, then barreled into my lane. Taping the breaks, I pulled into my proper lane before I hit the oncoming car that barreled past me, blaring its horn. The idiot behind me added his horn to the cacophony as I cut into the limited space they'd left between our bumpers.

"That was close," Katelin remarked.

The pickup in front of me stopped in the middle of the road, forcing me to slam on my breaks. A huge bear of a man got out and walked towards me. He was red-faced and had the looks of a brawler.

"What the fuck is your problem? You almost killed me back there!" he screamed.

"Killed you? It was my right of way. You cut me off! I had to swerve to miss you." I shouted back. Maybe not the smartest thing, but I'd learned to never let a bully win. They just come back. Hurt them, and even if you lose the fight, they'll leave you alone, so you win the war.

"Get out of that car. I'll show you right of way." The thug balled up his fists. The driver behind me leaned on their horn.

I opened my door and stepped out. My head came up to the thug's chin, but I kept my actions slow and calm. I'm no martial artist, but Cathy had shown me some moves, plus my Mum's father had taught me a little of the combat arms he'd learned in the Air Force. I took a fighting stance and mentally pushed fear and doubt towards the thug. I was vaguely aware of Katelin calling the cops on her cellphone.

The idiot behind us blared their horn again.

"Shall we spend the night in jail for assault, or just drive away?" I asked calmly.

A thunderous 'Woof' issued from my car's back seat.

The thug looked non-pulsed. Big men aren't accustomed to being challenged. Usually, their size intimidates. I'd spent my childhood being bullied by those bigger than me. Simply put, I stopped caring. That, plus Morgana's warning, had an effect.

"Fuck you, asshole." The big man stomped back to his car.

The horn from behind sounded again. "Move it," yelled a woman's voice.

I returned to my car as the truck pulled away.

"What in Tuonetar's name was that about?" asked Katelin.

"I have a suspicion. Call back 911 and let them know the crisis is averted." I pulled away to a chorus of horn blasts. A minute later, I pulled into the Hamilton Cemetery and stopped my car.

"Why are we stopping?" Katelin looked at me curiously.

"I have a suspicion." I stepped out of my car and moved to where Ellen had stood during her talk with Katelin. Katelin joined me. I pointed to the passenger side's back-side panel. There in black permanent marker was drawn a sigil. Two X s with slashes through them, the second slash extending to an e shape.

"Oh crap, I'm sorry, Ray. She must have done it while we talked. What does it mean?"

"You're the expert on Finnish practice."

"I... The X usually means elemental forces.

"The slash could be earthing or negating," I added.

"The e shape?"

"Don't know." I put my hand over the sigil and felt its energies. It was a calling of some kind. A curse. I felt it drawing things in and projecting fear towards me. It was a nasty, minor enchantment meant to weaken an opponent by building up their fear through encounters with outside forces.

"How could she have done it so fast? Elly isn't good at magic." Katelin felt the symbol then jerked away as if stung. "It feels like Cecilia, but she wasn't there."

I thought, but not for very long. "The ink in the marker carried the enchantment. The symbols directed the power. Say what you will. Your mother-in-law is good at what she does."

"Just what she does isn't very nice," Katelin added.

I smiled at her. "Wolverine is my favourite male Marvel character."

"Who's your favourite female?"

"Shadow Cat."

"My high school crush." Katelin smiled.

"Mine too." I returned her grin.

A dog that stood by an elderly man at one of the gravestones started towards us at a run. The man sped after it at a shambling pace.

I rubbed at the sigil, confirming it was permanent marker. I was getting pissed off. You don't mess with someone's ride. It's just rude!

The dog closed on us, crouching and growling. Morgana barked a warning from my back seat.

"Stand down, child of Anubis. In the name of your Lord, I command you, go in peace and leave us be." I pushed with my mind while I met the dog's gaze. At the same time, I mentally extended a shield over the dog blocking the sigil's effect.

The dog stopped growling and looked confused.

The old man came up to us, huffing and puffing. "What the hell are you doing to my dog? I'll call the police on you. I will."

Morgana growled and barked, pressing her nose against the glass of my window.

"Your dog charged us. Just take it and go." I stared the old guy down.

He sniffed, put the leash on the confused animal and walked away.

"I need to neutralize this thing before it gets me in more trouble." I rubbed at the marker, but it wouldn't come off. Popping my trunk, I got the bottle of emergency water I kept there.

What? Burns, heat exhaustion, radiator leaks, dirty hands, making holy water on the fly, a litre or two of water is a handy thing.

I grabbed a 4x4 dressing from my first aid kit and wet it, scrubbing at the sigil. It smeared a little but wouldn't come off.

"Ray, someone with a leaf blower is walking this way," Katelin warned me.

I took a mental inventory of what I had on hand and grabbed a bottle of disinfectant from my first aid kit. I used it to wet the sigil and scrubbed. The e shape began to blur, then the line broke, marked by a clean spot on the side of my car. I felt the line of the energies snap like an elastic.

"You here to visit a grave?" demanded the man with the leaf blower. He was of average height, middle-aged, dressed in workman's clothing.

"Some jerk marked up my car, and I didn't notice until I was on the road. You know what it's like. Get the stuff off fast, and it will come clean. Let it set, and you're stuck until you repaint."

The gardener looked sceptical then nodded. "Try rubbing alcohol. Good luck with it."

I spoke softly. "Katelin, do you know what's going on with
the revenant your coven raised last Samhain?"

Katelin looked shocked and jerked her hands away from
mine. "Revenant, what do you mean?"

"A mystical agent of vengeance, your coven created one
using the ethereal pattern of your sister as a template. That
was the 'justice' spell you told me about." I kept my tone

non-judgmental.

"We didn't, I… How can you know?" Katelin looked like a startled deer.

I sighed. "I'll tell you what I know. You used Maryann's ethereal pattern to create a spiritual agent of vengeance that your group targeted on men they viewed as abusive. What I suspect you don't know is you trapped Maryann's astral self in the process."

Katelin shook her head and wrung her hands in distress. "No. No. Cecilia said it was just taking the energies left in the body to make those boys feel how much harm they did. I wouldn't. I couldn't trap her spirit. I love my sister. I couldn't have killed those boys. They committed suicide. They were obviously unstable they—"

"Were driven to kill themselves by the revenant." I tried to look understanding, but there was no good way to say it.

"You're lying. You have to be. Why are you saying this?"Katelin jerked to her feet and backed away from me.

"Because it's true." I dipped my head and gave her space. "Maryann's spirit is maintaining the ethereal pattern. Her spirit is cut off from the astral world at large, imprisoned in a shell of rage, malice and guilt. Two things once in contact remain in contact. You have to know the law of contagion. Someone is feeding Maryann's spirit a steady diet of rage and hate. She's not really responsible for what the ethereal form has done. It's like pumping a person full of Meth and tossing them on the street."

Katelin looked at me with confusion, anger, denial and dawning comprehension. Things she had ignored were starting to make sense.

"You're saying we killed those boys. I couldn't. The others were victims too," blurted Katelin.

"I can show you a list of suicides linked to sex offenders' lawyers and judges over the last year. I suspect that some of the other women may have been consciously targeting the revenant."

"No! I don't believe you!"

"Katelin." I fell silent as she grabbed her purse off my coffee table and swept from my apartment.

I waited up, but as midnight pulled around, I went to bed. Sleeping was another matter.

The next afternoon, I pulled into my parking lot to find Katelin waiting by my building's door. She was in the same clothes as the previous night.

I parked and raced to her. "Katelin."

"Ray… Oh Goddess, Ray, what have I done?"Katelin looked and sounded distraught.

I hugged her. "Let's go up to my place."

She nodded.

When we reached my apartment, she moved straight to the kitchen table and sat. I think she wanted a physical barrier between us.

Wringing her hands and staring at the tabletop, she began to speak. "I spent most of the night walking. Trying to think. Ray, I don't want to believe you. If I do, I'm a killer."

I took a seat opposite her and let her words spill out.

"Not that those three bastards didn't deserve worse and that judge with a sentence like that. But the lawyers were just doing their jobs. Though they still should have thought more about how it would affect Maryann. I…" Katelin took a deep breath. "I won't apologize for that. They killed my sister, the lot of them."

"I'm not asking you to. Ma'at will have her judgment, and that isn't what I'm about. The revenant has exceeded the purpose it was built for. It absorbed so much energy, it's taken on a quasi-life and is killing to sustain itself." I rushed to lay out my case before Katelin could run off again. "Worse yet, someone is leeching off the revenant. They're taking the energies of the revenant's kills for their own purposes, forcing Maryann to feed more. The revenant has broadened its list of enemies to encompass anything male. It tried to kill my boss, who admittedly is a sleaze ball, but he's no rapist."

Katelin took a deep breath and hung her head. "Cecilia, it's why she's lived so long. Gentle Mielikki, what have I done?”

I took Katelin’s hand across the table. “You, like most of the women involved, sought justice in an unjust world. Whether you intended to force the abusers to confess or to kill them, I don’t think most of you wanted to kill innocents. But right now, that’s not important. Right now, today, all we can do is stop this thing, so it never kills again, and free Maryann’s spirit, so she can ascend to the astral level she belongs in.”

“How?”

That was the question I didn’t have an answer to. We spent the rest of that evening with Katelin talking while I added an occasional prompt to keep the information flowing. I learned a lot about the revenant and my new lover that evening. Not all of it reassuring. When we went to bed, I just held her. Sometimes that’s more important than passion.

The next day I called in sick to work. I had too much to do. I dropped Katelin off at the University then drove to Ways to Wisdom, an occult supply shop that has been operating on Barton Street longer than I can remember. I don’t often buy paraphernalia, but they had what I needed, and I didn’t have time to make what I had to. I purchased two specialty candles in the forms of a naked man in green and a naked woman in blue. Both were about twenty-five centimetres tall. Coming home, I crossed paths with Cathy in the building’s hallway. She glowered at me and didn’t return my, “Hi.”

In my apartment, I prepared my temple, took a ritual bath and donned my ritual robe. All far less impressive than it sounds.

Preparing the temple room consisted of picking out the God form statues I’d be using for my first rite and positioning them on the primary altar, changing the colour of the altar candles to match the God forms, vacuuming and dusting. I tend to spill a lot of salt on the floor, and how so many of Sekmara’s toy mouse collection found its way into my ritual space, I’m not sure. The fuzzy mice and a couple of bouncy balls were accumulated in front of the Bast statue. I had to wonder if my cat had something going on I wasn’t aware of.

The ritual bath is taken in blessed saltwater. You take time to cast off the everyday and focus your thoughts. Get rid of the earworms and still the emotions. People do this all the time without realising it when they want to stress down and pamper themselves.

My ritual robe consisted of a T-tunic made from a white bed sheet with a gold sash around the waist. In my tradition, the sash colour varies with the primary deity. In Wicca, they use a braid, and the colours vary with the tradition of the practitioner and the level of priesthood to which they have obtained.

This all played to the psychology of the practitioner. The pomp and ceremony made me feel empowered, so I was empowered.

The first right was a making. After setting my temple wards and invoking the Gods, I sat holding the statues, visualizing energy flowing into them. Standing, I presented the first statue to the east.

"Citizens of Duamutef, salamanders of the east from which great Ra rises with a banner of flame. This is not a thing of wax I hold but the essence of the feminine. The essence of woman. Let her power flow in the eyes of those who would do ill, making them as blind in perception as they are in understanding. So mote it be."

I repeated the charge for the other elements, facing in the directions associated by the Egyptians with each. Water to the south, from where the Nile flows. Air to the West, from whence comes the evening breeze. Earth to the North, where the rocky desert lays. Other traditions and practitioners use other associations. These work for me, and there are three legitimate ways to assign elemental correspondences that I know of. I then consecrated the masculine statue.

After that, I scribed symbols into the back of the feminine candle with my ritual knife.

The Rune Tir, the astrological symbols for Mars and Venus combined, both under the headdress of Hathor/Sekhmet.

With my mind focused, I lit the male candle, dripping the

wax onto part of the symbols.

The Rune Tir, the prime masculine, became Lagu, the prime feminine, as I filled in a line. The combined Mars-Venus was filled with colour from the masculine candle and the horns on the headdress of Hathor were filled in. I fashioned a uraeus serpent to surround the solar disk tying it to Ra.

As a final touch, I folded the facecloth I'd used to soak up the blood at the pool into a crude kilt and secured it to the female statue with wax dripped from the male. I then wrapped the female figure in silk and put out the male candle.

Dismissing the forces and opening my circle was followed by lunch and another ritual bath. The second ritual was the more important of the two, because if I could break the link to Katelin, there were good odds I could end the revenant. Only if I couldn't would my statue come into play. I couldn't be sure the enchantment on the statue would work. The lunar quarter had arrived. I was expecting a call from my early warning system just after sunset. Maryann would be hungry.

Katelin left school early and let herself into my apartment. I'd given her Cathy's old key for the duration.

"Ray?" her voice was tentative.

"In the temple. I've drawn you a ritual bath." I called out.

She came into my temple room barefoot but still in street clothes. "I… I really hope you're wrong, but, thank you in case you're right." She kissed me. That kiss said a thousand things about the now and about two lovers in a complex situation over half a century before. She slipped out of the temple. A minute later, I heard her settling into the tub. I laid on the floor and let my mind focus. Yes, I can do the lotus posture, but it makes my bad knee ache. That distracts me from concentration, so why make life hard on myself?

The sun was well behind the building on the other side of the parking lot but hadn't set when Katelin entered the temple room. Her robe was, like mine, a T-tunic, only hers, had a keyhole neck outlined in trim depicting gold elk on a burgundy background. The braided cord around her waist told me she was a second degree Wiccan and the robe itself was a dark-leaf green. I approved as both a wizard and a man of how she looked. It suited her on many levels.

"Be welcome to this temple of the Gods in all their many faces and forms. Bring thee no malice or harm to this sacred place and find thee naught here save what ye bring." I greeted her with a kiss then traced the eye of Horus over her third eye with my finger.

Katelin smiled. "Wizards, always with the fancy talk. I come purified to this circle." She cupped my cheek.

Setting the wards for ritual and summoning the elements and invoking the God forms took only minutes, and then I sat on the floor as Katelin lay with her head in my lap.

Closing my eyes, I lay my hand on her forehead and let our auras mingle and merge. It wasn't as smooth as the many times I'd done it with Cathy, but after a couple of hitches, our energy systems meshed. To say it was better than sex ignores the fact that sex is the physical allegory to this spiritual practice. Emotions blended; personal barriers dropped. She poked around in my mind, my spirit and evidently liked what she found. She was warm and sweet, though more than a little scattered. I 'looked' further and could feel the blind spot where Katelin wouldn't let herself see. The walls of grief and denial, of emotional distance that swirled around a lump of red-gold force over her heart chakra. Her energies tried to pull me/us away from the blind spot. As egotistical as it may sound, my will was the stronger. If I'd been doing this with Cathy, I couldn't have forced the issue.

We followed the edge of those energies and found the line of force stretching to Maryann's grave. I could feel the energies beginning to quicken and pulse. Sunset would be soon. I focused on Katelin's end of the connection and let pure gold energy flow against the red gold of grief-riddled, obsessive love.

"Think of something happy about Maryann. Sometime when you just enjoyed each other, and it was good," I spoke aloud.

Katelin took a deep breath, and I felt her slip deeper into relaxation as she followed my instructions. Flashes of images came to me. A sunny day, the air autumn crisp. A deer bounded into a field, then another and another. Fully a dozen deer gather in front of us, then they pause to graze. There is wonder, joy and excitement. I/we love the little girl. I/we know that she loves me/us. Maryann is so taken with the dear she hardly moves, just watches them with wonder. I/we hug her from behind. In the entire universe, there is only that moment and us.

"Stay focused," I say aloud.

Carefully, I let that pure memory touch the tainted gold of the line. At the same time, I elevated the level to the astral. The corrupted love energies yielded to the pure, opening a hole in the wall of denial. Katelin can see the line, sense where it starts and ends. As important, for an instant, she can follow it to the astral level, where Maryann's astral form is trapped in a shell of rage and hate. The pure wonder of that moment touches the imprisoned spirit, and she remembers.

"Katelin, help me. Take me home. I don't like it here. Help me!" Maryann's astral form projects the whole concept in an instant as she tastes the first comfort she's known in over a year. Then the headless swan attacks, casting us out. I/we get a vision of the headless swan beating at me/us with its wings and hear the odd flute-birdcall sound.

The shock of being so violently expelled broke the connection between Katelin and I, even as it slammed us out of the trance. The enhanced wards around the temple stop any other negative effects, as the God forces I invoked to aid in the spell rush in to prevent and rectify any real harm. You have to love it when you have the time to do proper ritual.

Katelin and I opened our eyes. A long moment passed while she lifted her head from my lap and then wordlessly kissed me. This type of magic is, as I've said, intimate. We blessed my temple in the most primal of ways, enacting symbolically the union of the projective and receptive forces that formed creation. As we lay together, I wished it could last forever, but duty demanded otherwise.

"We need to go." Katelin looked me in the eye. "I have to walk Morgana, and it's the lunar quarter. I have to fix things for Maryann."

"We have to fix things." I touched her cheek and drew her in for a kiss.

I opened the circle, thanking and dismissing the Gods and elementals that had assisted us. Moments after, we're in street clothes heading out the door. I had my silk-wrapped candle in hand.

"I hope Morgana is alright," said Katelin as we neared my car.

"Ellen has been feeding her. Morgana will like your walk. I'll need to stay close to the revenant's grave, so it will give you some time alone with Morgana."

We climbed into my car and stared out the window.

"This is silly," Katelin looked at me.

"What?"

"You know what."

"Umm, honestly, I don't?" My tone added veracity to my statement.

"I should talk to her. The revenant is based on Maryann. She's my sister. If I could talk to her, maybe I could get her to stop." Katelin sounded hopeful.

I shook my head. "Cecilia has a lot of control, and the revenant has expanded on the core that is your sister."

"It's still worth trying." Katelin insisted.

I started the car. One thing I've learned from Cathy is not to argue with a woman once they make up their minds. All one can do is fix the mess afterwards.

"Have Morgana with you as a ground. She'll protect you if you need it."

Katelin nodded. I saw it out of the corner of my eye.

We reached Katelin's house just before sunset. We had barely collected Morgana and walked up to Maryann's grave from the Grindstone Marshes Trail parking lot when I felt a rush of heat through my body. My early warning system had gone off.

Katelin wandered off with Morgana as I paced the area around the grave with my enchanted walking stick. Unwrapping the female candle, I placed it against the headstone and lit it.

"Let the hunter see only what cannot be hunted!" I placed a hurricane shade around the candle and stepped back.

Minutes passed. A translucent form coalesced over the grave. Bands of grey stretched up from the candle, mingling with the Maryann energies.

"Who are you?" demanded the shade.

I took a deep breath before I answered. "You can call me, Rachael." The glamour from the candle would make me look female, but I didn't want to push my luck. Why make it harder on a spell than you have to?

The shade lost all interest in me and sat on the grave. A headless, white swan appeared on her lap, and she gently stroked it. The swan gave off a series of fluting/bird song sounds.

Maryann looked up at me. "This is my friend Snowy. He's like me. Someone took his head, and he can't see. He'd like his head back. It makes him very sad. Can you give him his head?"

"Do you know where it is?" I asked.

Maryann continued to stroke the bird. "It isn't far, but the mean woman won't let us go to it. It's in her place. Branches and leaves are all Snowy ever gets to see now. Please bring Snowy his head. It would make him happy. Snowy isn't like human men. He is good and nice. We should help him."

"I'll try to find Snowy's head. Would you like to talk with your sister?"

"Sister… Katie." The revenant crinkled its brow in thought. Something was fighting its way down from the astral, some aspect of self at odds with the energies of vengeance and hate that powered the apparition. "Katie. My sister. She's sad. So sad. She doesn't love me when I'm angry, it makes her sad. Why is she so sad?"

"She misses you."

"I'm hungry. The bad man didn't let me eat. I'm so very hungry. The mean woman steals my food. I eat, but I don't get to keep it, and it hurts. It…"

My eyes strayed to the candle. It was burning incredibly fast and wouldn't last long.

"Katelin," I called loud enough to be heard across the graveyard. I'd been working it out for a while. Then the realisation came to me full force. The enchantment was too powerful to defeat head-on. My only hope was to tackle the elements of it one at a time. Weaken it until it could finally be snapped. Breaking the lines had been the first step. Keeping the revenant from feeding was also part of it. Now, the swan.

In the Finish tradition, the swan moves freely between the land of the living and the dead. When it dips its head under the water, it is said to be looking into the land of the dead. Decapitating the swan had symbolically built the astral walls around Maryann's spiritual form, cutting her off from all but the line to the revenant that was controlled by my opponent. Returning the head to where the body had been left might free the swan's spirit, removing the defender of the bubble of rage and hate encasing Maryann's spirit.

"Where is Snowy's head?" I asked.

"Close. He hears water flowing over rocks, and the leaves are green. An owl flies over sometimes, and once he saw an eagle. There are ants so many ants. They used to bite him, and it hurt, but not anymore, not anymore." Maryann continued to pet the phantom bird. I saw the sweet young woman that the thugs had shattered. It changed nothing. I prayed even harder that Ma'at would not hold the actions of the revenant against the karma of the girl.

I felt a gentle warmth touch my heart at this and was reassured.

"What is it?" Katelin and Morgana raced to my side.

"Katelin, sit and close your eyes, breath deep, relax and quiet your thoughts. There is someone here to speak to you," I instructed.

Katelin bit her lip as she sat on the grass beside the grave. After a moment, Katelin spoke aloud, "Ann."

The revenant stayed on its grave.

"Katie. I'm hungry, but there is nothing to eat." The candle sparked and seemed to melt faster.

"Ann, you have to listen. It's wrong to kill men. It's bad."

The revenant wrinkled its brow. "They hurt me. I—"

"Ann, why did you take the pills?"

"I didn't. It was dark, so dark. I hurt so much." The shade seemed to sob.

"The day you left me, what happened?" pleaded Katelin.

"The mean old lady was visiting. She brought me ice cream. It tasted funny, but I ate it anyway because she was trying to be nice. I didn't want to die. If I died, they won!" Maryann lifted her face and gazed at her sister. "But look who won. They paid for what they did to me! They will all pay for what they did!"

The sweet, sad girl transformed into a ghoulish agent of vengeance. Her delicate features became harsh and cadaverous. Her voice like Cecilia's.

"How can you defend them? How can you?" snapped the revenant.

The candle flame leapt as the ethereal shade fought against the illusion. Morgana barked in warning and laid her chin on Katelin's shoulder. Full night descended.

Maryann stood on the grave and then screamed, buckling over and flickering lighter and darker. A line of black energy flowed from her to the west. I stood watching, not knowing what to do, then I heard a growl.

Morgana looked around and growled menacingly in reply.

"Morgana. Protect Katelin! I'll try and draw it off," I ordered.

Morgana looked at me. The exact meaning of the words was probably lost on her, but the essence registered. I was new to her pack, but I was doing what a good pack member did, protecting her alpha. We all understand things through our own filters. Dogs, wolves and cats, no less than humans.

Morgana gave a "Woof" and I ran towards the Grindstone Marshes Trail.

I should have known better. I'd rather swim five kilometres than run one. I had to slow to a walk before I was halfway to the parking lot. My knee throbbed.

Boosting my shields, I kept walking until I reached my car. A dragonfly buzzed past my ear. The growling got louder. I glanced back seeing nothing, but knowing I was hunted.

My foe was only in spirit, but what is done to the spirit will soon find a way to manifest in the physical. Being mauled by a bear or hit by a truck, the end result is much the same.

Opening my trunk, I pulled out my travelling magic kit and found the bottle of salt I kept there.

The growling sound continued as I walked around my car, sprinkling the salt. I didn't expect it to be effective, but if it slowed her down, that would help. I'd have cast a circle, but I didn't have the time, so I sat in my passenger seat, clutched my crook and flail and tried to relax.

First, I imagined Sekmara lounging on my bed in our apartment. "Help protect Katelin," I thought and sent a mental image of my cat standing beside Katelin in a glowing circle of light beside Maryann's grave. I held the thought, hoping Sekmara would receive the message and that if she did receive it, she'd deem it important enough to interrupt her nap. She is wonderful, but she is a cat. They have their own set of priorities.

I then focused on saving my own skin. Bear is a powerful totem animal in most traditions, epically in the Finnish. There was a vast pool of astral energy built up around the symbology of the bear. I had to face that. To make matters worse, I suspected that Cecilia had taken on the form of bear as an animal projection, so she could personally direct the energy. Then the cherry on top, she was drawing energy out of Maryann. In short, her batteries were a lot bigger than mine.

I closed my physical eyes and watched with my spiritual vision as a massive she-bear came to the edge of the sprinkled salt and sniffed the ground. She was huge and shaggy with wicked claws and yellowing dagger-like teeth. Part of me was thrown back to the cave, fearing that the tribe could be destroyed by this beast, which I both revered and feared. I swallowed down my beating heart and focused my thoughts.

I'm not the greatest astral projector in the world, but for once, my body seemed to take the hint and stopped distracting me with its problems. Good on you, body. I'll eat a salad. Ra's beak, I'll even eat two.

I slipped free of my physical form and drifted out of the car window on the side opposite the bear. It looked at me, and its lips pulled back from its teeth in an almost human smile.

"Cecilia, this is not right. Go back to your body."

The bear started around the scattered salt to my side of the car. Before she could reach me, I leapt into the air and spread my arms, picturing a new form. As an ethereal falcon, I swept into the air.

I was barely into the ethereal plane. The drag back to my body was intense, but I held the falcon form, circling up. Cecilia made a gruffing sound and then shambled towards Maryann's grave, where Katelin and Morgana waited.

Would the old hag kill Katelin? Probably not. Katelin was a line tying Maryann to the earth, but there are degrees of injury that could be inflicted without affecting that line. Would she kill Morgana? A shudder ran through me, without a doubt!

I dropped to the ground and took on the black jaguar form that had served me a year before when I faced the Goddess of the Nukekubi. A nasty fight where my allies barely saved me from my own arrogance.

Bounding forward, I slashed my claws against the bear's back thigh.

Cecilia turned and swatted at me, but I was already racing back. She growled and chased me into the woods.

I ran. Did I mention before she was bigger than me? Yes, in the ethereal, size is a matter of focus and energy, but I wasn't comfortable enough in my animal forms to fully access their archetypal powers. Long and short, I wasn't good enough to draw the energy needed to become gigantic in my animal forms.

The legend of Gwion Bach and Cerridwen raced through my mind. Not much help. With my singing voice, me being reborn as a bard wouldn't do anybody any good.

Cecilia gained on me. I leapt into a tree, trying to keep my human consciousness out of the way and letting the form govern my movements as I climbed. Harder than you'd think for a control freak like me.

Cecilia shook the tree. On the physical, random wind gusts bent the trunk back and forth. On the ethereal, I held on with one paw as I was thrown around like a rag doll.

I managed to place my hind legs against the trunk and sprung away, imagining myself back at the opening of the trail.

Cecilia was better than I thought. She appeared behind me. I raced to the bay that projected into the edge of the marsh area and leapt into the water.

Cecilia followed.

The water was only centimetres deep, the bottom muddy, making running difficult, but I had a plan. Problem was it all depended on Cecilia being focused on one tradition and the limitations that could engender.

She was on my heels when the bottom of the lake dropped off beneath me. With an effort of will, I shifted. Where there had been a jaguar, now there was an orca. A flip of my tail and the bear was far behind. She sped after me as I swam through the harbour towards the passage to the open lake. I kept to the sequential perception of time-space and distance because the goal was to distract my enemy. Cecilia took the bait, and I led her further from Katelin and Morgana. Unlike in the physical world, the bear could keep up with my orca. The apparent forms were only ways to conceptualize the energies and actions. On the physical, my body still lay in my passenger seat, and… Yes, if I focused, I could hear a drumbeat. Cecilia had someone helping her maintain her place in the spirit form.

I filled my spirit lungs and dove, trying to lose her. It all depended on how accustomed she was to working in her animal form. Technically, neither one of us needed to breathe, but old habits die hard. She followed me, unconcerned about the water, my luck!

I sped through the passage under the Skyway into Lake Ontario. Below me, two phantom ships seemed to fight against a storm. I couldn't stop to watch. Cecilia was on my tail flukes. I felt a pull from my body. Something was happening with it that needed my attention.

The clock was ticking. Once I returned, Cecilia would be free to go after Katelin and Morgana.

I kept swimming, then, just as Cecilia was about to bite my fluke, I let my body slam me back into it.

Slamming back in is never a pleasant experience. I sat up gasping with a nose clogged with mucus. Scrambling, I found the box of tissues I kept in the car and blew. Seconds later, I could breathe again.

The bear was gone, and I could make a guess where.

Getting in the driver's seat, I sped to the closest point to Maryann's grave, stopped the car and got out.

What I saw made me look twice, even though I'm used to the weirdness of astral sight.

Morgana in the physical and Sekmara as a translucent shade the size of a Siberian tiger flanked Katelin, who stood holding her athame, facing the bear. The candle on the grave was burnt out. Maryann was gone.

The spirit bear growled and swatted, but the familiars carried the day, worrying Cecilia with hit and run tactics. My cat, my dear little love, had heeded my call and come. Never say to me, it's just a cat! Katelin cast energy at the beast. I'm sure she sensed something hostile, but she wasn't able to 'see' its form.

With a roar, Cecilia vanished. She probably had to blow her nose or go to the bathroom or anyone of the other trials this flesh is heir to.

Sekmara gave me a long-suffering look and vanished. I hobbled to Katelin's side as Morgana pressed up against her legs.

"Ray. The candle went out," warned Katelin.

"I know. Are you alright?" I leaned heavily on my walking stick. I felt like I'd tried a lake swim. Everything ached.

Katelin nodded and looked determined. "Cecilia killed Maryann."

"Yes."

"So that she could make the revenant?"

"Probably."

"I'm going to kill that bitch!" There was a fire in Katelin's voice that could level forests.

Morgana woofed.

"Sorry." Katelin patted the huge dog's side. "Morgana can't go back there."

"I know." It was a matter of fact with no need for discussion.

I turned to the candle on the grave, which was now a pile of warm wax.

"She went that way." Katelin pointed towards Hamilton. "She, it, wasn't my sister. I thought she might be when I first saw her. First talked to her, but…"

I put an arm around Katelin's shoulders.

"That thing, I hoped that Maryann would be there. I thought… It's just a prison. Vengeance, hunger, rage, keeping my sister trapped. We have to break the link and let her spirit move on," said Katelin as she pressed into me, seeking comfort.

"We will."

"Are we going to try and stop it tonight?" Katelin looked me in the eye.

"Where? How? We lost this round. Someone will die. It happens. I hate it, but it happens." I kept my voice even though, in truth, I wanted to hit something and embark on a tirade of profanity that would offend at least three pantheons.

Collecting the wax and hurricane shade from the grave, we packed Morgana into my car and headed for my apartment.

Chapter 16

Animals In The Mix

WANT TO HEAR a sick joke? What do you get when you put an Irish wolfhound, an entitled house cat, a wizard, and an identity challenged lesbian into a two-bedroom apartment? I think I answered the question.

When we reached my apartment, Morgana decided that the elevator triggered her claustrophobia. Seeing a dog the size of a small pony completely freaked out is not a comfortable situation, especially when you're trapped with her in a two-metre by a metre and a half box.

Opening my door, Sekmara took one look at the dog and puffed out to near double her size, then hissed like Apep himself had come calling and flew into the temple room. If her feet touched the ground once in the hallway, I didn't see it. Apparently, the alliance they had declared on the spiritual level didn't extend to the physical.

Morgana bounded into my living room and went directly to my couch, knocking over my coffee table during her transit. Katelin walked in and collapsed onto my recliner. I took the wax from the candle to my temple room, where Sekmara had perched herself on top of a bookshelf and glowered down at me.

"What else could I do? It wasn't safe to leave her with Cecilia." I looked imploringly up at my cat.

The *merwow merowo* grumble growl, coupled with two glowing accusatory eyes, told me what I could do with my explanations and apologies. The suggestion sounded exceedingly painful.

"It's just for a day or two until we can work something out."

Sekmara turned her back to me and lashed her tail.

I left the wax on my altar and went to the kitchen. Katelin had taken out my big mixing bowl and was filling it with water.

"Right, on the balcony. I'll leave the door open for her," I said.

"That isn't safe. Burglars climb up the outside and slip in. I heard about it on the radio," objected Katelin.

I stepped into my living room and glanced at where Morgana lay drooling on my couch. Evidently, the arm was a little too hard, so she'd pushed one of my throw pillows up under her head. It just happened to be the one I favoured when I lay on the couch.

I rolled my eyes. "I'll take my chances that the burglars aren't suicidal."

"We'll have to get her kibble in the morning." Katelin carried the water towards the balcony. I rushed to open the sliding door for her. Morgana watched us but didn't deign to rise.

I went to bed only to be joined by Katelin and Sekmara a few minutes later. Sekmara drew the line when Morgana tapped into the room. A quick swat across the nose and a growl left no doubt in anyone's mind who was on the top of the pecking order. After I put Band-Aids on the scratches on my chest from where her ladyship had used me as a launching pad for her attack, I finally got to sleep.

The next day I had to go to work. Katelin ran out while I made coffee and got a small bag of dog food from the corner store. We set up my second largest bowl beside the water bowl, and I, with a sense of dread, left the apartment.

When I came home, it was quiet. Too quiet. Ice gripped my heart. I loved my kitty, and I'd left her with a behemoth. Yes, I trusted in her to have the sense to stay on the high ground. I'd even set up a litter box, food and water station on the top of my dresser, above Morgana's reach. Still, I was worried.

It was with relief, astonishment and a brooding premonition of doom that I looked into my bedroom. Stretched across the bed was Morgana, with Sekmara half lying against her, casually taking a bath. They both spared me a look as if the butler had walked in at an inopportune moment.

Sitting on my couch, which now smelled of dog, I turned on the TV and brought up the early news.

"Two inmates at the Hamilton-Wentworth Detention Centre facility were found dead this morning," announced the local anchor.

I turned the television off. I knew without having to do a divination that Maryann had fed and would be more powerful than ever.

The door opened. Katelin came in, carrying a jumbo-sized bag of dog food.

"Did you hear?" she asked.

"About the two prisoners?" I moved to take the bag from her.

"It was on the radio. I think it worked, at least a little."Katelin sounded a bit self-satisfied.

"What did?" I was interrupted by a mad scramble of claws on the floor and a mass of shaggy hair colliding into Katelin.

"Who's a good girl," and such followed before Katelin retrieved Morgana's lead from my kitchen counter and clipped it to the dog's collar. "Time for our walk."

She led the way out the door. As it seemed the only way I'd get a timely report, I followed. Morgana refused to enter the elevator, forcing us to take the stairs. My knee, still none too happy with me, was already complaining.

We hit the street and crossed to the nearby park and schoolyard.

"So, what worked? As far as I can see, last night was a disaster." I watched as people stared at the couple with the huge dog and made way before us.

"I talked to Maryann and told her she should only go after really bad men, like prisoners and criminals. It's what the revenant was made to do initially. I thought that I could get her back on track. You know, minimize the damage. I'd read about two rapists that were in the Hamilton-Wentworth Detention Centre. I suggested that they would be a good target. Maryann must have taken the instructions to heart."

"You targeted her?" I observed.

"Better that than her going after some guy who's just out for a consensual good time." Katelin paused while Morgana squatted. "Here," she passed me a plastic bag. "Pick that up for me."

I was reminded of one of the many reasons that, while I like dogs, I prefer cats. I also realised that Katelin was still part of the problem. Whether she knew it or not, she, at some level, approved of Maryann's actions. Katelin still wanted vengeance, maybe not against all men, but against a scummy percentage. I couldn't fault her. I wanted them locked up as well, but there was no oversight. The big problem with guilty until proven innocent is it makes us all guilty. Philosophical musings aside, Katelin's attitude strengthened the link holding the revenant to the earth plane, which made my job harder. I reviewed the previous night's battles as I walked to the trash and dropped in something that could have been left behind by a horse.

If breaking the lines tying the ethereal to the earth plane had gone as far as it could, then I had to work at it from the other end, freeing the astral form so that the revenant lost the core of its pattern. But how? Of course, Maryann, the version that reflected more truly what she had been in life, had given me the answer. Snowy was the key, now to find it and put it in the lock.

We finished Morgana's walk, by which point there were scent marks all around the park declaring, I'm big, I'm here, don't mess. You have to respect the clarity of animal communication.

Back in the apartment, Katelin filled Morgana's food bowl while I gave Sekmara a special treat of tuna in water. I saved it for special occasions because of the crystals in the bladder thing, but she had gone above and beyond the call the previous night.

Later, Katelin and I sat at the kitchen table over a hastily thrown together spaghetti dinner. The couch was taken by Morgana.

"It's amazing that you can cook," remarked Katelin.

"I learned in self-defence. My mother's cooking could gag a maggot. She's in complete denial about it."

"I'd like to meet your parents."

I felt a lurch go through me. I wanted to protect Katelin. The last thing we needed was my mother going on about grandchildren and my father acting like I had made some kind of score because Katelin was of African heritage. I could handle it if he made a fuss because she was beautiful, intelligent, and sweet. "One disaster at a time," I answered.

"You know, if I can target Maryann—"

"It would still leave her astral form, her real form, trapped in the bubble of rage and hate." My voice was flat and no-nonsense. I had to cut that train of thought off.

Katelin looked at the table. "It's just… it was nice to talk with her. What I mean is, the core of the revenant is based on her. It felt like I was with her. I… You don't know what it's like!"

"Yes, I do. More than you can guess." I missed my grandfather, sometimes more than others, but always. It was like a sore spot in my mouth that I couldn't keep from brushing my tongue against.

Katelin looked at me with compassion. "Baggage."

"Steamer trunks. We all have it. I've been thinking. You worked with Cecilia. Correct me if I'm wrong. Sacred trees are big in the Finnish system, right?" I let my voice lighten.

"Very big. The old hag had one someplace. She said it was a major source of her power."

I nodded. "That might prove useful. How much do you know about Cecilia?"

"Not much, really. She never liked to talk around me, if it wasn't issuing a command or criticizing something. Now to learn that she killed my sister...." Katelin started to cry. Circling the table, I held her.

Long minutes later, I was back in my seat. "Katelin, I know it's hard, but anything you can tell me would help."

"The whole know your enemy and know yourself, thing." Katelin whipped her puffy eyes with a tissue.

"The Art of War is ninety percent common sense." I held the box of tissues out to her.

Katelin took a deep breath and waved away the tissue, her voice becoming firm. "If it helps us get that bitch, I'll tell you anything I know.

"She was born in Finland. Her parents were killed by the Russians when they invaded during the winter war, and she went to live with an uncle in the country around Vyborg. She was just a baby when it happened. She doesn't even remember her parents."

"Vyborg?" I asked.

"A city, the Russians took it after they helped the Finns push the Nazi's out. I think that's when she first learned about the art. After the war, the Russians took over the area that her uncle lived in. She ran away when she was no older than Maryann. She lied about her age and worked as a waitress until she found a man that was going to Canada. She seduced him, and they emigrated. All she ever said was that she hated him and how he could never earn enough to give them the life she deserved."

"Not surprising. Was he Ellen's father?"

"I think so. Cecilia had Elly late. Elly's father was mauled by a bear and died before she ever got to know him, but there was insurance. Elly says that Cecilia had some 'girlfriends' when she was growing up, but never anything serious. That's about all I know."

"It's a start." I took Katelin's hand and kissed her knuckles. I now knew more about my foe than she did me. That was a good thing.

The next evening found Katelin, Morgana and me at the Royal Botanical Gardens Arboretum. This area was composed of a grassy area on the upper flat and a forest surrounding the north side of the Coots Paradise inlet. The trees covered the steep slopes that led down to the water. It was one of my favourite spots because, if you ignored the traffic sounds, you could imagine yourself in Northern Ontario. It was also wonderful because there weren't as many bugs as in Northern Ontario. Importantly, given Cecilia's age, it was the easiest access of any of the nearby forested areas that fit the information of where Snowy's head might be. A pair of bald eagles had made Coots Paradise their nesting ground. As well, several streams crossed the area in their race to the lake.

I'd tried scrying the area and using a pendulum with no luck. The reason for this was two-fold. One: pendulum work didn't like giving me locations. Two: Cecilia likely had a glamour to deflect prying eyes cast over her sacred tree.

With no other options, we had to physically investigate the region. We followed the trail down to the water then up along the streams.

"It won't be on a public trail. I know she had a place because she and Elly would go there, but I was never invited." Katelin slapped a mosquito that landed on her neck.

"I know it's a haystack, but at least we know it is the haystack," I replied optimistically.

Morgana woofed and stared ahead.

A deer bounded away. Katelin and I clutched Morgana's leash to keep the dog from following.

After a tug of war, that nearly tossed me to the ground, I turned to Katelin. "Still think we could let her off the lead?"

"Okay, smarty pants." Katelin kissed me. I took a moment to hold her. She had been hesitant about showing affection to me in public. It was nice. Then we were back to the hunt.

The first night we lost the light before we found anything.

The next night I had to work a pool rental. Say what you will. The Lions Club members are nice folk who care about their community.

The evening after that, Katelin, Morgana and I were back in the woods. I opened my mind and could feel life all around me. I thought of Cecilia and Ellen, but they were lost in the swarms of people who used the trails. Then I had a thought.

"Katelin, take Morgana. I need to focus."

"What are you trying to do?"

I proceeded along the trail to where a commemorative bench had been constructed overlooking the inlet. The little clearing surrounding the bench was sun-dappled with a wall of thick underbrush between the surrounding trees.

"We've been looking for where the tree is. I'm going to try and look for where it isn't."

"O…kay." Katelin stared at me like I had two heads.

I took a seat on the bench. "It's a good bet that Cecilia cast a concealing glamour around the tree. Not to be trite, but something like a somebody else's problem field."

Katelin shook her head. "*Hitchhikers Guide to the Galaxy*, really?"

"You have to admit, it's a good description of a cloaking glamour."

"Fair enough." Katelin nodded. "We'll stand guard."

Morgana looked at Katelin, and I could practically hear the words. "Yeah, right, Muggins will stand guard, and you'll try and look important."

I settled on the bench and took deep, slow breaths. My thoughts stilled as peace filled me. I let myself become the woods. My mind quested in a spiral, feeling the energies. Out of the several places where enchantments had been worked recently, there was only one that my mind shied away from. It wasn't so much a barrier, as I simply didn't want to acknowledge that the spot existed. It was west by northwest.

I opened my eyes to find that the autumn evening was drawing in and that a dragonfly hovered less than a metre from my face. "Tomorrow, we search the pine woods at the back of the arboretum."

"Woof," Morgana's replied, always happy to walk a new trail.

"You found it?" asked Katelin.

"I think I know where to look now. But not in the dark."

Katelin nodded, and we took the quickest trail back to the parking lot.

I got home to music blaring through the floor above. Cathy had taken to turning up the volume on her stereo and stomping around like an angry ox. In a way, it was a testament to the fact that she still cared because why else would she want to punish me. On the other hand, it was childish, mean spirited, and selfish. All of which went to remind me why I had to hold my ground if I didn't want to be a lap dog.

"The bitch is at it again," commented Katelin.

"If it runs late, I'll talk to her." I sat on the couch. "Your turn to cook."

Katelin looked at me with those big brown eyes. "Could I maybe swap washing up?"

"Only if out of a tin is good enough. I'm beat."

"Chunky Beef Vegetable soup," Katelin smiled.

I went to get the tins with the full knowledge that washing up meant leaving the bowls in the sink so Kama could do them tomorrow. I'm no neat freak, but Katelin carried a dislike of housework to a whole new level.

After dinner came *Red Dwarf*. Watching Rimmer reminded me that I should check on Carl. He was back at work and seemed none the worse for his ordeal, but it was still good to follow up. Katelin laughed like a hyena at a comedy club. It was a little grating. When she moved out, I knew what she'd be getting as a housewarming gift. Not my copy, but I was sure I could find a disk set.

Later still, we were in my bed. I held her. It was nice, but I could sense a distance.

Katelin had an early class the next morning, so I had an hour to kill before work. On a whim, I put dragonfly into Google and started skimming. I nodded as I watched conflicting accounts of the symbology. While I liked them, and much of the lore saw them as positive, the Finnish system saw them as negative and a harbinger of doom. It fit with why they. were showing up so often around me. Cecilia was trying to use them to put me off and probably spy on me. My perception of them was so counter to hers that they had the opposite effect. This brought a smile to my face.

That evening, Katelin, Morgana and I were in the pine woods. The wind whipped through the branches. I could feel a subtle pressure at the back of my neck. We followed the main trail, which made a big loop through the woods.

"She was wearing a skirt so short it looked like a shoelace. I mean, really, you have to look, and she has a set of legs!" remarked Katelin.

"Sorry I missed the show," I replied absently as I tried to focus on the energies around me. Don't get me wrong, I'm a guy. I don't see anything wrong with appreciating the female form. I also have been known to comment on a woman's physical attributes, but I try to do it in the context of talking about a human being. I've always found the Hubba Hubba oww baby type of comments embarrassing, even when they came from other men. To hear my girlfriend objectify women in that way just seemed wrong. I've always said there was a world of difference between, 'she has great legs,' and 'I'd love to stroke those stems.' Basically, if I'd be ashamed if the lady in question heard me say it, then I try not to say it.

"You know if we—" began Katelin

I held up my hand. Katelin silenced. The pressure at the back of my head had peeked and then lessened. I took a step back. The pressure increased. On the ground, there was a trail where the underbrush was pushed aside.

"Morgana." The big dog looked at me. "Find Ellen's trail."

Morgana looked at me. I opened my thoughts and

pictured Ellen in my mind's eye. I then made a sniffing sound. Morgana barked, wagged her tail and sniffed the ground. A moment later, she barked again and pulled me down the side trail.

The pressure in my brain became a throbbing pain. I upped my shield, and it helped.

"This can't be it. The terrain is too rough for Cecilia. We should go." Katelin's voice was strained.

I felt the desire to go, a pressing need to leave. But I knew it was another protection. An area of negative emotion infused into the boundary around the sacred tree. It felt like the shell of anger and hate surrounding Maryann's astral form only impressed into a physical medium.

"Ray, are you listing to me? We need to go." Katelin sounded near panic.

"It's just another defence," I explained. Explaining to Katelin was becoming an irritant. Sometimes she was more trouble than she was worth. I hadn't counted on her moving in permanently when I offered to put her up for a few days. The sex had been interesting, for a while, it was new, and that was always interesting, but even that was getting bland. We just weren't connecting.

"Ray! Do what you like. I'm taking Morgana and getting out of here. This isn't right." Katelin glowered at me.

I took a deep breath and fought to hold my temper. "You can do what you want, but I need Morgana's nose, and I'm heading on."

"You can't steal my dog!" Katelin moved to snatch the leash out of my hand. I pulled it away and found myself staring into a snarling maw of canine teeth.

"You aren't the boss of me or my dog!" Katelin blurted, snatching the leash out of my hand.

I felt an urge to knock Katelin down and show her who was boss.

"We're going home!" Katelin snapped as Morgana snarled. My hands clenched into fists. I wanted to hit Katelin, to put the bitch in her place and show her dog who was the real

Alpha in this pride. I started gathering power, and then a screech caused me to glance up. There was a hawk in the branches of a nearby tree. The animal of Lord Ra looked at me.

Rage boiled in me.

"I'm going!" Katelin stalked off.

I watched her backside and wanted to knock her down and take her. Not from desire or a drive for unity but from a need to dominate, to control, to own. The hawk cried again, and part of me yelled, "Stop!"

Closing my eyes, I pushed down on the rage. I sought the emotions out and found that, while they were tied to minor annoyances in my psyche, the intensity of them wasn't mine. I followed them to their source and saw bands of violet, red and black snaking up from the ground. Increasing the output of my heart and mind chakra, I drove the dark energies out of me. Kneeling, I brushed away at the dirt and found a black stone with the image of a serpent painted on it.

"Apep by any other name is still a nasty piece of work," I whispered. Pulling out my pocketknife, I opened the utility blade and started scraping at the image of the snake.

Energies lashed around me, trying to enhance my rage, trying to break my will and pull out the darkness that exists in us all. I didn't know what the Finns called the force, but it was an old foe. The oldest foe that Ra symbolically stands against each morning so the new day can begin, the serpent that Bast helps her great grandfather defeat so that life can grow.

"I strike the snake, I tear the snake, I rend the snake, that Apep must fall and Keppra will rise bringing light to the skies," I spoke the charge of the morning sun from the winter solstice ritual to focus my power. Golden energy flowed down my arms and out my hands cutting through the mystical aspect of the spell as my knife scraped away the physical.

The rage kept trying to get in, but I would not be controlled. My knife slipped, cutting my fingertip. I dislike blood rite for many reasons, mostly that people use it stupidly. A nick is enough and never slice into your palm. The risk of tendon damage is too high. It is also stupid to cripple yourself with pain before going into battle. That said, blood rites can be powerful. I stroked my life's blood over the stone.

"From my heart, I deny you, serpent. From my soul, I cast thee down. In the name of Ra, I banish thee back to the chaos that is thy own. By Bast, I rend thee dispersing your power."

The enchantment snapped. It was like bands of energy flew back from it. I could now 'see' the energies with my Sight. They formed a C shape around an ancient, half-dead tree. I knew without looking that if I dug at the ends of that C shape, I'd find other rocks like the one I'd just dug up. Cecilia was a master in her Craft, and she had had time to build her sacred sanctuary.

I took a deep breath and pushed on. Cecilia would know that someone had broken her defensive enchantment. Odds were, she would come running. Having just expended the massive energy necessary to break the warding, I didn't look forward to facing her.

I approached the tree. Beyond it was a deep channel with a stream at its bottom. I lay my hands against the trunk and opened my mind. I felt pain and hopelessness from a wise old tree, despairing that its power was turned to evil. I also felt the terminus of the green line that led to the revenant.

The tree was half-dead. Insects had left it riddled with holes. The upper section was lightning split. The wood around the strike was scorched. Withered leaves sprouted from the branches. The feeling was there, 'Let me die. Let the wheel turn.' The ancient tree had seen the pale skins come to the land. It had known fire and drought. It had seen its seeds spread out, sprout and grow to maturity. I mentally quested, picturing a swan's skull in my mind. With a sense of relief, I felt an energy that drew my gaze up the tree. I began to climb. It was slow going, but I reached the cavity left by the lighting and ensuing fire years before.

Reluctantly, I reached in, hoping that I wouldn't disturb a resident critter. I felt things crawling on my hand and grimaced as stinging bites tortured my skin. I felt something hard. I pulled it out and took a moment to brush the ants away. It was a wristwatch bound with wire to, what I later learned was, a bear's tooth. Corrosion covered the metal, and the leather strap had rotted away.

"This I claim for the one it was taken from. All lines that bind it against the will of its true owner be broken!" I spoke the words as I pocketed the watch.

I felt a sensation like a cord breaking. The tree seemed to sigh in relief. How long Cecilia had maintained her enchantments, I couldn't tell. She'd only been in the area a year or two, so the tree was a fairly recent receptacle, but she could have transferred the items that fixed her spells from another place of power. I was sure this tree disliked having its sacred power twisted to the uses she had put them to.

I reached into the hole again. My fingers crossed another object. I pulled out a corroded athame with a crescent moon guard and a full moon pommel. The blade pulsed with power. I slipped it through my belt to work on later because the potential backlash from breaking the ties on it could be dangerous without proper preparation. Common sense isn't chicken; it's smart. I said before, I fight to win, not to be a macho show off, ultimately doomed to fail.

I reached in again and felt several things that were all too large or too small to be my quarry, and then I felt it, hard and smooth. Extracting it, I saw that I held a swan's skull picked clean of flesh by the ants.

By now, the skin of my hand was one big bite and beginning to swell. Also, the last of the day painted the horizon scarlet.

I scrambled out of the tree and started back to the main trail, being careful to pass through the deactivated section of the warding.

An incredible lethargy assailed me. All I wanted to do was lie down and sleep. Turning, I saw bands of my energy flowing back to the tree. The tree was a victim, but that didn't change the enchantments that had been laid upon it. The tree was feeding off me. A final attack to secure the grove.

I'd have been a fool not to have come prepared. Stroking the eye of Horus, I'd added to my regular jewellery, I imagined a flaming wall slicing across the bands of energy. I could feel the tree fighting against the enchantment, and between us, we snapped the bands. I started to feel better.

"I will be back to release you, my leafy friend," I spoke aloud.

The tree seemed to wave at me.

I stumbled out onto the main trail. The sun had set, and the path was dark. There is something primal and scary about the woods at night. I wasn't immune. Fortunately, my night vision is on the upper end of human capacity. Between it and auric sight, I could still make out the path ahead of me.

I saw glowing eyes approaching down the trail and had to push down the urge to run. The beast stalked closer, and I saw a shadowy figure behind the first. My mind jumped to Lady Hecate and one of her hounds. I stopped and braced myself for an attack.

"I come in peace and service and would leave in peace." Sure, there wasn't a quaver in my voice.

A bark that could topple trees sounded then a cry of, "Morgana, no," as the dark figure lurched ahead. A second later, I was nearly bowled over by seventy kilograms of shaggy beast that seemed intent on licking my face in a doggy apology.

I laughed in relief as Katelin bowled into me. My knee twisted, and I yelped, pulling her into a hug more to stay up-right than for the pleasure of doing so.

"I'm so sorry. Something came over me, and I just—"

I kissed her, silencing the apology. Morgana proceeded to wrap around us with her leash and press her head into my hand. I lost my balance, and Katelin and I did a controlled fall onto the trail. Into a puddle, I might add. The emotional release was too much, and I began laughing hysterically despite the throbbing in my knee and the water soaking my pants.

Katelin looked at me in the dark and added her hyena

cackle to my own. Morgana licked my face and splashed in the water.

Several minutes passed before we quieted. The golden energy of laughter had permeated the woods, dispelling the last of the negative enchantments that had clung to us.

"Are you okay?" Katelin's expression was lost in the dark, but her voice was full of concern.

"It was a nasty bit of work. I opened a path to her sacred tree. I have what I need."

"I got to the car and realised that you had the keys. Then I started to think… I'm sorry for what I said."

I kissed her and cupped her cheek. "So am I, for what I said. Cecilia is one nasty piece of work, and I don't think that Maryann is her first trip to the unpleasant side of the Craft. That spell was a piece of art. Fowl and disgusting, but magnificent in its power and skill."

"Let's go home and get dry," suggested Katelin.

I was too tired to react to Katelin's use of home.

Another kiss, then we untangled ourselves from Morgana's lead. Morgana was content to lie on a dry patch of the trail, secure in the knowledge that she was the biggest predator in the area and that nothing would take a swipe at her, except for my cat, of course, and she wasn't there.

Back on our feet, we moved through the night to the large meadow that bordered the suburb. Without the tree cover, there was more light.

We approached the parking area just as a pair of head-lights swept over my car. Ellen's Mazda Miata pulled into the lot. Two people climbed out.

"Mother, it's too dark to follow the trail. We should come back tomorrow." Ellen's voice came through the night.

"Are you a child to fear the dark? When I was a girl, we wouldn't even call this dark. I've spoiled you. Can't you do this one thing for your mother? After all I've done for you." Cecilia's voice was harsh and bitter.

"Ray," began Katelin.

I put my hand on her arm and nodded. Barely visible in

the dark, I guided her down a side trail. Morgana followed silently.

"This is the *Myrrysmies'* car. He is meddling again. I will have to put an end to his interference," hissed Cecilia.

"Should I slash his tires?" asked Ellen.

"Silly girl. He may be a meddlesome pest, but he knows his business. I can see the protections he has put on that decrepit scrap pile. You might deflate his tires, but your arm would be broken for your trouble within the day. Now, come, we must see what harm he has done my tree."

A flashlight's beam cut the night as the two women marched down the trail.

When they were well past our hiding spot, Katelin and I stood and went to my car.

"Scrap pile. She doesn't know what she's talking about." I patted my skateboard with an attitude. Morgana woofed as Katelin held open the backdoor for her, and then the big dog settled herself, spreading partially dried mud over my seat. Katelin took the passenger seat, adding dirt to the front. I completed the mess as I sat.

Chapter 17

Battle Of The Wood

BACK AT MY apartment, the first turn in the shower went to Morgana. Sekmara watched the process from the sink counter with a wide-eyed compassion. When the dog was mud-free, Katelin and I were soaked and couldn't decide who went next. Turns out that worked to my advantage, hers too, I'd like to think. Our shower took considerably longer than it had to. It was late when I secured my finds in my temple room and returned to my instant pizza. Katelin sat in a terrycloth housecoat on my couch with Morgana's head in her lap and Sekmara draped over her shoulders. My knee was swelling, so I collapsed into the easy chair.

"That thing is hideous," Katelin indicated my chair.

"It's comfortable, and I don't have to worry if I spill something on it." I closed my eyes.

"We should get you a new one."

"Why, this one knows where all my dents are."

"Ray..."

I opened my eyes and met Katelin's gaze.

"We're really doing this. Stopping the revenant." Katelin's voice was small and held mountains of sadness and regret.

"Freeing Maryann," I commented, knowing full well Katelin's mixed emotions. She lost her sister, and now, as twisted as the form was, in a way she could get her back. For only four days a month, and at the cost of human life for each day, and the price of her sister's spirit being imprisoned in a bubble of hate and rage. Nonetheless, she could talk to her, joke with her. I thought of my grandfather, what I wouldn't give. That was the point, the things I wouldn't give.

I clung to the memory, but I won't sacrifice others to have him back. I won't betray the reality of what he was, the essence of spirit that he is, to have him back.

I understood Katelin's confusion on many issues, but it didn't make any difference. I had to stop the revenant, or people would die. I had to free Maryann, or the energies of rage and hate would degrade her astral form, eventually transforming her into something demonic. The stakes were too high to lose this one.

"You don't have to come," I remarked.

"Big strong man protecting the weak woman." Katelin glowered at me.

"Katelin, I've done this kind of thing for years. It's not man/woman; it's experience and training. Cathy—"

"I don't want to hear about how great that bitch is."

"Fine, what do you want to hear?" I closed my eyes again.

"I… Don't you dare go passive-aggressive on me!" threatened Katelin.

"Katelin, what do you want? I can't let the revenant keep killing. I can't restore Maryann to life. All I can do is try to break the astral bubble around her spirit and let her move on. That will be hard enough with Cecilia in play. So, tell me, what do you want?" I once more met her gaze.

Katelin sighed. "I… This is hard. Death should be clean. An end, then you can start something new."

I shook my head. "It seldom is. Memory, regret, grief, they're all lines tying us to what was."

"I need to let her go, don't I? That's why you became my friend. You knew."Katelin stared at the floor and seemed to pull in on herself.

I nodded and spoke with weary neutrality. "You tie the revenant to the earth plane. You're the key anchor. The love you hold for Maryann, tainted by your grief, pain and regret, is a major element in the spell that ties the ethereal energies to the physical vibration. Maryann's astral form supplies the pattern, Cecilia directs and filters the energies, Ellen binds the overflow and grounds the excess, and you hold the revenant to the earth. The other lines helped but were all secondary. You're a prime. If you let go, the other lines will snap. Without the lines, the flow of energy that surrounds Maryann in the astral bubble of hate and rage will dissipate. The bubble will degrade and pop, freeing Maryann's astral form."

"I'm to blame for her suffering." Tears trickled down Katelin's cheeks.

"You didn't know." I projected all the reassurance I could muster.

"And now that I do?"

"You need to really let her go. Let yourself move on. Open your heart and remember the good times while letting the bad times and grief slip away."

"Is the hunt for the revenant why you, well—" Katelin left the question hanging.

Here honesty could be the best comfort, and I hoped the truth would carry through in my voice. "At first, you needed a friend. Yes, your connection to the revenant was a factor, but mostly you needed a friend, and our spirits remembered. I've told you this isn't our first time around."

"No fairy squadron. I still can believe I made that joke." Katelin smiled sadly. "We would have been good back then; from what little you've told me."

"Past life, different time, and I've told you as much as I know. Past lives are never all that clear, but I know I loved you. That and your need to get away from Ellen's abuse was why I asked you to stay here. No ulterior motives. The rest just happened. We both needed it for different reasons. I don't regret it, and I hope you don't." I stood up and limped across the room to stand beside her.

"Katelin, I loved you as Keith when I was Rick, and I love you now. I can't see where things will go. I know we have challenges, but I can promise this. I will always do my best for you."

Katelin looked up at me, and the corners of her mouth twitched. "I love you, too. Goddess, I wish you were a woman; it would be so much easier."

I cupped her cheek. "Tomorrow I have to prepare. The lunar quarter is coming. That will be my chance to free Snowy. What will come of that, we'll have to see? Are you ready?"

Katelin kissed my wrist. "I'll have to be."

The next day, after work, I went to my temple room and examined the items I'd liberated from the tree. Katelin had a night class, so I knew I wouldn't be disturbed.

Setting the circle, I sat in its centre and held the watch with the tooth. The energies were old and seemed to scream with agony and loss.

I used a pair of needle-nosed pliers to unwrap the wires binding the tooth and watch. I set the tooth aside in a wooden box and focused on the watch.

Standing, I moved to my altar and took salt from the salt dish.

"By the power of Hapi, I draw forth the pain, I banish the grief. I cleanse this watch that it may speak of brighter things."

With my Sight, I saw the salt crystals strike the watch and pull forth a mustard-yellow glow. For a second, the energy formed the shape of a bear. I had a good idea of why a bear was drawn to Ellen's father. The law of attraction, like attracts like. Cecilia had impressed a twisted version of the bear totem energies onto her husband. There is a brain parasite that drives bears into an insane furry. Cecilia's corruption had acted on the otherwise protective totem-like that parasite, causing it to draw infected bears to itself. The power to cure is the power to kill. The power to protect is the power to attack. The battle of Horus and Set rages in us all, no matter what our powers be. When the disgusting energy ceased to flow into the salt, I once more took the watch and sat on the floor.

Closing my eyes, I let my thoughts centre on the watch. First, the feel of it in my hands, and then deeper. I touched its energies.

Images came, a laughing blond woman—no, girl. Sexy in the way some girls are as they cross the cusp into womanhood. A seedy bar, desire, love? A grey sea, fields of wind-tossed wheat. Hope. A house… a country house. Simple but warm against the winter wind. Toil, depression, a screeching women's voice, the dizzy feel of too much drink. An infant wrapped in a blanket, placed in a crib. A heart filled with concern. The girl, now a woman, with crow's feet around her eyes and a drawn, gaunt face. She is suckling the infant. Across a gulf of years, I see Cecilia as she was. Papers fill my view. One word stands out, 'Insurance,' then a blank void. I've reached the place the toxic energy had filled. There was no more to feel. I tried to contact the spirit the watch belonged to, but it was gone on the wheel's turn. Perhaps even returned to life… no… returning, bound until I freed the watch and broke the ties to Cecilia. Why? A question for later.

"Killed him with magic for the insurance. You are a nasty piece of work, Cecilia."

I set the watch on my altar and moved onto the athame.

The energy here also ended in a morass of fear and despair. Using a rag and a bit of polish, I began physically cleaning the knife. I let my energies flow through it, showing it the respect a tool of the Craft deserves. The blade accepted my power like a baby bird accepting mealworms. I saw a woman with grey-streaked, black hair. She was hand in hand with a rugged looking man. The man faded, and Cecilia, maybe age fifty, took his place. A blond girl played in front of a decrepit farmhouse.

The image shifted, Cecilia in a circle, red and black energy flowing around her. She was beating her drum, which Katelin had identified for me as a Sami drum, and chanting. The language was probably Finnish. The man from before clutched his left arm someplace far away.

The athame was held forward in a woman's hand. A moment passed in indecision, and then a banishing pentacle was begun. Red and black energies lashed out, striking the athame's wielder. The athame dropped to the ground. Cecilia left her circle and retrieved the blade. A shell of malignancies surrounded the sacred knife and then the practitioner that wielded it, cutting them off from the magic of the universe.

I finish cleaning the athame, breaking the ties Cecilia put on it. In this world, or the next, a soul is freed to pursue the art and grow in spirit once more.

Now to the swan head. I touched it, opening my mind and spirit to the energies it contained.

Snowy nearly leapt upon my consciousness, desperate to be whole. I focused my energies, giving comfort. Images played in my mind. A snare, a mate left behind. Wings and feet bound with cloth then laid on the grave. A sharp knife against the throat and then blackness before the light. A ripping feeling. A sense of not being whole. Not alive, not dead, trapped, denied the freedom of the skies and the spirit. Ants, the feeling of ants devouring my flesh. The bonds of energy from the tree holding the spirit in place. Pain, sadness, rage.

I poured the gold of love into the spirit segment tied to the skull and set it where, if it had eyes, it could have looked out the window. There was a sense of gratitude. Cecilia had stolen innocent lives and bound spirits in a hellish astral pocket for her own ends. Good and evil are hard to define, but sometimes you know them when you see them. If I could, I would free the spirits and set a small corner of the universe to rights.

My final act was to take the wax from the female candle I used in my obscuring glamour and warm it in a brass bowl over a candle. As the wax became gummy, I moulded it onto the male candle, repairing and 'transforming' it into a female form. The symbolism was similar to the last time I'd done this but not as eloquent. I only needed the spell to last long enough for me to restore Snowy, which made things easier. What I finished with wasn't going to win any beauty contests, but with a bit of shaving, it was feminine enough symbolically for the spell to take. It would join the other items in my travelling kit that evening.

Katelin got home late and seemed ill at ease, but I didn't push.

The next evening, we drove to the Grindstone Marshes Trail parking lot next to the cemetery and walked Morgana up to Maryann's grave just before sunset. I had the duffle bag I used as my travelling magic kit slung over my shoulder. As we approached the grave, I noticed two figures walking towards us: Cecilia and Ellen. I swear I heard the theme from *The Good the Bad and the Ugly* playing in my head.

"It's them," said Katelin.

"Yup."

"What are we going to do?"

"What we came to do. It's your sister's grave. You take precedence." I undid the zipper on my magic kit and let my hand rest on the flail within it.

In the distance, Cecilia held her Sami drum in her hand.

Spell fight at the *Woodlawn Cemetery*. My hat might be a little grey, but I knew Cecilia's was black. I let go of my flail long enough to fish a stick of gum out of my pocket and slip it into my mouth. I had to have something to spit when the time came. Eastwood, eat your heart out.

We stopped walking and faced our adversaries across the grave.

"*Myrrysmies*." Cecilia dipped her head. We both had tasted the other's power and respected it.

"*Noita*." I spoke the word with respect, as it should be. I dipped my head, never losing eye contact.

"Kate." Ellen's voice had a pleading quality.

"Elly." Katelin sounded sad, but I didn't take my eyes off Cecilia.

"Why are you here?" demanded Cecilia.

"Need we be foolish? There are none who cannot see at least a little of the world beyond the everyday here." I kept my eyes on the old woman as I spoke.

She nodded, and her tone was reasonable. "You meddle where you do not belong, *Myrrysmies*. I'll give you this last chance to mind your own business."

"When magic is abused, it is my business. I am a son of the Netters. No matter the names they are called by, they are the forces of life's process. You stand against them, and so we are foes." I've said it before; I can be pompous with magic stuff.

"Because I will not go gently into that good night," argued Cecilia. "Because I rage against the dying of the light, I am against the light? Nonsense! By that reckoning, every healer is a foe of the wheel's turn."

Hey, just because she was an evil bitch doesn't mean she wasn't well-read.

"Because you throw others ahead of you in an attempt to stall the wheel. Because you've put your wants before others needs for a very long time. It's as if a doctor butchered healthy individuals to take organs for transplant. Your argument is false. And you have not only sacrificed the innocent for life."I spoke with conviction as I pulled the wristwatch out of my bag. I unwrapped the silk I'd used to insulate the watch and held it out towards Cecilia.

Her expression became venomous. "A bear ate him!"

"We both know the truth of that. Ellen, this is a gift from your father. I'd get it looked at before winding it." I held the watch out to Ellen, who glanced back and forth from Cecilia to me.

"He was a disappointment," spat Cecilia.

"He got you out of Finland and built a home for you," I countered.

"A home? I got to rot in that disgusting shack while he drank away our money. I deserved more! He gave me in death more than he ever did in life. Just as all men do." Cecilia sounded almost proud.

"What did you give him?" challenged Katelin.

"More than he deserved. Smelly brute, rutting like a pig. Of course, you've decided you like pigs now, whore! You were never much, so it's a small loss," snarled Cecilia.

Katelin's mouth fell open.

"Mother," whispered Ellen.

"Trust me, madam, speaking as a man, I'm more than happy you decided not to burden my gender with your company! No loss to us in that, in fact, a net gain." It was my turn to glower at the old hag. Don't ever go after my friends!

I continued in an even tone without taking my eyes off the old biddy. "Katelin, I think you and Ellen need to talk. Why don't you take Morgana for a walk together?"

Cecilia glanced at her daughter and gave a curt nod. "Yes, it is time for the grown-ups to talk. You're worse than useless to me here."

"Come on, Elly. It's time some things were said." Katelin took the watch from my hand and walked to her wife. Ellen accepted the watch. Katelin took her hand, leading her away behind Morgana.

"Yes, go and settle things between you," agreed Cecilia.

"And now it is the two of us," I remarked.

Cecilia nodded. "As it should be. They would only clutter our… discussions. My daughter has no skill in the art, and Katelin is little better. Besides, soon Maryann will rise, and Katelin could have proven a distraction for the shade. Can you face both me and my creation? Katelin still clings to the echo of that weak, little fool. Can you take that away from her?" Cecilia smirked.

"I'm not crippled by having known Maryann in life. I've only known the twisted thing you've made. As to you, I'm not crippled by loving you. I don't even like you. I won't hesitate." My smile was not pleasant.

"What are you saying?" Cecilia's voice may have held a trace of regret but only a trace.

I pulled the athame out of my bag. "She who wielded this blade's power tried to stop you from hurting the man she left to be with you. You bound her for it. She must have found something to love in you, and you stole her magic and killed her other love for her trouble."

"She should never have tried to stop me. His insurance would have bought us a proper house in the city. He was nothing." Cecilia's voice trembled as she looked at the athame.

"Is she still alive?" I asked.

Cecilia looked at the ground. "Not really, Alzheimer's."

"The death that is not death." For this, I had compassion even for Cecilia. Some things are so horrible for all involved that there is no room for malice regarding them.

Cecilia locked gazes with me. "She betrayed me. It's better than she deserves."

I felt the lash of rage against my shields just as my warning system for Maryann's rising went off.

"Now you die, *Myrrysmies*."

I smiled. As much as Cecilia was a psychopath, I knew my challenges had shaken her. She'd be off her game, and I had a couple of cards to play with the revenant.

In a show of bravado, I stepped onto the grave, pulling the candle from my bag.

Cecilia began to beat her Sami drum and glowered at me. The simplest thing would be for me to hit the old hag, but that would win the battle at the expense of losing the war, unless I was willing to kill her. I could just see trying to make that case of self-defence in the court system. The revenant was the target, and Maryann needed to see men as human once more. If I could end the ethereal manifestation, Cecilia, without her energy source, would soon follow, and to the world at large, it would have nothing to do with me.

"Let Maryann be as blind in seeming as she is in truth. Let her know not her prey by the power of Aset, so mote it be." Pulling a lighter from my pocket, I lit the candle.

Cecilia glowered at me. A passing occultist would probably think we were working together. A mundane might look twice and maybe call the cops. I stood so Cecilia would have to walk through me to reach the candle. Fishing a hurricane lantern cover out of my bag, I set it around the wax statue and flame.

"She will see through your trick, *Myrrysmies*. She's too smart to fall for it twice." Cecilia continued to beat her drum.

The candle flickered. I pushed my shield around it, creating a shell that blocked Cecilia's energy. It was almost like a game Cathy and I played. Light a candle one tries to make it burn brighter; one tries to make it burn smaller. Magic arm wrestling, only this time the stakes were higher than who had to do the dishes.

Maryann began to manifest on the grave at my feet. First, a pressure I felt in my chest and the back of my head. Then she took on the image of the sad, young woman gently stroking the headless swan.

"Attack him, I command you!" snapped Cecilia.

Maryann cowered as if she was about to be hit, and my candle burnt brighter. "Where is 'the him?' "

"I found Snowy's head. Remember you asked me to." I pulled the swan skull out of my bag and unwrapped its silk covering.

"No, you mustn't." Cecilia sounded panicked and lunged at me, moving the attack from mystical to physical.

I let her get a hit in against my back. For an old girl, she packed a wallop. Of course, she was all angles and points, which didn't help.

I bent towards the headless swan as the old hag kept up a series of blows and raked my back with her fingernails, all the time trying to snatch the skull away.

I gritted my teeth against the pain and held the skull to the end of the headless swan's neck.

"I return that which was taken. One made whole to re-join the wheel's turn. Free of bondage, free to fly."

Concentrating wasn't easy with an aged hell cat kicking the crap out of me. My kidneys would be bruised for sure. A kick to the back of my leg nearly dislocated my knee. Cecilia's screams almost drowned out my voice, but the intent of my words, the energy they held, was there.

The flute bird call of the headless swan stopped. Snowy

lifted his neck. The white bird's head was intact and attached to the end of the neck. The swan looked around.

"Snowy is happy. Thank you," whispered Maryann.

"What are you doing to my Mother?" demanded Ellen's voice as she raced to the grave. She must have heard Cecilia's screams.

"What am I doing to your Mother? I'm not the one throwing punches. Open your eyes," I replied as the old woman stepped away from me and started to sob.

Katelin and Morgana ran up.

"He attacked her!" accused Ellen.

"I didn't lay a hand on her."

The old woman fell into her daughter's arms.

"The skull, the skull," hissed Cecilia between sobs. In a strict sense, I didn't attack her, but there is a backlash when a spell like the one that bound Snowy is broken. It can be quite painful. Think of a migraine coupled with someone hitting you in the head with a hammer.

"Ray?" Katelin held Morgana back and surveyed the scene.

With the need to keep Cecilia away from the skull and candle mitigated, I poured my energy into Snowy completing the reattachment of the bird's spirit.

The revenant clapped in glee. "Look, Katie, Snowy is happy. Snowy is happy."

The spirit swan spread its wings and hissed. It moved its neck, looking at the beings around it. It dipped its neck at me, a beautiful, graceful gesture, then hissed at Katelin, who'd moved to my side. I stepped between the spirit bird and Katelin. "If thou would repay me, forgive this one. She was a tool used by others as much as you have been."

The swan hissed. Words are a human construct, a way of slicing reality into smaller and smaller bits that our limited minds can comprehend. The emotional message behind the words is universal. Snowy understood, 'my mate, my friend, leave mate alone, you hit me once, I still helped you.'

Snowy turned to Ellen and Cecilia. Cecilia scrambled away

from her daughter as the spirit swan hissed. Ellen shivered and went pale. Snowy fell upon her and began beating Ellen with his wings and pecking with his beak. The attack was on the ethereal and astral levels. On the physical, Ellen doubled over and grasped her stomach like she had cramps.

Cecilia backed away. I heard the sound of her Sami drum.

I'm sure Katelin could see a little more of the ethereal fight than Ellen.

Katelin turned to me. "Ray, stop this!"

All things considered, I was more concerned with how much my back hurt. Little old lady, my butt: a vicious psychopath with a sense of entitlement. As to Ellen, she'd hit someone I cared about and had been an enabler to a murderer. Maybe she deserved some slack because her mother was a nutzy bitch, but come on.

"Talk to Maryann. Tell her to let Snowy go home." I watched the white wings take revenge for nearly a year of torture. I doubted that Snowy had the juice to kill Ellen, but a few days down seemed more like justice to me than anything I should intervene in.

"Anny, tell Snowy to stop." Katelin addressed the spirit.

"Snowy's angry," said Maryann. "He didn't like having his head cut off. He didn't like being trapped with me. Snowy is my friend. Ellen was mean to him. The mean old lady hurt him. He wants to hurt them back."

"But that won't fix what happened." Katelin paused for a moment. I could almost see the thoughts racing through her mind as a truth she only half accepted sank in. "Vengeance won't make Snowy live again." Katelin started to cry. "You… he has to move on and find a new egg that he can make his own. Then he can grow up all over again. You have to help him move on. You have to…"

"But he's my friend." Maryann shimmered. With Snowy restored, the connection between the astral and the ethereal became more complete. More of the real Maryann came through. The astral form might begin exerting control instead of being just a baseline that restored the ethereal pattern.

I looked towards Cecilia, sitting on the ground with her eyes closed, beating her hand drum. "Set's nuts!" Read the myths. It's actually a good one. I saw an ethereal bear shuffling towards us.

"Maryann, if Snowy doesn't leave soon, he's going to have to fight a bear. He might get hurt," I spoke to the revenant.

"Snowy has been hurt enough," said Maryann.

I could see the flow of astral energy into the revenant. The line of hate and rage now had flecks of gold fighting against the current.

Maryann looked to the spirit bird. "Snowy, go find a new egg. You don't have to fight the bear. I love you, Snowy." What looked like tears appeared on the revenant's cheeks. The swan honked before touching its bill to the revenant's head and vanishing.

The bear lumbering towards us dissipated. I could only assume that Cecilia was running dry.

Ellen, holding her stomach, half staggered to her mother.

Cecilia glowered at us, stood and hobbled away with Ellen at her side. Headlights lit the road as a police car pulled into view.

"You're bad," spat Maryann.

I turned to see the revenant glowering at me.

"He's good, Anny. He helped Snowy. He's helping me. He made Ellen stop hitting me." Katelin stared at her sister.

I glanced at the candle. In all the confusion, it had been kicked over and gutted.

"I'm hungry," said Maryann.

"Anny, don't go," Katelin half-whispered. It was too late. I suppose the revenant recognised me as difficult prey from our previous encounters and went off in search of an easy snack

"What's this then?" demanded a portly officer who walked towards us.

"Sorry, officer." I moved to intercept him. Every step was a new experience in pain. "My friend's sister is interred here, and she's having a hard time dealing with the loss. We were trying to make contact." I pointed to the candle that had been melted enough that its human appearance was lost.

"The report said something about drums and a woman screaming." The cop eyed me sceptically.

"The drummer left. I think we're better off without her. She started screaming when I wouldn't let her put out the candle."

"Fine, keep it down. Your friend should see a counsellor if she's having a hard time. They can help."

I dredged up the energy to do an empathic push and smiled as I flooded the cop's aura with compassion. "I'll suggest it. We're done for tonight anyway."

"Whatever you do, keep it down. The neighbours freak easy after that weird satanic thing last year." The cop nodded and walked back to his car.

I rejoined Katelin by Maryann's grave.

"What now?" Katelin collected the wax and hurricane shade, putting them into an unused poop bag.

I shifted my shoulders and felt pain blossom on my back. "I think I take the win. Can you feel Maryann?"

Katelin closed her eyes. I was vaguely aware of the energy line stretching from her to the revenant. "Downtown, I think. She's hunting."

"Of course she is. Let's go home."

"But…"

"I need my ritual space. If we can track her, maybe we can stop the kill. It will take a while for the effect of freeing Snowy to fully manifest. The spell should start breaking down now, but I need to recharge, or I'll be toast."

Katelin nodded. "Do you want me to drive?"

"Please." Katelin and Morgana left to get my car. I used the athame to cut the sod over Maryann's grave and buried Snowy's skull. The astral bubble was now unguarded. The link between Maryann's astral form and the revenant should now run both ways as well. Mentally breaking the ties between me and the skull, I half stumbled to the side of the road.

— Chapter 18 —

Innocent Victim

BACK AT THE sanctum sanctorum: my apartment—so I like Dr Strange—I entered my temple and set the circle. I hoped I could summon and bind Maryann in a triangle of evocation while she was still distracted by the freeing of Snowy. That would bring the fight into my centre of power. When my back spasmed in the middle of invoking the earth elementals, I realised that I needed to care for myself before I could care for others. Closing the circle, I took a hot bath, which relieved the worst of my pain, though I was black and blue and ribboned with scratches. I could already imagine the comments from my co-workers.

Katelin helped apply antiseptic to the scratches. A clean shirt followed. By then, I figured my window of opportunity to capitalise on Maryann's confusion was over, so we hit the streets.

Now that Katelin had accepted that she was attached to Maryann, she could follow the revenant in a general manner. Compass directions may be cumbersome, but they were better than nothing.

It was nearly eleven at night when Katelin pulled my car into the Coot's Paradise Parking lot. Four older model vehicles were parked there. My back was a mosaic of pain. I climbed out of the car and leaned heavily on my cane, examining the line of large trees that bordered the side of the lot away from the lake. On the other side, the view of the marshy inlet was largely blocked by smaller trees.

Katelin moved to my side.

A glance showed that the other cars in the large lot were filled with couples in amorous embraces.

"Makes sense," remarked Katelin.

"What do you feel?"

Katelin closed her eyes and breathed deeply. A small part of me wanted to suggest we get back in the car and relive a scene from my teens with better results. I put the idea down.

Gods, Katelin looked good when she breathed deep.

"Up that sloping trail." Katelin pointed to a steep, one-lane path that led to a plateau of land at the parking lot's far end.

"It had to be up," I grumbled. Leaning on my cane, I limped across the parking lot. Getting over the security chain that separated the dirt natural area from the parking lot took me a moment. My right knee wouldn't bend. By the time I topped the plateau, I saw red blobs of pain energy drifting across my vision, and it was taking all my focus to stay upright. My breathing had become a steady series of hisses.

I paused, took a breath and listened. There was the sound of weeping.

"I'm sorry. I stopped when you told me to," spoke a tear-choked male voice.

Katelin pointed, and I hobbled forward over the large meadow that filled the top of the rise of land. Trees ringed the meadow, separating it from the inlet that looped around it on three sides. The cloudy sky made things dark enough that the tall grasses covering the ground blocked my vision.

When I had hobbled about fifteen metres, I saw a gangly teen male sitting on a blanket that he'd spread out. The blanket pushed down the grasses in the big clearing. The translucent form of Maryann sat beside him. Maryann looked as she had in life.

"It's the only way you can be sure you won't. It won't hurt. Just take the pills and let it happen. You'll never hurt anybody, and it is nice. You will never hurt anyone like they hurt you. You know what they say about people who were abused. They become abusers." Maryann spoke in a soothing voice.

"Will you stay with me? See me off," the youth half-whispered.

"I'll stay with you."

"Oh, crap!" I whispered. When I'd freed Snowy and strengthened the control of the astral spirit, I hadn't counted on making Maryann more dangerous. Compassion can be as damaging as hate, and it is far more insidious.

Focusing my will, I gathered up the pain energy in my aura and channelled it towards the revenant. She jumped like a scalded cat and landed well away from her prey.

"Maryann!" cried the boy who held a bottle of pills in his hand.

"I wouldn't listen to her, my friend. She does not have your best interests at heart," I announced. For a few seconds, my pain subsided as the levels rebuilt in my energy system.

"Who? What?" the boy looked at me with a startled expression.

"Katelin, talk to Maryann." I limped to the boy's blanket and lowered myself to sit beside him. "Hi, I'm Ray, hope you don't mind, but it's been a long night."

"I... what happened?" The youth had dishevelled dark hair and a pimply face. From the car in the parking lot, I was guessing seventeen, but he looked younger.

"You wouldn't believe me. Just take it that today the universe was on your side. What did she tell you?"

"Who?" The kid bit his lip.

"I won't think you're crazy." I smiled and pushed emotional reassurance into his aura. The kid's energy system seemed to latch onto me. Whether it was Maryann or life, this kid needed to talk bad.

"She... I was just hanging out, solo again. She sat down

next to me on a bench. I couldn't believe it. She's so pretty, and we talked. She said her name was Maryann. I said, 'like from *Gilligan's Island*.' That's how I remember names. I think of a TV show with a character name that was the same. It works, mostly. She didn't mind that I used a trick to remember her name. We talked about old TV shows. She's from out west. Then I drove her here. She seemed nervous and wanted to get out of the car. I think cars have bad memories for her. I got the blanket then we came up here to be alone. It was going great, then she pushed me away and said stop. I swear, I stopped! I don't want to be like… well."

"You've been abused," I filled in.

"It shows?" He sounded defeated.

"Not really. I overheard some of what you told Maryann."

"I don't want to do that to somebody else, but you know what they say, 'if you were abused, you will abuse.' " The youth hung his head.

I ignored my pane and lent certainty to my tone. "You know what I think. I think people usually go one of two ways. Either they abuse, or they are so enraged that they would never abuse and will fight against the abusers to protect others. You stopped when she told you to. That should tell you something about yourself."

The kid looked at me with an expression mixing surprise and hope. "Maybe. She kept saying the next time I wouldn't."

"I told you, she doesn't have your best interest at heart. What happened next?"

"I—I've been saving up pills. Ever since, well, you know. I don't want to be like that. I don't want to be gay either. Maryann told me I should take them. She said it was the only way to break the cycle. She said she'd help. She said that because I could stop, I must be gay." The kid sounded desperate and hurt. I bled for him a little. I'd hated being a teen.

"You stopped because you are a good person and take responsibility for your actions. That's being a man and has nothing to do with who you want to sleep with. It's okay no matter which way you swing, but it has nothing to do with how good a person you are." I reassured the youth.

"Thanks. Who are you?"

"A friend. It sounds like you need one. My girlfriend is trying to help Maryann." Clumsy I know, but the kid needed to hear that I had a girlfriend at that moment.

"Do you think I'll see her again?" His voice blended fear and a reluctant hope.

"Not if you're lucky, but there will be other girls. Just don't try and fall in love before you fall in like and treat them like people first and foremost. You'll do okay." I tried to sound wise. Maybe compared to the kid I was. A few years can make a lot of difference when you're young.

Katelin walked up to the edge of the blanket. "She's gone."

Between my stick and my good leg, I fought my way to my feet and faced my new friend. "You should head home. Find something you like and join a group that does it. That's the best place to meet girls. They may not be cheerleaders, but you'll have something to talk about. That's half the battle."

I hobbled to Katelin's side, and we started for the car.

Behind us, I heard a blanket being folded.

"I'll say it again. You would have made a great lesbian," commented Katelin.

"Mostly because I like women." I grimaced as I spoke, and it showed in my voice.

"You're done for tonight." Katelin eyed me with concern.

"Longer than that. I think we should go to the emergency."

The following day, I sat in my lounging chair, a set of crutches propped beside me. The anti-inflammatory drugs helped, but I still couldn't fit pants over my bloated knee. I had managed to get into a pair of loose legged shorts and a t-shirt. The energy manipulation work I'd done meant that I could hobble down the hall to the toilet if I had to. Want to? That was a different matter.

Sekmara lay across my lap, and the TV and DVD player

remotes were within reach, as were one of my magic texts, a fiction book and a university text on Anatomy. Katelin had queued up a Dresden Files disk before she went to class. Carl had told me I was letting him down when I phoned in sick. Honestly! Morgana lay on the couch, looking at me with huge puppy-dog eyes.

The apartment door creaked open. Morgana raced to the hallway.

"Get the fuck out of the way, you overgrown shag-mop. Ray, call off the dog?" It was Kama.

"Morgana, it's Kama, you know Kama. I'm in the living room." I commanded the dog in exasperated tones.

I turned to watch Morgana trot into the living room, followed by Kama and Cathy.

"What have you done to yourself this time?" demanded Cathy.

"Cath, what? Why?" I tried to get up and fell back with a hiss of agony.

"Katelin called me and asked me to check on you. I figured Cathy should know because she's in the same building as you." Kama strode to my side. "Fuck, your leg looks like something off an elephant."

"You should have seen the other guy."

"Who was the other guy?" Cathy had an expression on her face that said someone was going to die for this piece of work.

I cringed. "A little old lady. I really couldn't hit back. It's a tear in the meniscus."

"Macho twit," spat Cathy.

I smiled. "Cath… Thanks for coming."

Cathy looked at me. I wanted to hold her.

Cathy scowled. "Nothing has changed, but I don't quit on friends."

I nodded. Friends were better than nothing.

Between Kama arranging my apartment so I could get around easier and Cathy doing a load of energy work on my knee, by the time Katelin got in, I was pretty much set to function while I healed. Cathy left before Katelin arrived but promised to check up on me before she went to work the next day. Kama hung around to make dinner. Katelin came in and almost immediately took Morgana for her walk.

"Really nice," commented Kama.

"What?" I asked.

"You're fucking hurt, and she walks the fucking dog before she hardly says hello."

I shrugged, "Better than a puddle on the floor."

"I guess. Just… you deserve better." Kama let her hand rest on my shoulder. I could feel her concern. It was nice.

When Katelin came in, Kama raced out the door. Katelin settled on the couch. Morgana lay with her head in Katelin's lap.

"Kama made dinner. Spaghetti. She said to put the pans to soak, so the sauce doesn't stick," I opened.

"You'll be eating in your chair," Katelin's voice was flat.

"What's up?"

"Last night, do you think Maryann fed?" Katelin absently petted her dog. Sekmara lay on my lap, purring as I stroked her.

"Probably. It was only after midnight when she got away from us."

"That wasn't my fault!" Katelin glowered at me.

"Didn't say it was." I may have sounded a little defensive. It's hard to be nice when you're in pain.

"I'm sorry. I… Ray, we never really defined things. Are we monogamous?" Katelin blushed.

I sighed, "We never spoke the words or made any promises. Is it an issue?"

"Yes… No… I don't know. Yesterday when Ellen and I walked Morgana, there were a lot of old feelings. And there is this really cute girl in my Theories of Gender and Sexuality class who has been giving off a vibe. I mean, she is a sweet piece."Katelin's blush deepened.

"As are you." I had thought about this possibility. I would have been a fool not to. "I will give as good as I receive. I won't repeat the mistake I made with Cathy. Katelin, I've told you, I love you, and I stand by that, but I'll never be treated like a lapdog again. Maybe we can find a woman that likes both. Not really my preference, but I'm realist enough to know it's an option." I smiled, thought of moving, then thought better of it.

"Gods, I feel like I'm in an episode of Lost Girl." Katelin rolled her eyes.

I snorted with mirth. "As long as I get to be wolf."

Katelin shook her head. "All we're going through and I'm blathering about stuff like this. I'll get the spaghetti."

The next day, I filled Cathy in on the revenant. She sat on my couch shaking her head and humming and hawing in all the right places. For my part, my old lounger was doing more to keep my pain in check than pain pills ever could.

"It sounds like Katelin is a lightweight," Cathy said when I was finished filling her in.

"She can hold her own, most of the time. Cath, Cecilia is in a class by herself. The Nukekubi was more powerful but also more limited. For a general mystic, with the full bag of tricks, Cecilia takes the cake." I know I sounded worried.

"Could you just let the revenant fade out on its own? Now that the swan isn't locking the astral bubble in place, it shouldn't take that long." Cathy moved to my side and touched my arm. It was the first time she'd actually touched me, aside from healing, since our breakup.

"It's at least one death every quarter moon. I saw it on the news today. A convicted paedophile hanged himself in his parent's basement the same night I freed Snowy, and you can bet that Cecilia took the lion's share of the kill's energy." I sighed in frustration.

"No great loss, and you can't know that the case is related," said Cathy.

I shook my head. "Maybe, or maybe the poor bugger hooked up with a girl he met in a bar who said she was a junior. Problem was it turned out to be in high school, not college. It happens, and it's not necessarily the guy's fault. Asking for ID isn't really an option. Look at Kama; depending on how she dresses, she could say she was anything from fourteen to twenty-two, and nobody will bat an eye."

"You have to envy the Asian genetics for that," Cathy smirked.

"The kill was only a kilometre away from here. The revenant hunts in proximity to one of its existing anchors. Thanks to me, there are only four left, and Katelin is one of them." I laid my hand on Cathy's. I'd missed her. I'd missed the camaraderie, the way we got each other on so many levels.

Cathy smiled. "I've got to run. Barrie's in town. I promised him dinner."

And there it was. "Katelin will be home soon. I should be okay."

Cathy left with a sad backward glance.

The next day I was recovered enough to drive, so I spent it with my parents. I'm a masochist! I have to be. The willow tree looked like it had a green afro from where new shoots had sprung out of the trunk. Its energies embraced me when I touched it, all things forgiven and accepted. I think it realised that removing the overburden probably bought it a year or more of life. You have to love trees. I thought of Cecilia's sacred tree, twisted to foul uses, and it made me want to cry. I remembered to borrow my dad's bucksaw before I left.

I beat Katelin home. Moving into my temple room, I set the wards and lied down. Breathing deeply, I eased out of my body. The pull of my injuries tried to force me back. I knew I wouldn't be able to resist it for long. Focusing on Maryann, I found my astral self beside her grave. The sun shined down onto it. There were faint tracings left from all the spell work that had centred on the site but nothing active. I reached for the astral and found myself floating in a void with a bubble of black and red energy before me. I drifted to the bubble. Nothing tried to stop me. Visualizing a blade of golden energy in my hand, I carefully sliced the bubble.

Red and black energy poured out, dissipating in the void. Maryann's astral form, appearing in a human shape covered in a layer of black and red, emerged. The line to the ethereal revenant still tied Maryann's astral form, but she was no longer encased. It was an effect like a human-shaped helium balloon bobbing at the end of a plastic tube carrying coloured light back and forth along its length.

Maryann's astral eyes snapped open, and she glowered at me. "Don't touch me!"

"I won't." I drifted back.

"I… You helped Snowy." The spirits 'voice' was quizzical as if the concept of a man helping was foreign to her.

"Yes."

The veil of anger and pain parted a little as if it was dissolving in water.

"You're a man."

"Yes." I kept my 'tone' neutral, simply confirming the observation.

"Men are evil… Men hurt me."Rage tinted the spirit's communication.

"But a woman killed you. People are what they are. You need to move on, Maryann, for the sake of your sister." I projected reassurance into the exchange.

"Katie… You're friends with Katie." The 'voice was once more questioning.

"Yes."

"Ellen was wrong to hit her. You shouldn't hit people you love." Maryann nodded.

"Yes."

Maryann closed her eyes. Black and red flowed up from her connection to the ethereal, fighting against the revelations that were trying to penetrate through from her spirit.

"You should go. I'm getting angry. Nobody loves me when I'm angry, not even Katie." The sense of the words held an honest warning. She didn't want to hurt me but knew when the rage came, she wouldn't be able to help herself.

I nodded as a little more of the drama fell into place. The stages of grief. As much as she loved Maryann, Katelin had difficulty dealing with the girl's anger. Heck, she had a hard time dealing with mine. She tended to shut down and become emotionally distant whenever I got peeved about something. Maryann must have seen Katelin's reaction as conditional love, which became part of forming the revenant.

I was preparing to leave when I had a thought. Focusing my will, I touched the astral energies around me. I saw in my mind a kitten. I knew it, I felt it, I shaped it in the image of all the kittens I'd had over the years.

"Oh, Lady Bast, lend this creation the form of thy minions. Let it stand as a gentle companion to one here bound. In love, I ask, and in love, I pray ye answer."

The astral energy stirred, and out of it appeared a kitten. I knew it wasn't a real kitten. Given time and energy, I could have summoned the spirit of a cat in the name of Lady Bast, but it would have been overkill, and I was already fading from my injuries.

In a magical sense, the proto-kitten I called forth was like one of those toys they advertise that come when you clap. But it was soft, and it purred, and it had one purpose, to keep Maryann entertained, to show her love. This was one of the many positive uses of an artificial elemental. The kitten was born of my energy. I filled it from my heart chakra. Taking the love I felt for Katelin and extending it to her sister.

"A kitten," breathed Maryann's astral form.

I slipped away from her and back into my body.

I lay on the floor and wondered if peeing myself would be better than moving. Dignity finally won the day, but not by much.

Katelin got home late, having gone for coffee with the hotty from her class. I was too tired and in too much pain to care.

The next day consisted of me catching up on my coursework. Cathy dropped by to do more energy work on my knee and then left before we could really talk. The emotional ground between us was full of land mines. I felt better for her healing. Katelin came in with Chinese takeout, and we made an evening of it.

Chapter 19

Showdown At Voodlawn

THE FOLLOWING MORNING, I made my way back to Cecilia's sacred tree. My knee still hurt, but I was careful and brought my walking stick. I'd broken the obscuring glamour for me, so it had no effect. The emotional barrier of hate and rage had been jury-rigged back into existence. Cecilia had taken the energy leads from the two stones bordering the gap I made and stretched them to one another, making the spell's field of effect a horseshoe shape with a weaker band of energy closing the open end. Nice work for a quick job, but Cecilia wasn't the only one who could be clever. Knowing what I faced, I'd come prepared with a bag of earthing powder. A mix of salt, ground volcanic rock and other things chosen to earth unwanted energies, my own recipe, which was quite effective against things that use spiritual energy as a power source.

I moved to one end of the weakened part of the spell and sprinkled the earthing powder onto the ground. "By Lord Hapi, the son of Horus, I ground this energy. Let it dissipate within the earth and return as the powers of life and love."

The energies of the spell pulled into the earth. I moved to the other end and repeated the procedure.

The weak part of the spell snapped open. I limped to the ancient tree. Laying my hand on it, I opened my mind. The tree acknowledged me and seemed happy to 'see' me. It still hurt from the uses it was being put to.

I climbed the tree as high as I could with any assurance of not breaking a branch and falling. Unslinging my father's bow saw, I put it on the dead wood and started cutting. Bad memories of slogging through tonnes of firewood with the blasted saw assailed me, but I kept going.

The dead branch fell away, taking with it a host of negative enchantments. I moved to another branch.

Nearly three hours later, the insect riddled dead branches were largely on the ground. I was sweat-soaked and covered in sawdust. The glamour had dissuaded anyone from noticing me, so no Royal Botanical Garden officials had interrupted my work. Scrambling to the lighting-struck hole, I pulled on a work glove I'd kept in my pocket and reached in and extracted half a dozen things in various states of decay and enough ants to supply the banquet at an aardvark convention.

It was while I did this that Cecilia attacked.

A wall of red energy slammed into my shields as the sound of a Sami drum filled my ears.

I paused in my physical work and focused. My shield held. I'd added an inner layer just for this occasion. Tearing the outer shield free, I visualised it as a mirror and folded it in on itself, driving it back along the path of the attack and sealing it around my opponent. The attack paused, leaving me time to clamber to the ground. I hissed as my knee took the strain of a bad landing.

Another wave of attack came. It was a mix of muddy red and green that permeated the woods around me. Mosquitoes swarmed me, and I stumbled into a thorny vine. The ants from the tree colony started crawling up my pants legs. Individually, any of the things wasn't that devastating; collectively, they were extremely painful. Given that the ants didn't get all the way up my leg, things could have been worse.

Opening my pouch of grounding powder, I sprinkled its

remaining contents onto the earth.

"By Hapi son of Horus, by Unnefur, God of the green, by the netters who administer the natural world, I ground these malignant powers. I dispel them and call on the green to resume its natural course."

I heard a growling sound and turned to see a coyote stalk up to the hate barrier around the tree. It was a mangy beast with a grey pelt and a lean, hungry look. Energies danced around its head, and I recognised Cecilia's work. The coyote snarled at me. I lifted my walking stick like a club.

"Son of Anubis. In the name of thy species lord, I call thee depart. We have no argument. Be not a pack member without status to follow the dictates of another." I pushed with my will to back up the words while encasing the coyote in an orb of blue energy to cut of Cecilia's influence.

The coyote snarled.

I made myself look bigger and prepared to strike if the animal sprang. There was no way I could outrun it, but if I could convince it to go after easier prey, I wouldn't have to. That made me think. I pictured Morgana in my mind. In the image, I stood beside her to give a concept of scale. I added the idea that she was part of my pack and would be displeased should harm come to me. I let the concept reach out and touch the coyote. Then I envisioned Morgana showing me a subservient display. Rolling on her back, belly and neck exposed. I was dominant. In Morgana's mind, I'm sure the ranking went Sekmara, Katelin, me, her, then the rest of the world. Sekmara approves of this list.

The coyote looked startled. Taking a chance, I bared my teeth and took a step forward, brandishing my walking stick.

With Cecilia's influence cut off, the coyote gave a final snarl then stepped back, leaving the rage barrier's field of effect. It shook its head then ran away in search of easier game.

I opened to the tree again. If you've ever had chronic pain and woken up to not being in pain, then you know what I sensed. The old tree wasn't free of Cecilia's taint, but it was much closer. I sensed the will to live rekindling as its living trunk became aware of the weight it no longer had to support. I felt its gratitude. Mentally, I envisioned the green link to the revenant snapping. The tree was more than happy to oblige.

I heard the Sami drum as another wave of attack hit me— hopelessness and depression. My shields blunted it, but, in the end, I just ignored it. I was a past master at that. The old biddy would have to do better than dredging up something I'd faced on and off since my teens.

Never let it show because people will use it against you. It doesn't matter how emotionally draining it was.

I had work to do, and I knew how to push through depression. So, I let that old crone have a victory that wasn't a victory. It would keep her occupied.

I turned to the downed branches, cutting them into pieces the length of my forearm. All the time I visualised Cecilia's energies flowing back to her as I broke her links to the tree. "You will die, you will die, you will die, you will die." I chanted as I sawed, letting her darkness pass through me and return to its source. Not a death curse, a simple affirmation of the inevitable truth that lent fear to her heart.

It was late afternoon when I finished stacking the firewood for later retrieval. I hobbled out of the largely cleansed sacred clearing carrying a bundle of twigs that could represent the broken connections to the tree.

I got home to find Katelin huddled on the couch with Morgana and Sekmara, tears trickling from her eyes.

"What's wrong? What happened?" I hobbled to her side.

"She called. She was awful!" Katelin managed to get the words out between sobs.

"Who called?" I sat beside her and put my arms around her.

"Ellen. I don't know how she got your number, but she did. I'd just come home from class. The phone rang. I… she started nice, and then she got mean. She called me a slut. She said I was helping you kill her mother. That I was empowering rapists and abusers. She just went on and on. I wanted to hang up, but I couldn't. It was awful. Sekmara knocked the phone on the floor. It must have bumped the button because it hung up."

I stroked my cat. "Good girl." I then turned my attention to the phone. Katelin had left it on the floor. Lines of force writhed around it. "Ra's beak! I never thought of that."

Of necessity, things passed through my apartment's wards, the phone line being one of them. The enchantment was a simple compulsion to not hang up, probably sent along the line during the 'nice' part of the conversation. The actual attack had been the words. "Cecilia is sneakier than I gave her credit." Out of habit, I returned the phone to its place on the end table and hung up the receiver.

"How could Ellen say those things?" Katelin sniffled.

"Probably her mother more than Ellen. Katelin, I may be shooting myself in the foot here, but cut Ellen a lot of slack until her mother is out of the way. Often, I think Ellen, literally, isn't herself."

Katelin nodded. The phone rang, and she moved to pick it up.

I caught her wrist. "Let me."

With a deep breath and a blast of directed energy, I cleansed the phone of the enchantment then picked it up.

"Hello."

"I want to talk to Kate," demanded Ellen's voice.

"I think not." I could feel energy trickling into the phone.

"She's my wife," snapped Ellen.

"She's not a punching bag. Call back when your mother isn't around." I hung up.

Katelin watched me with wide eyes. "Thank you." She fell back into my arms.

"Any time," I told her and meant it. I had my suspicions about where Katelin and I were headed as a couple, but it didn't matter. She was one of my people. That didn't change just because a romance ended. Whether she knew it or not, she had a guardian for life. Sir Galahad snickered at me from the sidelines. Jerk!

Katelin took Morgana for a walk.

I slipped into my temple room and, using a pair of Katelin's earrings to form the link, projected a shield around her. It turned out to be a good idea as I felt several attacks bounce off it. Cecilia was getting desperate.

The following day was quiet with a sense of menace. It was the last chance to store up energy before the lunar quarter. Cathy came by and did another healing while Katelin was out. She also gave me a snowflake obsidian on a chain and told me she was taking the next day off to help. I let her have my key, just in case. She didn't give me hers, but then there wasn't an immediate use for it.

I was walking almost normally. That night involved a Red Dwarf marathon for Katelin and me. The laughter was as empowering as any trance or spell I could have done.

The next day, I listened to more of the Kalevala and prepared. Katelin came home early, and we drove to the revenant's grave for Morgana's walk. A funeral was being conducted within sight of the grave. It wouldn't be a battleground that night. Ellen stood by Maryann's grave, looking downcast. Katelin and I walked up to her with Morgana, who head-butted Ellen in an affectionate way. Katelin and my issues with the woman didn't change the fact that she was part of Morgana's pack.

"Ellen?" Katelin greeted her wife coolly.

"I came alone. I… I was apologising to Maryann for what Mother did to her. I never knew. I didn't want to believe it. Mother doesn't know I'm here. I'm sorry I said those things on the phone. I honestly called to talk, and then I got so angry. I'm going to go into therapy. I don't like who I've become." Ellen absently petted the huge dog as she spoke.

Katelin hesitated, then moved forward and hugged Ellen.

Ellen began to sob. Katelin closed her eyes and held her wife, giving comfort. I accepted then that Katelin and I was a passing thing, not that I wouldn't enjoy it while it was still good, but with Cecilia and Maryann out of the way, Ellen would return to the woman Katelin fell in love with. In any case, it opened a possibility for me. I closed my eyes, feeling the link between the revenant and Ellen. It was weaker, a shadow of the conduit of rage it had been. Taking my walking stick, I focused on it and made a slashing motion visualising a line of energy slicing the link. The link broke. I felt the revenant stir in its grave, but the late autumn sunshine held it trapped.

Ellen gasped and pushed away from Katelin to glower at me. "What did you do?"

"Freed you. Your mother was using you to contain and maintain the revenant's rage. That line is broken."

"My mother will die without the spell." Ellen looked at me with a mix of anger, query and almost hope.

"Yes, and with it, the killing goes on, and she'll still die. It will just take a little longer. How many men should die so that she can have a few extra months? The spell your group cast was perverted into something I doubt any of you intended." I kept my voice even, neither comforting nor accusatory.

"Elly, we started out to make things right, but Maryann… The revenant is killing the innocent. That's not what any of us ever intended, and my sister's spirit is trapped by the spell."

Ellen sighed. Without the link to Maryann, she was clearing the background rage that had plagued her for months. She looked me in the eye and spoke with a tired resolve. "You're a son of a bitch!"

"No argument, but when did you meet my mother?" I shot Ellen my best impish grin.

Ellen almost smiled back. "Thank you for looking after Kate." Ellen turned to Katelin. "Mother is expecting me. I left her by her sacred tree. I pretended to have forgotten her Sami drum." Ellen wearily sighed, "You can guess what she was like about that."

Ellen turned to me. "I'm going for a drive. I'm not a sensitive, like you and Kate. Mother told me I took after my father. With what I grew up with, I think I didn't want to be. I do know right and wrong. I won't go to the tree until midnight. Keep Kate safe, and don't hurt my mother any more than you have to. Despite everything, she's still my mother."

I nodded. "I will do no more than I need to."

Ellen started walking away. Katelin looked at me, and I gave her a nod. Oddly, I could separate my emotions when it came to Katelin. Something I have never managed with Cathy.

Katelin ran after her wife and caught her by the arm.

"Elly, Ray and I have an understanding. If you're really in counselling, call me after, well… when Cecilia isn't a factor. We can go for coffee."

A moment passed ,and then the two women embraced and kissed.

"I love you. No matter what I've done, that never changed." Ellen slipped from Katelin's embraced and walked up the street.

"I love you too," Katelin called after her before walking back to me.

"The tree is Cecilia's place of power. It doesn't like her, but that only mitigates the situation," I observed.

"So, what do we do?" There was a tremor in Katelin's voice.

"We end this. I've nibbled away at the spell all I can. Now it's Cecilia or me, and Apep take the loser."

We arrived at the arboretum's back parking area just as the sun was setting. My early warning system went off as I got out of the car. Maryann was rising.

Katelin, her face a mask of concern, climbed out of the car and let Morgana out of the back seat.

Collecting my gear from my trunk, the three of us started down the trail. Dusk deepened. I could feel a malignancy in the woods at odds with their usual welcoming nature.

Katelin walked beside me. She grasped my arm and pulled me to a stop. "I want to let Maryann go, but I just can't. I keep remembering her, and I want her back so much."

I patted her hand. "Freeing her astral form is the best we can do. The revenant isn't Maryann, not really."

Katelin looked at the ground. "A twisted caricature made

in Cecilia's image. I know. It just that—"

I barely had time to enhance the shields around us when the revenant swept down the trail. It took the form of a glowing red and black cloud and seemed to be screaming.

My shields held against the first attack, but the backlash sent a bolt of pain through my head.

"It's coming back," warned Katelin.

"By Usire and Aset, I command thee halt and return to the grave from whence thou came." I gestured with my hand held in the posture of the sacred bull.

The energies flickered but didn't depart.

"Maryann, stop this!" ordered Katelin.

The energies paused and coalesced, taking on the appearance of the young woman. She held a kitten in her hands.

"Katie, where am I? Why am I so angry?" The revenant sounded confused.

My betting was that the manifestation that attacked us was strictly ethereal and that the connection to the astral had been inactive until Katelin called Maryann's name. I focused my thoughts. Only three lines of energy flowed from the apparition. The one reaching to the astral was awash with colours and seemed to pulse as they shuttled back and forth between the astral and the ethereal. Maryann, the true spirit, was trying to take control. The line to Katelin was now a near gold shade with only flecks of the corrupted energies of guilt and grief. The line to Cecilia was red and black, feeding into the revenant as the colours of a dirty rainbow flowed back to Cecilia.

"It's alright, Maryann. Ray and I will help you." Katelin's voice sounded soothing.

"He's bad. He's a man!" The shade of Maryann grasped her head. "I'm hungry." She looked at me and drifted closer.

"I'm your friend. I helped Snowy. I gave you the kitten." I spoke aloud.

"I'm hungry. The mean lady says I have to. I don't want—"

"Don't listen to Cecilia. She's bad," said Katelin.

"Where's Ellen? Ellen drinks the angry. I… I'm hungry."

Maryann closed on me just as several things happened at once. A bear appeared on the trail in front of me. A line of energy opened up from the snowflake obsidian pendant Cathy had given me into my heart chakra, and I smelled Cathy's perfume. Katelin let Morgana off her lead. The huge dog charged the spirit bear, worrying it as if it was a physical one. Katelin moved to stand between Maryann and me.

"You take Cecilia. It's time I had a serious talk with my sister." Katelin's heart chakra glowed with a warm, pure light that flooded out along the link between her and Maryann.

I glanced at the revenant, red and black pushed from one side and gold from the other, like some metaphysical arm-wrestling match.

I focused my will on Cecilia and walked slowly to the sacred tree. Waves of attack struck my shield, hissing and popping like acid thrown against a limestone wall, but with Cathy's power added to my own, I built the shields from within, allowing the attack to shuffle off. When I reached the tree, I saw Cecilia sitting on the ground alone. A tired, dying, old woman at the end of a life defined by selfishness. She was drawing in the energy from all her protections. The obscuring glamour around the tree was gone, as was the power from the anger stones. All amassed into her active reserves. This was her last stand.

"*Myrrysmies*, I warned you!" she snapped.

"And I you. Let it go. Spend the time you have left making it right with Ellen. The revenant is through. You must know that. With the astral component released, it will dissipate. Is a month or two more of life for you worth the lives of eight or nine people?"

"Eight or nine men. It is worth thousands!" Cecilia released a blast of red and black energy at me. It hit my shields and stuck like burning tar scorching my defences. As the energy of her attack pushed in, a wave of pain swept through me. All my injuries and mild chronic problems flared up, making it hard to concentrate. Distracting me from the fight at hand. I pulled the energy Cathy sent away from my outer shield and shaped it into an inner barrier close to my skin. My outer shield was almost gone. I shed it like a snake shedding its skin, tossing the energies into the earth, taking Cecilia's attack into the ground with it. Cathy's energies protected me against Cecilia's next, less potent attack while I re-established my own shield.

Setting my duffel on the ground, I opened it. Cecilia paused in her efforts to fry my brain to muster power. She evidently realised what I'd come in knowing. Anything less than a focused high energy attack from either of us was nothing more than fireworks. Setting my duffle on the ground, I pulled out my crook and flail and held them crossed over my chest in the pharaoh posture. I felt a chill run up my spine.

I dove out of Maryann's way into the thick underbrush flanking the pathway to the grove. The revenant, looking as Maryann had in life, shot past me to hover half a meter off the ground beside Cecilia in the grove around the sacred tree.

"Kill him," hissed Cecilia as she gestured towards me.

The revenant hesitated, giving me time to regain my feet.

The lines coming off Maryann blazed with multi-coloured energies.

Taking up the pharaoh posture and envisioning the shell of hardened concentrated auric energy that is a mystical shield around me, I spoke to the revenant. "Maryann, what do you want?"

Maryann hovered, seeming to consider.

"I order you," Cecilia screeched. Red and black energies flowed up the line from her.

"You're not my mother!" Maryann's expression filled with the rage and rebellion of a teenage girl ordered by a disrespected authority figure to do something she didn't want to.

"By Khonsu banisher of demons and the powers of the ennead of Heliopolis, I hereby break this line, freeing the spirit to find its rest." I slashed down with my flail envisioning a blazing knife of golden fire cutting across the line connecting

Maryann to Cecilia. The power of the Gods flowed through me, enhancing my efforts.

The line resisted for a second, then snapped. In that second, a blast of red and black energy slammed against my newly reformed shield, causing me to fall back to sit in a puddle on the trail. Despite the hit and the icy water soaking my neither regions, I held my concentration.

Cecilia howled in pain as the line to the revenant fizzled away like a string touched by a flame. She sent a blast of energy towards me that shattered the new outer shield I'd forged and carried through to the inner layer I'd sculpted from Cathy's power. In my mind's eye, I saw Cathy in my temple room collapsing to her knees, clutching her head. The wards around her deflected much of the attack, but not all.

The power of the grove blinked out for a moment as the tree sought to recover the energies drained by Cecilia's attack. Considering the force that attack represented, Cath and I got off light with migraines.

Still in the puddle, I reached down mentally, calling on the powers of earth and water, drawing them in and envisioning an oblong shell of blue and brown surrounding me. Nature obliged me and flooded power through me. I scrambled to my feet, building my power all the time.

The grove came back to life as new energy flooded in from the surrounding environment to fill its depletion. Only this energy was free of Cecilia's taint.

Cecilia stood, breathing hard. Her age-spotted skin was pulled tight against her bone rack frame. The black dress she wore pulled against her with every random breeze. Her teeth bared in a snarl while her face filled with fury. The eyes, black pits in the night, nearly caught me with a spell to steal my power and make it her own, but I refused to meet them, so the spell couldn't lock onto me. Cecilia looked more demon than human.

Katelin and Morgana ran into the clearing under the tree. "Maryann got away from me," gasped Katelin.

Red and black poured out of the severed line from

Maryann, who still hovered in the grove, as the gold of Katelin's love pushed the energies of anger and hate away. Cecilia drew those red and black energies to herself before they could dissipate, like a black hole sucking in energy from all sides.

Cecilia glowered at me as I borrowed power from the earth and water to reconstruct my defences. I knew she was readying another blow, and I was on my own. The last attack had knocked Cathy out of the fight, and Katelin was busy with Maryann. Cecilia still had the hoarded might of a lifetime of selfishness and greed.

I managed to erect a thin blue shield of my own power under the shell of earth and water energies before my foe could ready another blast.

A thought came to me. This battle was all about reserves. I'd taken hit after hit, letting Cecilia push the offensive to wear her down. Now it was time to cut off another of her batteries. "Let her go, my friend. The hurtful one can't punish you anymore." I spoke to the tree. It seemed to pull in its energies, leaving Cecilia bereft.

Cecilia held up her hand and called, "*Minulle koirani!*"

A growling sound came from the surrounding woods as the coyote from before stalked towards me.

"*Viimeistele hänet, yönmetsästäjä!*" snapped Cecilia.

The coyote lunged at me. I raised my arms in a defensive pose. Morgana bounded into the air, slamming into the coyote, driving it to the ground. The huge dog and the coyote tore at each other, snapping and snarling. Morganna had size and strength, but she'd had a gentle life that hadn't taught her to fight. The coyote had hard experience and cunning with a wiry strength and savagery born of living rough.

Still, Morgana held her own, the love and loyalty to her pack lending her strength beyond the physical.

"*Ärsyttävä mut!*" Cecilia raised a hand in preparation for throwing a spell at Morganna.

"Lord Anubis, I call you that the wheel will turn," I spoke the words and summoned death. Each second we die and are reborn. That energy is in us all. I called the seeds of my own death, accepting they were there and would someday manifest, gifting my foe with that energy. She tried to deny the gift, but she wasn't prepared to block a gift of energy when she'd put so much effort into ripping energy from everyone and everything around her. The spells that she used to extend her life crumbled as her physical form became too decrepit to support her spirit drawing power.

Cecilia gasped and collapsed into a heap.

Free of Cecilia's influence, the coyote took off at a run. Morgana let out a howl that said as much as words, "That's right, you better run, and don't come back because I'll be waiting!"

Katelin gazed at her sister, now a ghost in the classical sense.

Nearly a minute passed in silence while I gathered my power and prepared a defence incase Cecilia was playing possum.

Cecilia lifted her face and hissed. "You've killed me."

"Nature did that. I just stopped you stealing others lives to delay the inevitable." I focussed my full attention on her.

Cecilia scowled. "She will leave you. She is not a lover of men."

"Yes, but she loves, and that *is* enough." I had no compassion for Cecilia that night. She'd hurt too many people, too many people I loved.

The old woman glowered at me.

"Ray, Maryann and I are going for a walk," said Katelin.

I half turned so I could look at Katelin and still keep an eye on Cecilia. "Katelin, she can't stay on the material plane."

"I know she has to go, but the link to the ethereal won't dissipate until sunrise, even I know that. I'm going to spend some time with my sister."Katelin spoke with a quiet assurance that bore no dispute.

I nodded.

Maryann drifted up in front of me and smiled. "Thank you," I heard her whisper before she, Katelin and Morgana headed back to the main trail.

Cecilia cackled.

"What are you laughing about?"I asked.

"A little vengeance, *Myrrysmies*."

I let it go. An hour or so of playing prison guard later, Ellen arrived and, for lack of other help being available, I carried Cecilia to the parking lot. With the revenant no longer feeding her energy and the expenditure of the last battle, Cecilia was fading fast. Her objections to me carrying her fell on deaf ears. It was either let me carry her or die in the dirt. The specks of colour in her black aura were almost extinguished.

I settled Cecilia in the passenger seat of Ellen's Miata and stepped back.

"Thank you," said Ellen. She got in the car and drove away.

<h1 style="text-align:center">Epilogue</h1>

RESSED IN A black robe, Dan carried the ritual sword around the circle's outer edge, setting the wards with a dignity worthy of the warrior Gods of old. Returning to his place in the circle's east, he laid the sword on the altar.

Beth, who was High Priestess for the rite, waited before the altar. She wore a simple, black robe. With Dan's return, she addressed the congregation.

"We are gathered to celebrate Samhain, the new year of the Celts, and the start of winter. It is also the night when the barrier between the worlds is thinnest. Let the beloved dead come to you in love, make amends or simply share the joy of their company. A symbolic feast has been prepared for you to share."

I glanced at the two small plates before me. I hoped, as I had for fifteen years, that the one I longed to see would visit.

Beth continued. "Speak in silence, for the dead have no need of words. Treasure this time. I will chime a bell when it is time to begin, then again when it is time to bid our guests goodbye, and a third time when the rite is done. Be blessed with the love that binds all things together."

Beth chimed the bell, and all fell silent as Dan settled in a chair and began breathing deeply, lending his power to the dead that they might manifest.

I glanced around the dingy, upper-story room of the coffee shop. The flickering candlelight and well-placed shrouds turned it into a magical cave. Cathy sat beside Shawn on the opposite side of the circle. She wore a black robe that suited the ritual but not her. Katelin sat beside me, eyes closed, her hands pressed against her belly.

The handmaiden, the assistant to the priest and priestess, a young Asian woman in a black robe with her long hair falling down her back, stepped in front of me, depositing a slice of pomegranate on my plate. I'd already set a blueberry tart there and a small piece of banana bread. They had been my grandfather's favourites.

Reverently, I divided the food and placed a sample of each on the visitor's plate. Then I waited.

Along the ring of people attending to my right sat Ellen. Her eyes kept straying to Katelin. Ellen's aura was brighter than I remembered, but her expression had a lost quality. As I watched, a wispy cloud of muted colours settled before her. I'd probably have to do some cleanup work to clear Cecilia's spirit, but with her deceased, that wouldn't be too bad.

I'd just about given up hope. Another year and he hadn't come. Could he be that angry that I didn't save him? Grandfather, don't you know I love you. I did all I could.

"Shh."

I heard the sound. I looked across the plate to where a transparent, beautiful, dark-haired woman had appeared. She looked younger than I remembered, maybe thirty and free of the cancer that had ravaged her body before her passing.

I almost spoke aloud but managed to only think the exclamation, *Gran!*

Ray Ray, he loves you, we both do. We are so proud of you. You are nearly ready. Hold on a little longer.

What?

I don't have much time. Don't give up hope, my Gran nodded in Cathy's direction. *And to each thing, a season, don't cling.* She nodded at Katelin.

Have you been well? One thing I know is the dead will only tell you what they want to.

The pain is gone. I have to go; your father is calling from another circle. Don't carry the world on your shoulders, Ray Ray. Just do what you can and try to have a giggle on the way.

Then she was gone. A long-dead cat from my childhood visited, and a friend of a friend I hardly knew desperate to have someone relay a message. Bloody Galahad said he'd do what he could. Finally, the third bell tolled, and the circle was opened.

Katelin drifted to Ellen's side and moments later told me they were going for coffee to talk because Ellen was having a hard time dealing with her mother's death. I let it go and drifted to a dark corner of the room. Cathy was, as usual, the life of the party. Shawn was chatting up some barely legal, Goth chick. Grandma and Dan sat with a group of other elders by the feast table.

A scrawny twenty-something man in a black robe, wearing a wolf's head pendant, tried to impress a pretty blond woman with an impromptu lecture of the occult nature of dogs and how they often played roles in the journey of the dead. Little lightning bolts of violet passed through his aura as he spoke. She looked like she needed saving.

Somebody turned on a portable speaker connected to their smartphone. The wolf howl opening to *Medicine Woman* by Gypsy blasted through the room.

I moved to the pretty blonde's side, "Sorry to interrupt, but would you like to dance?"

"I'd like that." She grabbed the social lifeline I offered her. "It's been interesting talking to you. Bye."

She took my hand and let me escort her to the dance floor while wolf pendant guy shot daggers at me with his eyes.

About the Author

Stephen B. Pearl is the author of several novels, including "Nukekubi," "Worlds Apart," "Revenant", and many published short stories

He lives in Hamilton, Ontario, Canada with his cats and his wife.

For more information about Stephen and his books:

www.stephenpearl.com

NUKEKUBI
By
Stephen B. Pearl

"…exciting…fast paced…you are going to enjoy Nukekubi."
- *Sizzling Hot Books*

Ray McAndrues, a lifeguard by profession, is not what he appears, for he can sense energies and perform magic. While doing a favour for his girlfriend and fellow mystic, Cathy, Ray discovers exactly what is causing the gruesome deaths of innocents.

Will Ray be able to find and destroy the Nukekubi before it can consume him and those he loves?

Available in paperback and ebook
Everywhere fine books are sold.

WORLDS APART
By
Stephen B. Pearl

"Worlds Apart is a very well written and touching love story. I could not put this book down." - *Bottles and Books Reviews*

Alcina, a Witch, is in a custody battle over her son, Tim, when a strange visitor from another Earth enters her life. Can Alcina save Tim, even with the help of her bizarre, intriguing visitor? Can Markus save his world with the aid of this alien enchantress, and what of the bond that grows between them? Can love triumph when you are Worlds Apart?

Available in paperback and ebook
Everywhere fine books are sold.

DREAMING THE GODDESS

An Anthology

Edited by Karen Dales

Available in paperback and ebook.

"... a passionately written, original collection of fresh, contemporary, Goddess mythology for our modern era. Each chapter is a pilgrimage to meet and get to know another embodiment of the Goddess and Her particular mysteries."
- *Dodie Graham McKay, author of* Earth Magic.

The Realm of the Goddess is vast. From mythology to legend to modern retellings, between these pages, you will experience Her Mysteries in original stories destined to become new mythology. Experience the Goddess in Her many guises, from Egypt to Nigeria, from Europe to the UK, from the Middle East to North America.

BOOKS

To see a full list of our amazing books,
please check our website:

www. darkdragonpublishing.com/books.html

All Books Available At The Following Retailers:
Amazon.ca
Amazon.com
Amazon.co.uk
Amazon.com.au
Barnes and Noble
Books A Million
Book Depository
Smashwords
Powell's Books
Chapters/Indigo

And other fine book retailers.